VERONA WITH LOVE

By

Deborah Rine

ISBN- 9781679989018

Verona with Love is dedicated to Marie-Juliette, Charles and Christopher, the joys of my life.

Books by Deborah Rine

Banner Bluff Mystery Series:
THE LAKE
FACE BLIND
DIVERGENT DEATHS

Contemporary Novel:
RAW GUILT

Emerald Coast Mystery Series:
THE GIRL ON 30A
ENVY ON 30A

Deborah Rine can be contacted at:
   www.deborah-rine-author.com
   http://dcrine.blogspot.com/
   Facebook and Twitter

Trovommi Amor del tutto disarmato
et aperta la via per gli occhi al core,
che di lagrime son fatti uscio et varco...

Francesco Petrarca (Petrarch)

Love found me all disarmed and found the way
was clear to reach my heart through my eyes
which have become the halls and doors of tears.

"True love bears all, endures all and triumphs!"
Dada Vaswani

Prologue   2019

I'll never know what came over me back then. I tossed my inhibitions to the wind and went with my emotions. There was nothing rational about it. I couldn't help myself. Or maybe that's just an excuse for the inexcusable. I was in love, or at least I thought I was. Passion, sex and over-the-top thrills: I've never felt anything like it since and I never will again. Certainly not at age 74. I was on a perpetual high for four months and then it all came crashing down.

We're on the plane on our way to Verona. I will be awarded a literary prize and perhaps given the keys to the city. My latest book was a love story set in Verona. Think Romeo and Juliet, with a modern-day twist. Verona with Love *has been a top best seller. Let's face it; we're all push-overs for suffering young lovers. A copy of the book is on my lap. My Giulietta sits gazing out at her beloved city.*

The children and I are in first class. Lucie is sitting next to me. She's got her earbuds in and is unavailable for conversation. She's listening to a podcast and frowning; her eyes are closed. She's an environmental sociologist and becomes impassioned about melting glaciers and polluted waters. I'm sure her podcast will get her riled up. She's often riled up.

My children are all in their forties now. They have vague memories of their life in Italy, but they wanted to come along and revisit the past. For each of them, the trip was scheduled at just the right time. They were able to leave their jobs, spouses and children and make a holiday of it. I will relish the time we'll spend together. It's not often that we are back together, our intimate little group.

As for me, I'm not sure why I agreed to this trip. Walking down the Corso Porta Nuova again will bring back memories both joyful and painful. Will I visit Cerro? Maybe yes. Maybe no.

Chapter 1   1975

We made our way to Verona by way of Paris. We'd taken the *Queen Elizabeth II* from New York across the Atlantic. It was late May and the crossing had been stormy. There are pictures of the children out on deck wearing blue windbreakers, being buffeted by the wind. My father-in-law came to meet us in Le Havre where we landed. Henri's family were thrilled that we were relocating to Europe. We spent a few days in Paris, having lunches and dinners with friends and family. Then we began the drive down to Verona.

Our possessions were in the bowels of a freighter and we wouldn't see them for three or four months. However, we'd brought over our car, a yellow Volkswagen station wagon. I remember seeing it swing back and forth as it was maneuvered into the ship's hold. The chief advantage to that car was that the engine was in the back under the rear platform, so the front hood opened up as a trunk. You've got to remember that this was before seatbelts, so kids were free to roam the car. In my ignorance of child safety, I loved the fact that the boys could roll around and play with their toys on the back platform, while their sister played with her dolls on the back seat. If they got tired, they just stretched out and fell asleep. It seemed great at the time.

Henri was taking a position at an Italian ice cream plant, Gelati Bianchi. It was partly owned by Robertson's Foods, an American

3

multinational firm. The company had part ownership in Gelati Bianchi. Henri would serve as comptroller as well as oversee the venture for the Americans. This would prove to be a difficult task because of Giancarlo Bianchi, the Italian owner of the company. Bianchi ruled his plant like an irascible Napoleon. He wanted the Americans' money, but he didn't want their oversight.

The original plan was to rent a cottage on the Lago di Garda for the summer and then look for an apartment in Verona in the fall. I was told the weather would be warm and sunny, so I packed summer clothes with a couple of sweaters for the kids and myself. But instead of a house on the lake, a colleague at the ice cream plant had suggested renting a cottage in Cerro Veronese, a village in the Lessine Hills above Verona.

Italians believe that for children to grow strong and healthy, they need to spend a month in the mountains and a month at the seaside each summer. Their lungs need the purified mountain air and the salty sea breezes. Considering Italy's geography and topography, this goal was easy to accomplish. Someone had convinced Henri that the Lessine Hills would do marvels for our children.

As we zigzagged up the mountain, the children were fighting. They weren't interested in the view. They'd been cooped up too long in the car.

"Mommy, tell Papa to stop going back and forth. Everything's falling on the floor," Lucie complained. Her neatly arranged dolls had taken a nosedive with each hairpin turn.

From the way back where the boys were rolling around, Marc screamed, "Mommy, Timmy is banging into me. I don't want him to touch me."

"Come here, Timmy, honey. Come sit on Mommy's lap." I stretched out my arms.

Grinning, he tried to climb over the back seat and fell onto his sister, who screeched as though mortally wounded. I reached around and pulled him forward. Timmy was two and a half, with bright blue eyes, strawberry blond curls, pink cheeks and a huggable, chubby body. I pulled him onto my lap as we went around another sharp turn.

I glanced over at Henri. He had a neat profile with a straight nose and thin lips. His dark hair was carefully coiffed, a little longer than usual. He had both hands on the wheel and was frowning as we neared another turn. Henri was concentrating on the road. He had this annoying ability to block out the children when they were at their worst. This was a blessing at times and an irritation at others. But then, as I gazed down the steep slope, I was glad his eyes were on the road. Timmy was patting my cheeks with his chubby palms and laughing.

"Mommy, mommy lovey dovey," Timmy sang as he patted my cheeks and giggled into my eyes.

"How much longer?" Lucie whined.

"Ouch, I banged my head," Marc complained and burst into tears.

"Lie down flat, so you won't roll around," I said.

"I hate this trip," Lucie said.

After ten more long minutes, we came out on a valley of sorts. We pulled over to the side of the road, and Henri took out the directions he had scribbled down the previous evening when he called Signor Moretti, the owner of the cottage we were renting. After studying the paper, he handed me the torn sheet. I looked down but couldn't make out his scribble.

"Look, kids, we're almost there," I said, my voice full of excitement. All was silent now in the back of the car.

We drove another quarter mile in the narrow valley. To the left was a paved road that led up to the village of Cerro perched on the peak of a hill. To the right was an unpaved road climbing up a grassy hill dotted with houses here and there. We turned to the right. After passing two gravel roads, we turned left onto a narrow, unpaved lane.

We passed a couple of cottages, one hidden by tall cypress trees and a metal fence, another was built on the slope below the street with a sharply pitched driveway leading down to its garage. Further along, we arrived at our summer cottage. The white stucco house was set back from the road and ringed by a metal fence. It too was built on a sharp incline and was surrounded by empty land. Little did I know then what would transpire in that cottage; that my life would be changed forever.

The gate was open, and a car was parked in the driveway. As we drove up, Signor Moretti, his wife and daughter emerged from a dark blue Fiat. We pulled in beside them. The children tumbled out of the car and began to run around. I had to rein them in, so they could say a proper greeting. We'd practiced *"Buongiorno"* on the way in the car. Miraculously, they all remembered and shook hands, even Timmy. Signora Moretti and her daughter beamed down at them.

Signor Moretti had grey hair, a slight build and friendly eyes. He wore a grey tweed jacket, knit vest and a fedora at a jaunty angle. Signora Moretti was plump with short greying hair. Her eyes twinkled, and smile wrinkles radiated from her mouth. She was wearing a knit twin set, dark skirt, thick stockings and sensible shoes. As I would learn, this turned out to be her uniform.

Their daughter Elena was a sturdy woman of about thirty-five or forty. She was hampered by a club foot that turned inward, and wore a specially designed shoe. Luckily, the children didn't notice and make comments. I thought about the fact that she was probably a baby during WWII and undoubtedly there had been no possibility of medical help back then. Elena was dressed in the same uniform as her mother: twin set and dark skirt. A quiet smile graced her lips.

Henri's Italian was quite good, and he discussed the ins and outs of the house as we took a tour. Signora Moretti, Elena and I did a lot of smiling at each other. I tried a few simple sentences and they continued to smile. Maybe I wasn't making much sense.

The cottage was built of cement blocks covered by stucco with stone trim. On the ground floor was a garage, bedroom with a double bed, armoire and a bathroom. A washing machine was hooked up to the tub. Since the house was on a slope, you accessed the main floor by an exterior metal stairway. There was a wide terrace across the front of the house. Lucie and Marc raced up the stairs. Timmy reached up and took Elena's hand as we followed along. He beamed up at her and a smile flooded her face. It's amazing how the attention of a child can bring such happiness. As she held on to the banister and clumped her way up the stairs, Timmy chatted to her unintelligibly about dinosaurs.

The cottage wasn't large. The main room had French doors that opened onto the terrace. Signor Moretti unhooked the heavy metal shutters and pushed them back. There was a lovely view of the village of Cerro Veronese, perched on top of the hill across the valley. Beyond that were snow-covered mountains. The furnishings were modest and not terribly comfortable. There was a rectangular wooden table with eight straight-backed chairs, a matching sideboard with dishes for eight, a tired-looking sofa and a TV with rabbit ears. We would learn that TV reception was hit or miss up here in the foothills.

The kitchen contained a small fridge, cook stove and the basic necessities to prepare a meal. Here too, a set of French doors opened out to the terrace. I pulled the doors open and looked across the valley at the mountains beyond. I loved the thought of cooking with this poetic view right outside my door. We were certainly a long way from our Evanston, Illinois apartment and the flat Midwest prairies.

"Mommy, we're all going to sleep together. Won't that be fun? Come see, Mommy," Lucie yelled.

At the back of the house were two bedrooms separated by a bath. One room contained two single beds, a crib and an armoire. When we went in, we found Lucie lying on one bed, her eyes closed. She had one of her baby-dolls beside her and looked angelic with her blond curls spread out on the pillow. Marc and Timmy were jumping up and down on the other bed and giggling. Henri strode over and yanked them off.

"What are you doing? You do *not* jump on beds," he said, his voice tightly controlled. Then he turned to Signor Moretti and began to apologize for his unmannered children. Now, the boys were in tears and the Moretti family looked chagrined.

I went over and picked Timmy up. He sobbed into my shoulder while Marc bolted out of the room. I could hear him clattering down the stairs outside. He did not like to be disciplined publicly, and particularly not by his father.

In the other bedroom was a double bed with attached bedside tables and an armoire. There wasn't much room to put things, but we didn't have that many possessions. The tiled bathroom in between the bedrooms contained a toilet, bidet, sink and a small tub. There was a single shelf for toiletries. Everything was spotlessly clean. As we made our brief tour, I smiled at Signora Moretti and repeated over and over that everything was "*molto bello*."

That evening we went down the hill to a restaurant with the Morettis. On the terrace, in front of the restaurant, we could see the lights of Verona in the valley below. There was pasta, polenta, grilled meats and a myriad of other dishes. Since it was Sunday evening, other families were dining at adjacent tables. Soon our children were chasing around with other little kids. It was relaxing

9

because no one got uptight about laughing or crying children. As we ate, I learned that the proprietor of the trattoria was a relative of the Morettis. In the months to come, our lives would become intrinsically entwined with their friends and relatives.

Chapter 2

It was freezing that first night in our new abode. It was May. Spring was slow coming up in the hills. We didn't have sufficient blankets for the unheated house, and I'd packed light summer clothing and summer pajamas for the kids. But in spite of the cold, everyone slept soundly in their pajamas, socks and sweaters.

The next morning, Henri left before seven. He was determined to make a good impression in these first days on the job. As I would learn, the owner of the plant, Signor Bianchi, demanded allegiance from his minions. Like a mafia boss, he expected his employees to be present when he was in residence. Usually Henri was a self-possessed individual with an assertive personality. But I could sense that Signor Bianchi held a certain sway.

My job that morning was to find something for breakfast and walk into the village to purchase *una bombola di gas*—a gas tank. Once we had the tank, we would have hot water and gas for the stove…but no heating. Signor Moretti had given me directions to the *bombola* store the night before, but I'd been too tired to retain what he'd said.

The children woke up thrilled at their new little house. They raced around the main room, chasing each other and giggling.

"Come on, let's get dressed and get some breakfast," I said.

"Why can't we have breakfast here?" Marc said. His straight brown hair hung over his right eye and his normally pale cheeks were pink from running.

"Because I can't cook anything yet. We have to go get the *bombola di gas*," I sang.

All three of them started to giggle and began to run around the table singing, "bombola, bombola, bombola." I trapped Timmy and carried him into the bedroom, where I changed his diaper and got him dressed. Meanwhile, Lucie pulled on some shorts and a tee-shirt.

"Honey, you're going to freeze. Let's put on some long pants."

After lots of negotiating, all of us were dressed. I insisted they put on two sweaters and a windbreaker. Henri had left with the car, so my only form of transportation was my trusty stroller that could accommodate three children on flat ground. But in these hills, it would be a real workout to push even one toddler up and down the steep slope.

Outside the air was chilly. We started down the hill. I looked at the house below ours. The metal shutters were locked shut, like tightly closed eyes. No one was living there or in the house on our side of the lane with all the cypress trees. We were very much alone. Thinking back on those times, I marvel at the fact that I had no phone, no car and no neighbors. Yet I had no sense of fear. What if a child had fallen and I'd needed a doctor? I was truly in the hands of fate.

At the end of the lane, we took the track down to the main road that zigzagged its way up from the valley below. Lucie and Marc skipped down the hill and I held tight to the stroller, so it wouldn't go rolling down. We crossed the main road. There wasn't any traffic that early in the season. A café was located just a short walk up the opposite slope. I parked the stroller by the front door, and we went in. The interior was dark and smoky, with a musty odor of wine and coffee. At a couple of tables, old guys were having espressos probably laced with grappa. I stood uncertainly at the door, Timmy in my arms and the other two clinging to my skirt. The café was deadly silent. Then a cheerful, roly-poly lady came out from behind a curtain and bustled over. She ushered us to a table in the corner. In my broken Italian I ordered hot chocolate for the children and café latte for me. We soon had our hot drinks and a basket of fresh bread and homemade apricot jam. Conversation began again around us. As the children chattered and giggled, everyone in the café turned to smile at us. Italians love beautiful women, but they love cute children even more.

After breakfast we started up the hill into the village. It was still early, and the few shops weren't open yet. I asked a couple of people where one could buy a *bombola*. They shrugged or gave me an unintelligible answer. At that point I could understand a lot of Italian, but in Cerro, many people spoke a local dialect that I couldn't decipher. We wandered up the narrow streets. The village was not prosperous. Many buildings seemed in disrepair. There was a large cobblestone piazza in front of the church, but no one was about. I was feeling a little panicky. The day before, Signor Moretti had assured me the bombola man would be easy to find.

At the top of the hill we came upon an open esplanade and a decrepit children's playground. The view gave on another steep valley and the snowy Dolomites in the distance. The playground equipment was old and rusted. Red poppies grew in the crevices between the broken cement blocks. There was one functional swing, so the kids took turns. Then they hopped around from one flat chunk of cement to another. Lucie picked a poppy bouquet for me as I pushed her little brother on the swing.

I remember I was dressed in a new white blouse and a blue cotton pleated skirt with a matching jacket. Before I left Chicago, I thought I needed this tailored ensemble for my new, exciting life in Italy. Looking around at the broken-down playground equipment and the bleak village, I felt terrifically over-dressed and terribly foolish. Then I looked up and noticed the dilapidated building across the lane. A large sign on the wall read *Bombole di gas. Urrà!*

Chapter 3

After paying for and arranging delivery of the gas tank, we began the trek back home. We stopped at several shops. The vegetables at the greengrocer were past their prime: wilted lettuce and brown-spotted beans. I bought some so-so carrots, spring peas-in-the-pod and an onion. At the grocers we found boxed milk, ground coffee, hot chocolate powder, eggs, spaghetti, bottled tomato sauce, butter, a chunk of parmigiana and sliced ham. The children were fascinated at the butcher shop with the rabbits and chickens hanging on hooks by the door. I bought a whole gutted chicken complete with feet. This was a far cry from the packages of chicken parts I found at the grocery store back home. Lastly, we went to the bakery for a thick loaf of country bread.

By now, the kids were getting tired and hungry. Lucie and Marc were poking each other. Timmy didn't want to stay in the stroller and was crying bloody murder. The woman at the counter had pity on me and handed each of the children a round cookie with sugar sprinkles. This brought instant silence and big smiles. With some prompting, they all said *grazie*. I gave the woman my biggest smile.

On the way home there was barely enough room for Timmy in the stroller. I was glad when he wanted to get out. Slowly, we made our way up the sharp incline to our lane. Just as we arrived, the *bombola* man showed up. He installed the large gas tank in a special alcove outside the garage. It had a padlocked door. Then he came upstairs and checked the water heaters and the stove. Rather than a large water heater as we have in the US, these appliances had a series of coils running back and forth over the gas flame. When the hot water was turned on, the gas was ignited and heated the water as it ran through the coils. It was hot water on demand.

We had ham sandwiches for lunch. Then the boys went down for a nap. They were both exhausted. Lucie and I cuddled on the sofa with a blanket and some books. I read to her. Then she dozed off. I didn't want to awaken her, so I sat still and gazed out at the village and the mountains beyond. There was still a winter tarnish to the hills with spots of greenery here and there. I wondered at our isolation. The few houses nearby were all empty, their shutters tightly closed. Henri had assured me that in the summer this was a popular place. I wondered when summer would begin.

That afternoon, it was warmish and sunny. The children clambered down the metal stairs to the driveway below. It was wide enough to permit easy parking for a couple of cars. For the children it was a wide-open playground. Lucie and Marc played ball while Timmy toddled around with Lolly, his beloved teddy bear. I made a tour of the house. In back was a laundry line and an uneven lawn that sloped up. In one corner I noticed a tilled area where someone had planted a small garden. Sharp green spikes were forcing their way up through the inhospitable earth. I knew practically nothing about gardening, but maybe delicious vegetables would emerge in a month or so.

I looked up the hill. Way above us I saw a large chalet perched on an outcropping. I thought I saw movement on the terrace, but I couldn't be sure. Finally, a sign of life! It would be nice to know I had a neighbor. Maybe the children and I would take a hike up there one of these days. I turned and looked at our cottage. Given the steep slope the house was built on, the bedroom and bathroom windows were at ground-level. I could easily peer into our bedroom. I'd left the bed unmade and the suitcases were open on the floor. The children's room was littered with clothes and toys. Time to put some organization into our new lives.

Later, I brought a large bowl and the peapods outside. We sat on the ground in the driveway and popped peas into the bowl. The kids saw this as a game. Timmy was our courier who chased down the wayward peas and dropped them in the bowl. Until that day my kids thought peas came in square frozen packages or round cans. Who knew peas grew in these clever little parcels?

I managed to cut up the chicken with a dull knife and cook the pieces in butter and olive oil. After dinner and a wash, we sat on the small sofa, Timmy on my lap and Marc and Lucie on each side. I read through five of the ten books we had. When Timmy's head began to loll on my chest, I carried him into bed. He was out like a light. I tucked in the other two. Then I began to sing. We went through my usual repertoire: Down at the Station, Rock-a-Bye

17

Baby, Mommy Loves the Dear Little Girl/Boy. Ten minutes later, Lucie and Marc were zonked.

I went around the cottage and closed the metal shutters and made sure the front door was locked. During the day, I hadn't felt alone, but tonight in the dark and with the children asleep, I realized how isolated we were. There was no telephone and no way to contact anybody if something happened. I shook myself. These fears would lead me nowhere. I went into the kitchen, made up a plate for Henri and did the dishes. Then I sat on the sofa wrapped in a blanket. I was too tired to read. Finally, I went to bed wearing my nightgown, cotton pants, two pairs of socks and a long sweater. Henri came home when I was dead to the world. I was vaguely aware of his presence when he slipped into bed.

In the morning, I awoke to the sound of running water. Henri was shaving. We spoke in whispers.

"Henri, do you think you could come home early today? I need help with the shopping. We need a bunch of stuff, and…"

Henri didn't stop shaving. I watched as the blade slid smoothly down his cheek. "Kate, I cannot come home early. I have just started my job. What's Bianchi going to think if I skip out early?"

"It's just that it's hard with only a stroller and the kids…"

"They're going to have to learn to walk."

"We also need warmer clothes and some blankets. It's freezing in here." I was shivering with my bare feet on the tile floor.

He rinsed off the razor. "This weekend we'll drive down to Verona and get what you need."

Henri was gone ten minutes later. I took a bath, dressed in jeans, a blouse and a couple of sweaters. The children were still asleep. When I opened the shutters, I was met by dark clouds that seemed to be hovering right outside the window. In the kitchen, I took down the little espresso pot and figured out how it worked. A few minutes later after the mini Mount Vesuvius bubbled up in the pot, I had a strong cup of espresso with a splash of warm milk. I sat down at the table and gazed out at the grey foggy day. The village across the valley was invisible. As I sipped my coffee, it began to rain. Raindrops drummed on the roof and pinged on the terrace. What was I going to do with the children today?

Chapter 4

As it turned out, it rained off and on for five days. I tried every game I knew and invented some more. We put sheets and covers over the dining table and the kids spent hours inside their cave. We raced the Matchbox cars down chairback ramps. Lucie's dolls had a tea party and Marc and Timmy were invited. I read our ten books a hundred times. On Thursday afternoon, the weather cleared up a bit. We needed milk and other basic necessities. I lured the kids down the mountain with the promise of an ice cream bar. I'd noticed that the café-bar where we'd eaten breakfast the first day had a Gelati Bianchi ice cream freezer. Marc and Lucie skipped down the hill and Timmy sat in the stroller and clapped his hands. With a chocolate-covered ice cream bar in hand, we walked up into the village. I bought a few items, before it began to sprinkle again. By the time we got home, it was pouring.

Henri arrived home each night after we were asleep. When I questioned him in the morning, he said the executive staff had dinner together every night. They were planning a new line of products and there was much to discuss. It was essential that he be there.

"You have to be patient, Kate. The weather will improve, and you and the kids can take hikes. They say there will be lots of families here in July, lots of other children to play with." Henri was making a neat knot in his tie. He looked annoyed.

I was annoyed, too. "That's well and good. But today, it's raining. I'm running out of warm, dry clothes…and I'm going stir crazy." I was pleading with him. I knew I looked tired and strung out. I wasn't being the docile and charming wife he expected.

He sighed, put his hands on my shoulders and looked into my eyes. "I can't do anything about the weather. I have to go to work. You wanted to come to Italy. Enjoy it." He kissed my forehead and tapped me under the chin. Then he left.

***

Friday was another rainy day. Earlier in the week I'd done some laundry and hung the wet clothes in the bathroom downstairs. Nothing had dried. In the morning, I brought up some of the wash and hung it around in the kitchen and main room. The children had been fighting all afternoon and Lucie and Marc were in time out, one in each bedroom. Timmy was sitting on my lap sucking his thumb. I hadn't washed or changed that morning. I had tomato sauce on my sweater and my blond hair was in a messy ponytail. Outside there was a gentle drizzle.

It was after five and I was contemplating another pasta and butter dinner when I heard a car honking outside. *Henri!* He'd come home early. Maybe we could go out for dinner. From the kitchen window, I looked down onto the courtyard. A car had pulled into the driveway, since I'd never bothered to close the gate. I opened the door and stepped out onto the terrace with Timmy balanced on my hip. As I watched, the four doors of the sedan opened up. Three children tumbled out of the back. A woman and a teenage girl emerged from the front.

The woman waved and shouted out, "Buongiorno, signora." She was short and sturdy with a mop of dark curly hair.

I waved back and shouted, "Buongiorno." Who could this be?

The woman charged around to the back of the car and opened up the trunk, shouting instructions to the kids like a drill sergeant. They lined up in back of the car and she piled items on their outstretched arms. Then they headed toward the stairs and up to the terrace. I stepped back as the little army entered the front room. They placed their items on the dining table, then headed back outside for more. There were warm blankets, gently used woolly sweaters, and sacks and boxes of foodstuffs.

The children came out of their bedroom and watched in wonder. The signora brought up the last load. I had tears in my eyes and rubbed them away with the palms of my hands. She placed a box containing four bottles of wine on the table and came over and gave me a sisterly hug. Then she hugged each of my children. Their little arms went around her waist. Instinctively, they knew this was a special person.

Signora Adriana Peron introduced herself and then her children: fourteen-year-old Maria; twelve-year-old Pietro, seven-year-old Chiara and five-year-old Antonio. They all had chestnut brown hair and almond eyes. My children studied them shyly. Then I introduced my kids. Timmy reached for Antonio's hand and pulled him towards the bedroom. Undoubtedly, he wanted to show off his Matchbox cars. Then Lucie gestured to Chiara.

"Come and see our room," she said in English. "We could play house."

Chiara didn't understand a word; but she followed along into the bedroom.

Adriana helped me put the food away, chattering all the time. I understood most of what she was saying. Apparently, her husband, Giuseppe, was the chief mechanic at the plant. He had come home to tell her we were camping out in this cottage. Adriana was horrified because it was still so cold. Her family had a vacation house not far from ours. But the Peron family came up here only for weekends until the mountain climate warmed up. In addition, their cottage had a wood-burning fireplace. She invited us for lunch on Sunday.

As we worked, I could hear the younger children giggling at each other in the bedroom. The older children, Pietro and Maria, helped stash things away under their mother's direction. The kitchen lacked enough cupboards and shelves, so we lined up boxes on top of the sideboard and under the sink. Along with basics like olive oil and flour, Adriana had brought fresh vegetables, wine, coffee, pasta and a banged-up aluminum pot containing a fragrant veal stew. My mouth watered when I lifted the lid. I kept saying, "Grazie, grazie," like a broken record. After we'd put things away and placed a blanket on each bed, we sat around the table on the hard, straight-backed chairs. I offered to make coffee, but Adriana refused.

"What do the children do all day?" Adriana asked.

I said, "*Giocare*," which means "to play." Then I rubbed my eyes and beat my fists to indicate that they cried and fought as well.

Adriana laughed and said they should go to the *asilo*.

I asked what an asilo was and she explained that it was a school for little children, a nursery school. She said the nuns ran an asilo in Cerro and we could probably enroll Lucie and Marc for the rest of the month of May as well as for the month of June. The two of us decided that the following morning, she would come and pick me up and take me to the monastery where the asilo was located.

That night we enjoyed the veal stew with rice, and I had two glasses of red wine. Later, we all slept like hibernating bears, under our warm covers.

Chapter 5

I must explain that for several years before we moved to Italy, Henri traveled back and forth to Europe on a regular basis. He spent six weeks away and one week back in Evanston. He worked at various plants that Robertson's Foods had acquired in several European countries. I had become independent in terms of managing finances and childcare. When Henri came home, we all had to readjust. The children had to reacquaint themselves with their father. Timmy would cry when his father picked him up. For a toddler, six weeks is a long absence.

It wasn't so great for our marriage, either. It took days for Henri and me to reconnect. When he first came home, he was nervous and edgy. Then he would calm down and relax. When I look back now, I can see our marriage was unraveling bit by bit. The romance was gone, and we didn't know how to reach each other across the deep chasm of estrangement.

The plan was for us to join Henri when he settled down to work in one European location. The previous October, we'd learned we would be moving to Italy. I asked around and found an Italian woman who agreed to give me some Italian lessons. I already spoke French and knew some Spanish, so I thought another Romance language wouldn't be that difficult to learn.

Maria Rosa lived in a small house on a quiet, shaded street. Her husband had been a police officer and had died several years before. She was from Naples and had met her husband when he'd been stationed at a US naval base near Naples. They'd had four children. Three were married and lived in other cities. Only an unmarried daughter lived with her and worked in Chicago.

Maria Rosa wore her thick, grey hair in a low bun at the back of her neck. She had snapping dark eyes and a pleasantly plump body. We sat at the kitchen table and drank small cups of espresso. Each week she would prepare a short article from one of the Italian magazines her sister sent her from Naples. Together we would dissect it and discuss it. I remember at the time, there was a vote about a law permitting divorce that many people wanted to overturn. It had only been instituted a few years earlier. In 1974 there was a movement to get rid of the law. We spent a long time discussing the pros, cons and effects of divorce. Maria Rosa explained that when a couple married in Italy, they married the entire extended family. Divorce meant destroying an intricate network of aunts, uncles and cousins. As I would later learn, many of the people we met in Italy obtained wine, polenta flour, jobs and vacation rentals through the extended family network. Divorce meant disconnecting all of those relationships.

We discussed movies, fashion and recipes. A couple of times we cooked together, making lasagna, pumpkin risotto and a fabulous tiramisù. Those days, I took home a delicious dish for dinner. This irregular language program turned out to be an excellent way to learn a new culture. Goodness knows, I wasn't fluent, but I understood a lot and had a basic knowledge of present-day Italian life.

***

The asilo was located on a side street about a fourth of the way up the hill to the village. A high wall stretched out on each side of a small arched wooden door. Adriana pulled a cord and we could hear a bell tinkle in the interior. Moments later, the door was opened by a tiny nun in a black habit and white wimple. I was holding Timmy in my arms and his big blue eyes studied the sister with fascination. Marc stepped back in trepidation. Lucie smiled and said, "We're here for school."

The nun smiled gently at the children. Adriana introduced us and explained that we would like to talk to the Mother Superior. There was some discussion that there was no school that day, but eventually the sister led us down a hallway. Adriana chatted away to the nun. We went through an open courtyard, where covered walkways surrounded a large grassy expanse. We walked down the passageway to the left and passed glass doors into various rooms. One room held small cots and cribs lined up. The next one served as a refectory, with child-sized tables and chairs. Another room was a playroom with toys lined up on shelves. This brought oohs and aahs from the children.

"Can we play in there, Mommy?" Lucie asked.

"I don't know. Let's wait until we talk to the *Madre Superiora*."

At the end of the covered passageway was another arched door. Our gentle guide knocked, listened and then opened the door. We were ushered into a sparse office. Behind a carved wooden table sat another nun, also in a black habit with a starched wimple. She looked up distractedly from a stack of papers. When she saw our little group, she immediately stood and came around from behind her desk. Her craggy face broke into a broad smile. She had a strong nose and wonderful, alert eyes. The little nun began to explain who we were, but Adriana interrupted her and stepped forward. She began to present our case.

The Madre Superiora listened and frowned. She looked down at Marc and Lucie, who looked up at her expectantly. She seemed to be concerned that the children spoke no Italian. Adriana kept on. More talk. More frowns. Then a smile, and the nun said, "*Va bene.*" (Okay.)

I understood that the children would start school on Monday. The school day began at 8:30 AM and lasted until 4 PM with lunch, snacks and a nap included. The financial arrangements were made, and we all shook hands. Madre Superiora patted the kids on their heads, and they beamed up at her. She had a magical aura that children naturally responded to.

I thanked and hugged Adriana when she dropped us off at our cottage. She waved me away and said she was glad to help, and that she thought the children would be happy at the asilo. That afternoon the sun came out for a few hours. I went out back and hung the damp laundry on the line. The kids played an elaborate game of house on the terrace while I swept out the cottage and washed the floors with a bucket and mop.

Before bedtime we settled down on the sofa, Marc and Lucie on each side of me and Timmy on my lap. I read a couple of stories that the children already knew well. After *Good Night Moon*, Lucie complained. "Mommy, I know this story. Don't we have any other books?"

"No, we've only got ten books in English. Once you've learned a little Italian, we can read some Italian books."

"Don't they have English books here?" Marc asked.

"No, honey. But after you've gone to your new school, you'll learn Italian and you'll like Italian books."

His face turned dark and disapproving. He made me think of his father. "I don't want everyone to speak Italian. I don't understand." He crossed his arms across his chest. He looked like a miniature Henri.

I sighed, put my arms around their shoulders and pulled them closer. "Let's read another book and then it will be time for bed." I started *Green Eggs and Ham* and pretty soon Lucie and Marc were reciting the words along with me while Timmy sucked his thumb.

Once they were all in bed, I rummaged around in one of the suitcases I hadn't completely unpacked. At the bottom, I found two blank notepads. I poured myself a glass of wine, wrapped myself in a blanket and sat down at the table. I began to write a story about a unicorn that moved to a strange land where horses and zebras lived.

They spoke a language he didn't understand and ate strange fruits from bing-bang trees. I added an ogre and developed my story.

I had never written a children's book before. I wrote novels and short stories for adults. In college, I'd had several stories published in *The Atlantic* and *The New Yorker*. My first novel had done pretty well. It was a coming-of-age story that resounded with the hippie world of the '60s. At the time, I was considered the latest sensation. I appeared on the TV morning shows and had many radio interviews. My second book came out shortly after I'd married Henri and before Lucie was born. It bombed, and I hadn't written anything since. Most days now, I was too busy with children and cooking and washing and cleaning. I felt as though my brain had dried up. But tonight, I could feel the flowering of my creative spirit.

After I'd completed my little masterpiece, I poured another glass of wine. Then I carefully printed a paragraph of the story at the top of each page. Using the children's Crayons, I did stick figure drawings to illustrate my chef-d'oeuvre. Tomorrow Lucie would have a new book. I went to bed feeling happy and relaxed.

At midnight, I was shocked awake. I had been deep in a unicorn dream of flowers and butterflies. Then I felt cold hands. Henri had pulled back the covers and was pushing up my nightgown. His hands groped my breasts and his mouth covered mine. His rancid breath tasted of garlic and alcohol.

I groaned and tried to push him away. "What are you doing?"

He had never been like this before. His lovemaking had always been controlled and predictable. Now, he was naked and breathing heavily. Without speaking he moved over and covered my body with his. Then he entered me, pumping hard into me. I whimpered, because I wasn't prepared, and it hurt. But he kept pushing and held me down with his hands squeezing my upper arms. When he'd finished, he rolled off of me and was instantly asleep. I felt as though I had been violated, raped by a stranger. I got up and went into the bathroom to wash. Back in bed, I lay trembling, clutching the edge of the bed.

Chapter 6

Sunday morning, we went to mass in the Cerro village church. It wasn't a terribly old church in European terms. It dated back to the nineteen-twenties. We sat on scratchy cane chairs. Henri and I separated the children by sitting in between them: Lucie, me, Timmy, Henri, Marc. This would avoid one child poking another and the inevitable cries. I was not a Catholic, but I had agreed to raise the children in the Catholic faith. I attended the services as a dutiful wife, but my heart wasn't in the repetitious words of the mass.

As we sat there, I glanced over at Henri. Neither one of us had mentioned last night. I felt embarrassed and angry. It hadn't been lovemaking. It had been rape, pure and simple. He sat there now looking pious and conventional. But last night, he had been a monster, taking advantage of me, like I was a whore. Now sitting there in church, I felt anger fill my mind... definitely not holy thoughts.

Henri and I had met in Paris. I spent a semester studying at the Sorbonne and met Henri in October. We took long walks along the Seine, kicking at the fallen leaves. We sat close together in cafés, smoking Gitanes and arguing existentialism and Zen metaphysics. We dined on steak frites in little bistros and drank copious amounts of red wine. We kissed under the streetlamps and always held hands. Henri was a careful lover, almost fastidious in his actions.

Who was this man who'd assaulted me last night? This morning I had bruises on my breasts like smudged fingerprints. I shuddered, remembering the feel of his hands groping me.

"Mommy, Mommy. I have to go potty," Timmy said.

"Now? Can't you wait?" I whispered.

"Now. Go now, Mommy."

I glanced at Henri. He was concentrating on the homily. I reached over and touched his arm. He shrugged me off and frowned. "Timmy has to go. I'm leaving," I whispered. I got up, balancing Timmy on my hip. I started to step over Lucie, but she got up and followed me, holding on to my skirt. I tried not to look at the disapproving parishioners as I made a beeline for the exit. As I pushed open the heavy, wooden door, I realized that Marc had followed along. With the kids in tow, I rushed towards a café across the square. But it was too late. Timmy couldn't hold it. I felt warm urine run down my dress, my legs, and sprinkle my shoes.

"Mommy, Timmy's going pee-pee all over you," Lucie screeched. Then she started to laugh and so did Marc. Timmy decided it was funny, too. We stood there in the middle of the cobblestoned piazza and laughed. Moments later, Henri appeared. He did not think it was funny. He looked around, clearly hoping no one was observing us.

"Kate, behave yourself. This is not respectable. People are looking." His French accent seemed especially strong.

Somehow this sent me off into gales of irrational laughter. The children looked up at me and they laughed, too. Timmy wiggled to get down and I placed him on the ground.

"I think you and Timothée had better walk home. I don't want that smell in the car." He grabbed Marc and Lucie's hands. "You two come with me."

But the two kids resisted. "I want to walk with Mommy," Lucie said.

"Me, too," Marc said.

"Are you sure?" I asked. "All the way down the hill and up the other side? Papa will drive you in the car."

They both nodded their assent. I glanced at Henri and shook my head in frustration. "I guess we'll walk."

He left and headed for the car. The children and I started our descent.

***

We arrived for lunch at the Peron cottage at one o'clock. We parked in a spot above the house and walked down a rocky path to an open space. The cottage resembled a chalet. It was constructed of dark wood. There was a wide terrace in front of a covered porch. Adriana's children and several other kids were playing a child's version of bocce ball with bright red and green balls. They waved to Lucie and Marc, who looked up at me as if asking permission. I shooed them towards the kids.

Adriana beckoned from an open French door. We entered directly into a long room. To the left was a staircase leading up to a balcony that ran the length of the back wall. Directly ahead was a long dining table with a kitchen beyond. To the right was a seating area and an open fireplace. A fire was smoldering, and a grate was balanced among the coals. Some chops were being grilled along with a row of mysterious yellow logs. Later, I would learn those were slices of cooked yellow polenta. In the kitchen area, two women were busy at the stove. A couple of men sat at the table with juice glasses of red wine before them; the same juice glasses we had at our cottage.

The men stood up and Adriana made the introductions. Of course, Henri already knew everyone. Both men worked at the Bianchi gelato plant in production. Adriana's husband, Giuseppe, was a small man with an open, friendly smile. He had thick dark hair that was greying at the temples. The other man was Francesco Ferrari. He had a florid complexion, thick moist lips and a rotund build. His eyes traveled over my body and then he smiled slowly. I stepped back involuntarily, as though burned with a cattle prod.

Adriana's mother was one of the women working in the kitchen. A heavier, greying version of Adriana, she had a brusque manner about her, but when it came to children she melted like a stick of butter in a hot skillet. She hugged me with one arm, wielding a wooden spoon with the other. She was stirring the *risi e bisi* that we would enjoy as a first course; a delicious creamy risotto with the addition of spring peas.

The other woman's name was Giulia. A dyed blond with dark eyes and a voluptuous body, she wore a green knit dress that accented her curves. She spoke to me slowly and loudly as though I were deaf or mentally deficient. This had happened with other people I'd met. Since my level of Italian was that of a child, I was treated like a child. And in fact, it was hard to make a potent, passionate argument with my minimal vocabulary. I smiled and responded with exaggerated slowness. Adriana looked over at me and rolled her eyes. She had already become my champion.

The children were called in for lunch and it was a raucous, joyous meal. After the risi e bisi, there were grilled meats, polenta, platters of sweet and sour cipollini, crispy lemony baby artichokes and many more sides. All of this was watered with quantities of wine poured from dark, unmarked bottles; undoubtedly from the vineyard of a second cousin of a cousin. Lucie was giggling with Chiara and eating voraciously. Marc sat quietly observing the people around the table with his dark eyes that so resembled his father's. He took small careful bites, not sure what he was consuming. Timmy walked around the table. Periodically, he was picked up and sat on La Mama's or Adriana's or my lap. He ate from everyone's plate and received lots of hugs and kisses.

After the apricot crostata, all the children left with Maria and Pietro, Adriana's two oldest, for a hike to the top of the hill. It was the first time I'd been sans children in months. After I'd helped to clear the table, La Mama and Adriana brought over espressos. The men added a generous dollop of grappa to theirs.

The men were discussing happenings at the plant. I strained to understand the gist of the conversation. There was talk about the ice cream freezers that were installed in bars and cafés in the south. I knew Gelati Bianchi provided the freezers free of charge, so the cafés would carry Bianchi ice cream bars rather than a competitor's. From what I could glean from the conversations, the Mafiosi who owned many of these establishments were demanding that Bianchi pay a fee for the placement of the freezers. As I understood it, there was little chance of negotiating with the Mafia. Apparently, Giancarlo Bianchi was furious and had spent Friday raging around the plant.

They discussed Giancarlo, who they seemed to admire as well as fear. He ran that place like a warlord. I turned to listen to Giulia and La Mama, who were discussing the children and the end of the school year. I listened abstractedly with one ear while still paying attention to the men's conversation. Henri was so close-mouthed that I felt I knew little about his job. I thought he might share more if I was more in the loop. Francesco was laughing and banging Henri on the back, his eyes gleaming with sly malevolence. Henri looked proud and then blushed when he saw I was frowning at him. Giuseppe looked uncomfortably at me. Then Adriana was at my side.

"Let's take a walk up the hill to find the children. Have you been up to the chapel?" she asked. "*Andiamo.*"

Giulia stayed behind. She was wearing stiletto heels and wouldn't be comfortable walking. I pulled on a heavy sweater and we left the house. The weather had cleared that morning and it was a sunny, cool afternoon. I told Adriana that we'd never walked up our hill before; always down and up, towards the village. She told me our hill had a name: Monte della Croce, because in the past there had been a wooden cross at the top. In the 1900s, Pope Leo XIII had agreed to the construction of a small church in that spot. It was dedicated to Christ the Redeemer. She described the carved wooden door that led inside to a tiny chapel. Behind the altar was a stairway that led to a balcony at the top, from which you could see Verona along the Adige River. On a clear day the Lago di Garda and even the Apennine Mountains were visible in the distance.

I nodded as we trudged up the incline. When she'd finished her explanation, I smiled. Then I changed the subject. "Does Giuseppe like working at Gelati Bianchi?"

"Yes, it is a good place to work. Good work conditions, good salary and Giuseppe feels that his job is secure." Adriana wasn't even breathing hard as we walked steadily upwards.

"Good," I said, and then tried to think how I would word my next question. "Does Giuseppe come home late?"

"Not usually, only if there's a problem with the equipment." At least, that's what I thought she said.

"Henri always comes home very late," I tried to say, fumbling my words. I stopped walking and took some deep breaths.

She frowned and said gently, "Giuseppe works in the factory. I think Giancarlo Bianchi requires the administrators to stay late."

"What do they do, so late?"

She began to walk again. "I don't know. You must ask your husband." I could tell she didn't want to continue this conversation.

We came around a bend and arrived at the top of Monte della Croce. There was a wide grassy area surrounding a small tower constructed of white stones. This must be the chapel. We found the older children hopping on a series of large rocks, playing King of the Mountain. Maria was tossing a ball with Timmy and Giulia's little girl. My children were having a wonderful time.

Chapter 7

The next few weeks took on a rhythm. Every morning Henri left before the children awoke. Later, when they were dressed, we had breakfast and left for the asilo. Unfortunately, it rained almost every day. I covered Timmy in plastic bags while he sat in the stroller. Lucie and Marc walked, hopped and skipped all the way. They never complained about the hike.

I learned that the little nun who welcomed us was Suor Maria Angelica. Both children beamed up at her when the door swung open. I never got a clear picture of what they did in that school, but the children were happy to be there. Having only Timmy home all day was both a blessing and a curse. Usually after I dropped off the older two, we went up the hill into the village where I would do a little shopping. Then we headed home. Timmy was only able to entertain himself for a short while. Then he would want me to play with him or read to him. What I wouldn't have given for an hour of *Sesame Street*. After lunch he took a nap, and I sat down and wrote children's stories or cooked. I'd been trying out new recipes from an Italian magazine. Using my dictionary, I translated the instructions. One day I even managed to bake some chocolate chip cookies from memory, since I didn't have a cookbook.

I remember one particularly wet, grey day. I arrived at the small grocery store after dropping off the older children. There were three crones standing together gossiping. When I entered with Timmy in my arms, all conversation stopped. In my memory the old women were all dressed in black with sturdy shoes. For a moment they evaluated *la signora Americana*. I ventured a smile. Then I asked the proprietor of the shop, in my best Italian: "How do you make minestrone?" Oh, my goodness, talk about the perfect icebreaker! There was an explosion of chitter-chatter from the crones:

"Signora, you start with onions, then add carrots, chopped fine and celery."

"I always put fava beans."

"Canned whole tomatoes."

"No, you need to use pureed tomatoes."

"I always begin with pancetta."

It went on like that for quite a while. They all wanted to help me and pretty soon they were passing Timmy around from one set of arms to another while he was happily licking a lollypop.

"*Che bel bambino.*" (What a beautiful little boy.)

I left the shop with bags of vegetables, a convoluted minestrone recipe and three new friends.

***

I grew used to being alone in the evenings. I relished the time to read or write without being disturbed. Once I'd closed and fastened the shutters and locked the front door, I felt safe. One evening, shortly after the children had fallen asleep, I rolled up in a blanket on the sofa, and began a short story about Glenda the frog. Glenda's back legs were too short, and she couldn't jump as far as her brothers and sisters. This caused embarrassment and unhappiness.

I was so involved with Glenda's problems that I didn't hear footsteps on the metal staircase outside. A knock on the door made me drop my pencil in surprise. Who could it be? Had Henri lost his key? I pushed off the blanket and hurried to the door. "Henri is that you?"

"*Buona sera*, signora. *É* Francesco...Francesco Ferrari," a deep voice responded.

Why would Francesco be here? *Something must have happened to Henri.* I yanked open the door. "Has something happened?"

Francesco was leaning against the door frame, dressed in a wrinkled suit, his tie loosened at the neck. There was a smirk on his flat face. To me at that moment he looked like one of Glenda's frog relatives, with his heavy-lidded bulging eyes and moist, thick lips. He slowly looked me up and down. I was barefoot, wearing jeans and a sweater, but he made me feel naked.

"No, signora, I came for a little visit, since I know Henri is very busy these days. You must be lonely."

"No, I'm fine...not lonely at all." I stood in the doorway, blocking his entrance.

"I brought a good bottle of wine. I thought we could have a glass." He held up the bottle.

"That was very thoughtful of you, but I don't really want a drink at this hour." I still hadn't moved from the door.

"Signora, I've come all this way. Let's sit down, have a glass of wine, then I'll go home."

What should I do? I didn't trust this man, but if Henri knew I hadn't been polite and invited Francesco in, he might be upset. I'd got the feeling Francesco was important to Henri's work. Finally, I relented. "Please come in."

Francesco stepped across the threshold and looked around. I suddenly felt embarrassed. There were toys on the floor, picture books on the sofa and dirty dinner dishes on the table. I hadn't gotten around to cleaning up yet. I rushed to the table, gathered the plates and piled them in the kitchen sink, making excuses all the while. Francesco followed me into the tiny kitchen, carrying the children's drinking glasses. He brushed up against me as he placed the glasses beside the sink. I cringed with distaste and moved away.

"Where would I find a bottle opener?" he asked.

I opened the drawer and handed it to him. While he pulled out the cork, I found two clean juice glasses. He poured each of us a full glass of wine. Henri wouldn't have approved of that. Wine should only reach halfway up the sides of a glass. But I guessed Francesco was not into niceties.

He walked over to the sofa and pushed the blanket to the side. I hastened to pick up the books and my notebook. Then I folded the blanket and put it on a chair. I could feel Francesco's eyes on me as I crossed the room. I took my glass and pulled out a chair on the other side of the table.

He patted the sofa. "Why don't you sit here. It's more comfortable."

Was this really happening? I was filled with disgust and a tinge of fear. I was alone with this man. What would I do if he tried to rape me?

"I'm very comfortable here. Thank you." I swept some breadcrumbs into my hand.

"Do you like living here? It's very primitive." He critically appraised the simple furnishings.

"It's fine for the summer. The children are happy." With my hands, I nervously smoothed out the wrinkles in the tablecloth.

"Come on, Kate. It's Kate, right?" Come over here and sit with me. Leave that tablecloth alone." He chuckled. "Do I make you nervous?"

"Yes, you do." I held my hands tight in my lap.

"I bet I can calm you down." His voice was low and sensual.

I looked over at him. He had downed his wine and was licking his lips. I shivered in disgust. He got up, went into the kitchen and filled his glass again. Then he came over to the table and put the glass down. He moved behind me, and suddenly I was filled with horror and fear. I would not let him touch me. I pushed back my chair, almost knocking him over, then I said in a hoarse whisper, "Get out of my house. Get away from me. Otherwise I'll tell Giancarlo Bianchi that you've attacked me."

He held up his hands and started to laugh, "Signora, calm down. It's nothing. I'll leave now if you wish."

"Yes, I wish…"

Moments later he was out the door. I fumbled with the lock and then I stood trembling, rubbing my forearms. From then on in the evenings, I kept the French rolling pin by my side. It would be almost as good a weapon as a baseball bat.

Chapter 8

The children had been enrolled in the nursery school for only a couple of weeks when they told me they'd been invited to a birthday party. At first, I didn't believe them. How could they understand a party invitation, when they spoke practically no Italian? When did they learn the word *compleanno* (birthday), and who would have invited them?

Later, when we got home, a short, heavyset woman with three children showed up at the gate. Her name was Gabriella Gallo. She wore work clothes and heavy boots, and had an open, honest face. The children all looked like their mother, with hazel eyes, light brown hair and shy smiles. My children were hopping around with excitement.

I invited them inside, but Gabriella said they had to get going. She reiterated the invitation for a birthday party the following afternoon, including Timmy and me. It was a celebration for the middle daughter, who would be six. I figured the older son must be about eight and the little boy was maybe four, like Marc.

"Where do you live?" I asked.

"Up there, the house right above yours." She pointed up the hill to the chalet, where I remembered seeing movement on the balcony that stretched along the front of the house.

The next day was Saturday, so the children were home from the *asilo*. In the morning, we walked up into the village and went to the *libreria* that sold newspapers and books. We bought a couple of children's books and a packet of Perugina chocolates. Back at home, they kept asking me what time it was. For them and for me, the morning seemed to crawl by. At last, three o'clock arrived and we set off. We climbed the hill towards the Redeemer Chapel Tower but veered off to the left halfway up. The kids weren't complaining about the hike…they were getting used to walking up steep hills. From the lane, we could look up at the chalet projecting out over us. The three Gallo children stood on the balcony, waving and shouting. Marc and Lucie started to run.

We entered the house by a side door off the driveway. Since the chalet was built on a sharp incline, the basement was fully above ground. The next floor where we entered had a kitchen at the back that looked out at ground level. The windows of the spacious family room in front framed the snow-covered mountains in the distance. A balcony wrapped around the façade. In front of the windows were several bamboo cages with parakeets and canaries flittering and chirping. My children were immediately drawn to the colorful birds. The other kids stood together, smiling shyly.

On a long wooden table was a simple, round yellow cake with six candles along with two bottles of orange pop. We gathered around the table and sang the familiar *Happy Birthday* tune in English and Italian: "*Tanti auguri a te…*" We fumbled with the words and laughed. I think the cake was made from polenta flour with the addition of currants. It was not super sweet and had a pleasing graininess.

Afterwards, the kids left to play. Along with the chirping birds, we learned there was a basket of puppies in the basement. My kids were in heaven. Gabriella and I had coffee and made an effort to communicate. I learned that she and her husband had an egg business. Somewhere around the other side of Monte della Croce, they owned a piece of land where there were hangars filled with hundreds of chickens. They gathered the eggs and sold them to shops in Verona. I believe neither she nor her husband had much formal education. They came from simple peasant stock but were clever and hardworking and had built themselves a thriving business.

I told her about Chicago and our life in the suburbs. Like many Italians, at that time, Chicago to Gabriella meant Al Capone, gangsters and crime. I explained about the beaches along Lake Michigan and the beautiful Chicago skyline. All this meant nothing to somebody who had lived their entire life in Cerro Veronese with short trips down to Verona. What I admired about Gabriella was that she did not have a provincial closed mind, but always seemed ready to learn something new.

The following Saturday, we were invited to visit the chicken farm. It was a mild day with no rain. The kids wore their blue windbreakers. I had on a cotton dress, sweater, raincoat and the brown leather hiking boots Adriana had leant me. They were well-worn and had belonged to her husband; not very elegant, but they fit with heavy socks. We hiked to the farm, taking a path around the back of our hill. The children were filled with excitement and gamboled along like baby lambs. We met Gabriella's family at an old abandoned farmhouse, a small cottage built of dark wood with only a few rooms. This was the original Gallo farmstead. Inside the dilapidated kitchen, I met Gabriella's husband, Matteo Gallo. He was short and stocky with a thatch of black hair that flopped down across his forehead.

After introductions, I was offered an espresso with a shot of grappa. I declined the grappa, but the espresso, prepared on the wood-burning stove, might have been the best I ever had. As we sipped our coffee, we chatted quietly. Matteo had a low, rumbly voice. When you talked with him, you found yourself speaking just above a whisper. I remember us laughing about their last name. *Gallo* means cockerel in Italian—perfect for a family that deals in chickens and eggs.

After coffee, we headed for the long hangars that housed the chickens. The hens were squeezed into tight pens, perhaps two or three chickens per pen. They all wore tiny blinders, so they couldn't peck at each other. A conveyor belt with chicken feed rolled along in front of their cages. Another conveyor belt underneath the cages carried away the feces. The noise was unbelievable. We all pitched in. Lucie and Marc helped gather the eggs with the other children. I helped Gabriella with a new shipment of baby chicks. Each one had to be picked up and held firmly while eyedrops were administered in each eye. I can still recall in horror the smell, the racket and the inhumane treatment of those poor chickens. It was the first time I'd observed industrial farming.

In spite of that, we came home with a dozen eggs, individually wrapped in newspaper, as well as a cut-up chicken. I had learned that after about a year and a half, the chickens no longer laid an acceptable quantity of eggs and so they were sold for meat. When the children were back outside, Gabriella killed the chicken, cleaned it and chopped it into pieces. She wrapped it in more newsprint and handed it to me with a big smile.

Chapter 9

The Sunday after our chicken farm expedition, we drove to church. Happily, the children were well behaved. Afterward, we did some shopping. I particularly wanted to purchase heavy items like potatoes, milk, and food in cans and jars. The trip home in the car, down the village hill and up Monte della Croce, was heaven. Usually it took us about thirty minutes walking if no one balked or cried, so, the five-minute car ride was a breeze.

For Sunday lunch, I fried the chicken pieces and made mashed potatoes. I never actually said what was on the menu. The kids picked up their crunchy pieces and ate appreciatively. I didn't want them to connect these tasty morsels with those poor chickens we'd seen the day before. Henri tut-tutted at their table manners. Usually I insisted that the older two use a fork or spoon, but fried chicken seemed different.

Being French, Henri was horrified by the fact that Americans sometimes picked up their food with their fingers. He was a master with his fork and knife. He even ate hamburgers with silverware. As he carefully deboned his piece of breast meat, he listened to the children talk about their trip to the chicken farm.

He turned to me. "Who are these people you're frequenting?"

I explained how I had met Gabriella, and about the birthday party.

"They don't sound like educated people. Should our children frequent their offspring?" Henri took a sip of wine.

"They're really nice, Papa," Lucie said.

"They have lots of chickens," Marc said.

"Yes, and puppies and canaries," Lucie added.

"I like puppies. I love puppies," Timmy said.

"I love puppies, too," Marc said while chewing a big bite of chicken.

Henri looked at him with revulsion. "Marc, you're disgusting. Please close your mouth when you are eating."

Marc immediately turned red with embarrassment. He was the most sensitive to Henri's disapproval, and this comment sliced through him like a knife. He dropped his chicken leg on his plate, got up and ran outside.

"Marc, come back here immediately!" Henri roared. He got up, pushing back his chair so hard it fell to the floor. He rushed to the open door, but Marc was already down the stairs and out into the lane. Henri came back, picked up his chair and sat down.

I sighed. "You've got to be a little more sensitive with him. He takes everything to heart."

"Sensitive? Really, Kate? If I didn't discipline these children, they would be running wild."

"I agree that learning good manners is important, but we were having a pleasant lunch. You ruined it."

"I ruined it? These unmannered children are the problem. You need to take them in hand." He took a small, neat bite of chicken and chewed slowly…his mouth closed.

Lucie was barely eating now. She was frozen, staring down at her plate. Timmy seemed oblivious to what was happening. He stirred his mashed potatoes with his spoon and sang to himself, "Puppies, puppies, I love puppies."

***

After lunch I put Timmy down for his nap. Then I did the dishes with Lucie's help. Marc hadn't returned, and I was worried about him.

"Henri, maybe you could go look for Marc? He still isn't back."

"He will be home soon. Let him cool down and then he can come and apologize to me."

"I don't know. It looks like it might start to rain again."

"Not now. I need you here, Kate."

Henri was seated at the dining room table with my ledger open before him. He had learned from his father that a good way to control household finances was to write down every expense. Each week, he gave me a sum of money, and I was expected to account for it in my ledger. Each Sunday, we sat down and went through my expenditures.

I hated the entire process, but I was a wimp. I never complained. Each day, I attempted to dutifully write down every loaf of bread or can of tomatoes, but I was lax and forgetful. Usually, I tried to make shopping lists and when I got home, I would know what I bought.

53

But half the time, shopping in the village, I couldn't make out the price of each item and the shopkeepers would mumble something unintelligible when I asked.

"What's this here? More milk?" Henri asked. "That seems like a lot this week."

"Oh, I made pudding. That takes four cups of milk."

"What's this?"

I stared at the scribble, trying to make it out. "Oh, that's for me...a feminine item." I knew Henri didn't want to hear about tampons.

We continued down the list of items and numbers. I knew my mother-in-law had to go through this same process. She told me once how she would fudge the numbers, so she'd have a secret stash of cash.

After that, Henri started to yawn. He needed his Sunday nap after being out late every night that week. I was feeling panicked about Marc, who still wasn't back. It had started to drizzle again, and he had run off in a tee-shirt and shorts. Lucie was seated on the sofa with a coloring book, filling in a drawing of Disney's Cinderella.

"Lucie, where do you think Marc could have gone? Do you have any idea?"

"Maybe he went up to see the puppies. Remember we were talking about puppies?"

"Okay, I'm going to hike up to Gabriella's and see if he's there." I pulled on my raincoat and started down the stairs. Before going out into the lane, I looked in the garage. Then I checked out the downstairs bedroom and bath. No Marc. On the way back outside, I glanced into the car. There he was, curled up on the back seat, fast asleep. He looked so small and fragile. His straight dark hair fell across his forehead and his dark lashes lay against his pale cheeks. Here was a beautiful, sleeping angel. Why couldn't his Papa relent and give him the love and approbation he so craved? I think I realized then that Henri projected his own fears and weaknesses onto his oldest son. He couldn't face what he saw.

Chapter 10

On July first, summer arrived right on schedule. It was suddenly warm and sunny every day. The children were out of school and things became slower and more relaxed. We had begun to settle into our mountain life. The children slept later and awoke to a lazy breakfast. In the mornings, they played around the house while I did housework. In the afternoon, we were out and about. Adriana Peron worked for a government agency and she stayed down in Verona during the week, as did her husband. Her mother, La Mama, moved to Cerro for the summer with her grandchildren. Some days, she and I took all the children for a hike to a mountain stream or up the hill to the chapel.

On Wednesdays, we met at the crossroads and went up into the village to shop at the market. The children giggled and raced each other. With the influx of vacationers, the village had taken on a new life. The quiet, empty streets were bustling with summer people. The shutters on the summer cottages were flung open and we heard laughter and music when we walked by. All the shops overflowed with merchandise. At the *Frutta e Verdura* shop, there was a large variety of fresh vegetables and small baskets of strawberries. The *Formaggeria/Latteria* had an abundant selection of cheeses and fresh milk. Pastries appeared in the *Panificcio/Pasticceria*, a shop that had only carried a few loaves of bread previously. People strolled on the main piazza or enjoyed an *aperitivo* seated in the sun. Cerro was an entirely different place from when we'd arrived in the rainy month of May.

La Mama had a sort of basket with wheels that she filled with groceries, and I had my stroller. As we went up and down the aisles of the market, she would suggest I buy certain unfamiliar vegetables and later she would explain how to prepare them. In the '70s, no one in the States had ever seen a red, sweet pepper. We only had green peppers back then. I was likewise unfamiliar with fennel or baby artichokes. Sometimes after our shopping adventure we would go back to the Perons' cottage and broil and sweat red peppers; or stuff zucchini with breadcrumbs, sausage and cheese; or prepare a Caprese salad or a platter of gnocchi. Then we would eat an early dinner. Afterwards, the children and I would walk home slowly in the waning light.

La Mama was a quiet person who exuded strength and calm. Being around her was like a soothing balm. She never asked me anything personal, but I found myself talking to her about my life, about the children, about my writing. I never mentioned Henri and she never asked about him. Sometimes I asked her advice. Her response was delivered with a dry sense of humor.

I remember I was frustrated with Timmy, who still needed diapers. I was having no success in potty-training him. She said, "How many twenty-year-olds, do you know, who still wear diapers? I wouldn't worry about it."

57

That made me chuckle. I just needed to put things in perspective.

***

Gabriella was not available that often. She and Matteo had their business to run. They usually took their children to the chicken barns during the day. The kids helped with the work and played there.

I invited them over for the day about once a week. They all played quite nicely. We had very few toys, but the children played for hours with sticks, pebbles, balls, paper and crayons. The downstairs bedroom became a store, a school or a house. I marveled at their creative imaginations. Poppies grew in profusion in our backyard. The children learned to peel away the outer petals. Then they pressed the black stigma at the center of the flower to the back of their hands or their cheeks, where it formed an intricate black stamp.

Sometimes, when Gabriella came back early, we would all climb the hill and hang out on the grassy area around the Redeemer Chapel Tower. I would bring chocolate sandwiches and lemonade and a blanket. Gabriella and I would knit and talk while the kids played.

I remember one heated political conversation. Gabriella and her husband were staunch Communists, and fully believed in the Marxist doctrine. Since they had been brought up living in near poverty, they saw the Communist ideology of economic equality through the elimination of private property as the necessary future of the country. It was incredible to me, because they were the poster children for a capitalist success story. Together they had grown a small chicken and egg business into a thriving affair. They sold the eggs and when the hens were no longer producing at an acceptable rate, they sold them for meat. I believe this sort of production was new in Italy at the time.

But Gabriella couldn't see herself as a member of the Christian Democrats, who'd been in power in Italy since WWII and the fall of Mussolini. The regime was often criticized for its financial scandals and corrupt politicians. To Gabriella they represented the lazy, entitled rich.

***

One day, Lucie came to complain about Marc. They were playing hide and seek among the rocks. Marc had disappeared and none of them could find him.

"He's cheating, Mommy. We've been calling, but he doesn't answer."

Feeling panicked, I jumped up, as did Gabriella. We started calling and hunting around. The only real danger was if Marc had tried to hide across the field, where there was a cliff and a sharp drop. I ran that way, hoping against hope that he hadn't fallen. Thankfully, when I looked over the edge, there was no little body clutching at the scrub grass.

Apart from the crevasses among the rocks, there really weren't many places to hide. Could he have run home because he was angry? We looked everywhere, and I grew more and more upset. Could someone have whisked him away? We'd seen a couple of hikers who were up there to enjoy the view of the mountains. But that had been some time ago.

We decided to start home and see if he was there. If worse came to worst, we could call the *polizia* from Gabriella's house. She had a phone. The children were quietly standing around looking worried. As I gathered up the blanket and my bag, I thought I heard Marc crying.

"Do you hear that? It's Marc. He's crying. We have to find him," I said to the other kids.

Gabriella headed over towards the chapel tower. Moments later, she beckoned to me. *"Vieni qui! È Marco."* (Come here. It's Marc.)

I rushed over to the door of the chapel. Now, I could hear Marc distinctly. The sound of his sobs made me happy and angry. "Come out now, Marc. You scared me to death," I yelled.

More sobs. "I can't get out. The door won't open."

I studied the wooden door. Its carved keyhole was large enough for a big, old-fashioned key. "How did you get in there?" I asked, with some irritation.

"I just pushed something with my finger and the door opened up." More sobs.

I studied the keyhole. He must have stuck his skinny little finger in the hole and pushed the bolt or latch. I thought for a second, and then I ran back and got a knitting needle. With some jiggling, I managed to push back the bolt and open the door. Marc fell into my arms. I hugged him and kissed the top of his head.

"Marc, don't you ever do that again." I choked back tears of relief and held him tight.

60

Chapter 11   2019

As the jet drones on towards Italy, I am unable to concentrate on the book on my iPad. My mind keeps wandering to the past. This seems to happen more and more lately. This trip is unearthing painful memories that I'd buried deep in my psyche.

I glance over at Lucie. She's fallen asleep, her mouth slightly open, her face relaxed. It isn't often I see her like this. The whimsical little girl who escaped into daydreams is an ardent activist these days. The current US government seems oblivious to climate change and the state of our planet. Lucie works tirelessly, trying to educate the nation about rising tides and polluted water. She's crisscrossed the country, speaking at schools, Rotary Clubs, women's groups and rallies. The rare times we've gotten together for lunch, she was rushed and tense. There was always a problem at work or at home that required her attention. Deep worry lines had forged their way between her brows. But now as she sleeps, her face looks smooth and lovely.

Lucie is married to Robert, a tall, skinny redhead. As a journalist, he travels the globe and reports on injustices around the world. He also runs a blog read by millions, dealing with human rights abuses. Robert is as passionate as his wife about his sphere of interest. He champions the underdog and writes with poignant fury. When they're together, Lucie and Robert argue incessantly, but never with malice. Fellow crusaders fill the house when they are home. It's a lively, intense and exhausting atmosphere. I can only take it for a short period of time.

Lucie's daughter, Chelsea, is a dreamer just like her mom was as a girl. At thirteen, Chelsea is tall and skinny like her dad, with thick strawberry blond hair and a sprinkling of freckles across her perfect nose. She's painfully unsure of herself and escapes to her bedroom when the house is vibrating with noise and people. Whenever she visits me, we curl up at each end of the sofa, drink tea and read, looking up now and then to smile at each other. Lucie loves her daughter, but she doesn't understand her. Chelsea's passivity annoys her. She feels the girl has no backbone and will never succeed in this world that requires fighting life's battles. Privately, I wonder if Chelsea's found a way to retreat from the constant upheaval that surrounds her.

Carson, Lucie's son, is a senior in high school. Tall, handsome and athletic, he's set to graduate at the top of his class. Several Ivy League schools sent him acceptance letters, and he's debating which college to choose. Carson is articulate and charismatic, qualities he uses as President of the Conservative Club at his school. Both Lucie and Robert were incensed at that: a conservative! How could their son embrace these archaic and static policies? At home, they argue with him constantly and he very effectively defends his views. Again, I think Carson has found a way to successfully navigate his world. His parents want him to think for himself...but to embrace their world view. In his independence, I think he longs for a more secure, more predictable and unilinear world. He makes

62

me think of Alex Keaton, the conservative kid on the show Family Ties *that was popular back in the '80s. I smile, remembering a quote from that show when the parents were discussing their conservative business-oriented son. It went something like, "Do you think maybe he was switched at birth and the Rockefellers have our kid?" Lucie and Robert could have uttered the same words.*

I lean back in my seat and close my eyes. Chelsea's sweet smile floats through my mind like a delicate butterfly.

Chapter 12

In the first week of August, Henri's parents arrived for a week-long visit. In the days before their arrival, I scrubbed and cleaned the downstairs bedroom and bath. I had let the children play down there and it needed a good once-over. The morning of their arrival, Lucie and I picked a big bunch of wildflowers. I placed some in a glass on the small table in their bedroom and another bunch in a blue pitcher on the dining room table.

They arrived at four in the afternoon. The children were bathed and nicely dressed. Lucie was wearing her favorite pink sundress and the boys were in shorts and pressed shirts. Henri had come home for lunch and strutted around the house inspecting our tiny domain. We were all excited. When the Peugeot appeared at our gate, Marc and Lucie ran down the stairs and Timmy toddled along behind, holding my hand. Henri raced down and pulled open the gate.

Henri's mother was out of the car in a flash. Françoise was a thin, elegant woman who exuded energy. Her dark hair was worn in a smooth French chignon. Her deep-set dark eyes glowed with life. She had a strict sense of proper decorum; but she was also quick to laugh and quick to anger. The children adored her. I think that was because she adored them. Françoise and Lucie seemed to share a special bond; although it was Marc who most resembled his grandmother physically with his straight dark hair, deep-set eyes and pallid skin. Lucie and Timmy had strawberry blond hair like me, blue-green eyes and rosy skin.

After Françoise hugged each of the children, she kissed Henri on both cheeks and hugged him briefly. Then she stepped back, holding him by the shoulders. She looked at him critically.

"You don't look well, Henri. Are you eating enough? Are you working too much?"

"*Non, Maman.* I'm feeling fine. I'm working hard but things are going well," he responded in French.

I looked over at Henri. In fact, she was right. His normally pale skin looked sallow in the bright sunshine. His eyes were shadowed with dark circles. In the last few weeks, I had rarely looked right at him. He was rarely home. He went to bed late and slept little. I assumed he ate well, going out to restaurants every night. What did I know? We were living separate lives in tandem, on parallel tracks.

Françoise gave me a hug and patted my cheek. "I am here to enjoy the Italian sunshine and help you out."

"We are all thrilled to have you. The children love their *Bonnemaman* and *Bonpapa*," I gushed.

Benoît, Henri's father, stood by the car. He smiled at me and we gave each other a three-cheek air kiss. Then he patted the children on their heads. "We found your house without a problem. This Michelin Guide did the trick." He held up the familiar dark, green guidebook.

Henri came around and hugged his father. "That's good. I thought you might get lost on the way up here. It's tricky."

Benoît looked critically at our cottage and inspected the surroundings. He was a quiet, thoughtful soul. As a history professor at the Sorbonne, he lived a life of study, reading and writing. When we visited their Paris apartment, he was usually hidden away in his office. With a receding hairline and curved shoulders, he looked older than he was. He always wore a comfortably worn suit and tie. His glasses were perched on the tip of his nose. He was Central Casting's archetype of the quintessential absentminded professor.

Françoise bent down and picked Timmy up, giving him a hug. Lucie took her hand and pulled her towards the downstairs bedroom. Henri and Benoît got the suitcases out of the car and followed them through the garage.

We had dinner at seven with the children. With suggestions from La Mama, the day before, I had prepared an antipasto platter, a creamy pasta dish, a green salad and peaches with sweetened mascarpone. Benoît ate with pleasure, but I don't think Françoise liked the pasta. Perhaps it was too heavy. The children were on their best behavior and, except for Timmy, they ate relatively neatly.

While I put the children to bed, Françoise did the dishes and the men talked. Both father and son worked hard to relate to each other. I don't think either one understood or cared about their different occupations. Henri had told me how much he'd hated his father's eternal lectures on the Renaissance or the Hundred Years' War when he was a child. On the other hand, his father was at a loss where company finances and marketing were concerned.

When I came back into the main room, Françoise had prepared coffee and Benoît had produced a bottle of Armagnac, his favorite *digestif*. He poured himself and Henri a small amount in clean juice glasses. When I saw the spotless kitchen, I thanked Françoise profusely. Then we both sat down. I poured coffee for Françoise and myself and added a lump of sugar to each of the cups.

Henri cleared his throat, "Papa, Maman, I'm hoping you can help us out next week."

"*Bien sur, mon chéri,*" Françoise said as she stirred her espresso.

I looked up at Henri questioningly. What was he proposing?

"We need to find an apartment in Verona for this fall. Lucie will be beginning school."

Both of his parents were frowning. I was perplexed and wondering where this was going.

"I've spoken to people at the plant. The best way to find a suitable apartment is to go door to door and talk to the doorman. They tell me he will know what is available in his building." Henri was leaning forward, wearing his most charming smile.

"How will you do that? You're too busy at the plant," I said.

"You're right, Kate. I can't take the time, but you can…if Maman will watch the kids." He avoided my eyes.

I glanced at Françoise. "I think that's asking a lot of your mother."

She was feeling energized. I could tell. She would like nothing better than to take over my children and my home. "I would be happy to help," she said.

I felt at a disadvantage. Henri had sprung this on his parents without even discussing it with me. "How am I going to get down to Verona every day, and where will I look for these apartments? I don't know the city at all." I could feel my face turning crimson.

Henri turned to his father. "Papa, I know this is asking a lot, but I wondered if you could drive Kate down to the city. I know you would love to visit the churches and historical monuments in Verona. There's the Piazza delle Erbe, the Arena and the Duomo…"

"Can't we find a realtor to help us? This sounds crazy, wandering the streets and knocking on doors." My voice had risen an octave.

In an annoyingly calm voice, Henri said, "People at the plant have given me a list of street names and neighborhoods. I've got it all marked out on a map."

I rolled my eyes.

"Now, Kathrine, you can certainly do this for Henri. He is far too busy at the factory to spend time searching for an apartment." Françoise patted my hand and smiled.

"Besides, you have been complaining that you're stuck here with the kids all day. This is a chance to escape. You should be grateful that my parents are willing to help," Henri said sarcastically.

"You have me here to take care of the children. It will give me such pleasure." Françoise patted my hand again.

I felt like yanking it away. "Of course, I am grateful for your help, but this method of apartment hunting seems ridiculous." I glowered at Henri.

"You need to adapt, my dear. When in Rome...or when in Verona." Françoise laughed at her little joke.

I looked over at Benoît. "Is this all right with you? Do you want to spend the day in Verona?"

"Yes, I think this is an excellent plan." Benoît rubbed his hands together in anticipation of visiting all the churches in Verona.

Chapter 13

We left at nine o'clock the next morning. I had studied the marked map and found two adjacent neighborhoods. I would begin my search there. Benoît dropped me off on a corner across from a nice-looking restaurant. We agreed to meet at the restaurant at one o'clock. I knew that all the shops would be closed from one to four. People took a leisurely lunch and perhaps a siesta. It would be inappropriate to bother a doorman during this three-hour break.

I set off. I entered a building and knocked on the glassed-in cage where the *portinaio* was located. I had practiced my request at home. I asked if there was an apartment available for a family of five. We needed three bedrooms, etc. The first fellow frowned at my accent and said there was nothing. Then he shut the door. Maybe he didn't like Americans? Maybe I hadn't made myself clear. I knocked on the door again. I could see him inside, sitting on a padded chair and reading the newspaper. With annoyance, he stood up and came to the door again.

"*Scusi, signore.* Do you know of any apartments available in the area?" I asked.

He frowned, rubbed his chin with his puffy hand. Then he said, "Maybe down at Number 53."

I continued down the street. There was nothing at 53 or 55 or 57. I was told over and over that there was nothing available. At twelve-thirty, I was back at the restaurant. I found a table in the shade and flopped down. I felt bushed and dejected. My apartment search was going nowhere. I ordered a Campari and soda and waited for Benoit. He arrived a few minutes later. We ordered lunch and Benoît entertained me with descriptions of the monuments and churches he had seen. He read from the Michelin Guide and added interesting tidbits.

I had rarely been alone with him. When Françoise was around, she controlled the conversation. With just the two of us, Benoît was voluble and entertaining. After lunch we strolled to a small chapel, the Santa Maria Antica chapel. Originally built in the 8th century, and rebuilt after an earthquake in the 12th, it was a gem. Then I took off in another direction, refreshed and ready to attack; but my afternoon was no more successful than the morning.

On the way home, we discussed my pitch. I didn't think it was *what* I said, but maybe because I was foreign. Then I thought about the expressions of all the doormen I'd talked to. I really felt they were telling the truth. There was nothing available.

When we got home, it was seven-thirty. The children were bathed and in their pajamas. They were just finishing their yogurt and fruit when we walked in. Françoise had everything under control. The children beamed up at me, but no one hopped up and rushed over to jump in my arms. They had barely missed me. I felt a little disgruntled, where I should have felt grateful. Françoise insisted on

71

putting them to bed while I set the table. The kids went down without a whimper.

Of course, Françoise had prepared a perfect meal: melon, followed by a lovely veal roast, crispy potatoes, perfectly cooked green beans and a crème caramel, Henri's favorite. How had she prepared all this and entertained the children? I felt like a total failure in comparison.

***

The following day was much the same. Benoît dropped me off in another neighborhood and we met for lunch. I visited one very dark and depressing apartment that would never do. As the afternoon drew to a close, I felt increasingly depressed. This house-hunting routine seemed incredibly ineffective.

That night, Henri did not come home for dinner. Françoise, Benoît and I had a quiet dinner together once the children were in bed. Françoise filled me in on all the family gossip. There was Henri's sister, Marie-Claire, who still wasn't married at thirty-five. Françoise was concerned that her daughter would never produce grandchildren. Marie-Claire worked in the bowels of the Louvre. From what I understood, she managed and cataloged specific parts of the museum's collection. She lived in a small studio on the other side of Paris and rarely visited her parents. I knew something was amiss there, but I'd never gotten to the heart of it.

Henri's brother, Jean-Pierre, was married to Claude. They had produced two perfect children, Martine and Laure. The girls were older than my three and from what Françoise reported, they were impeccable young ladies: attractive, well-mannered and straight-A students. That evening I heard a lot about what a wonderful mother Claude was. The message was that it would behoove me to follow her pristine example.

Henri's grandmother, Suzanne, was in a nursing home and suffered from dementia. I knew she and Françoise had never gotten along. Benoît had been his mother's pride and joy, and neither woman wanted to share him. In addition, during WWII they had lived together in the country when it was nearly impossible to find food, clothing or basic household goods. I'm sure this caused incredible stress.

More important, during the war, they had been on opposite sides of the Vichy-De Gaulle debate. The Vichy government at the time was a puppet of the Nazis. Suzanne felt it was important to get along with the Germans and she trusted Maréchal Pétain, who had been a leader in WWI. Françoise, on the other hand, had been active in the Resistance. She had even hidden a British pilot who'd been downed in the woods nearby. That fiery difference of opinion still smoldered years later.

That night, Françoise talked about how hard it was to find the time to visit her mother-in-law, and besides, Suzanne didn't even remember her. Benoît was quiet as a clam.

Françoise turned to him. "It's really up to you. This is your mother. You should be visiting her. Not me."

As she talked, I could see Benoît shrinking into himself. He was not a man to argue and I could see Françoise was trying to get a rise out of him. He stood up, excused himself and went out the door. We could hear him clanging down the metal stairs. Françoise carried our dishes into the kitchen. I followed with the serving platter.

"What did you do today with the children?" I asked in an upbeat tone.

"We went for a hike and picked some *myrtilles*." *Myrtilles* are small blueberries that grow in the Alps. "We made a small tart which they devoured at teatime." Françoise said.

"That sounds lovely." I pulled out the dishpan and began running the hot water.

"I also bought some material in town," Françoise added. She handed me the dishes and I plunged them into the hot water.

"Oh? What for?" I couldn't imagine what she would be sewing up here.

"I think you need a tablecloth and a proper set of napkins. I've begun hemming the tablecloth. If I don't finish the napkins, you can do them after we leave. The children need to have their individual napkins. We also bought some plastic napkin rings." She gestured to the neatly folded, blue-checkered material that lay on the sideboard. On top of it were a stack of brightly colored plastic rings.

"*Merci, c'est très gentil.*" (Thanks, that's so nice.) "We did need some linens." I had been using paper napkins, which were definitely not acceptable.

"*Avec plaisir.* My dear, you need to work at making a home for your husband and your children. I know you spend time writing your little stories, but your household will thrive when you devote yourself to domestic tasks."

I felt unfairly chastised. "Yes, I'm sure you're right, but we're kind of camping out here. All our stuff is on its way from the States."

She began to dry the dishes I placed in the green plastic dishrack. "How shall I put it; I think Henri is not happy. It's just a feeling I have." She paused, searching for words. "You need to provide a comfortable home for him."

I turned and looked into her eyes. "I would, if he came home at night. He's always gone."

Françoise shook her head, "Ah, Kate. All the more reason to provide the little niceties…"

I was seething, but I said nothing. We finished the dishes in silence.

***

The next morning, Henri left early, saying he would be home for dinner. At nine, Benoît and I headed down the hill to Verona. Today, we were quiet all the way down the mountain. I held onto the door handle as we went around the sharp curves. In town, Benoît dropped me off near the Arena on the Piazza Bra. This was on the edge of the old town. Across from the Roman Amphitheatre was a wide sidewalk with several restaurants. We agreed to meet there at one o'clock.

I walked out of the piazza under a Roman arch and down a broad avenue: Corso Porta Nuova. There was a lot of traffic; cars, scooters and tourist buses. I walked by a large *salumeria* bustling with shoppers. From the window, I could see salami and hams hanging from the ceiling. Two blocks further, I began my search. At the first apartment house, I received the usual rejection. One block further, I entered an airy marble-floored entryway. The *portinaio* was standing by the door, laughing with a tiny, wizened woman all dressed in black. He had a jovial expression with sparkling blue eyes. He wore a dark blue uniform.

They both smiled at me. I felt as though these were the first truly friendly smiles, I'd experienced that week.

"Buongiorno, signore, *Sto cercando un appartamento da affittare*." (I'm looking for an apartment to rent.)

"*Ma sì, certo* (Yes, for sure)," the portinaio said. "There's a very large apartment on the third floor. It just became available. Would you like to see it?"

My jaw dropped. I couldn't believe it! An apartment! Then I started to laugh. "Yes, I would love to see it."

The little lady patted my arm and said something I didn't catch. Then she left.

The doorman, Signor Colombo, took me down a short hall to the elevator. We rode up to the third floor in a well-maintained car. Upstairs, he pulled out some keys and opened a dark wood door. The apartment was perfect. There was a marble floored entryway. Straight ahead was a large living room/dining room with windows and a balcony that opened onto the Corso below. To the left, a short hallway led to a pantry and a large eat-in kitchen with a covered balcony outside. To the right of the front door was a library or den.

A hallway led into another corridor. The master bedroom occupied the corner of the building. Further down, two bedrooms and two large bathrooms gave onto a side street. The floors of the formal rooms were a creamy marble and the bedrooms had swallowtail parquet floors. The apartment was empty and ready to go. Later, I would be told this was a *signorile* apartment. *Signorile* means ladylike, gentlemanlike, luxurious, refined, elegant! I had hit the motherlode.

I went into Signor Colombo's office and called Henri. He agreed to come by and sign a promissory note later in the day. I left there skipping with happiness. I had a few hours before I was to meet Benoît, so I spent the time familiarizing myself with the neighborhood. Across the street was a little park. I saw old men sitting there reading the paper or chatting. By the entryway to the building was a bar/café, I hadn't noticed when I charged by. It seemed to be a favorite meeting place. I walked under the trees, along Corso Porta Nuova. Apartment houses lined the avenue with small shops on the ground floor. I would be able to purchase many of our daily needs right nearby.

I went back to the Piazza Bra and wandered down some of the little pedestrian streets. Luxurious shops displayed elegant clothes, designer jewelry, antiques, high-end foodstuffs. I strolled along behind beautifully dressed women, walking arm in arm. With my tired pink flowered dress, I felt like a country bumpkin.

Benoît was settled at a table on the piazza. He looked up at my beaming face. "You found something?"

"Yes, I found a wonderful apartment. Henri will visit it this afternoon and sign some papers. We could walk over there now, but I think the doorman will be off duty."

"Well then, let's have a celebratory lunch."

Chapter 14

Before returning home, I ran back along one of the little streets where I had seen a pastry shop. I bought a cake and a bottle of spumante. That night, we would have a party.

Henri arrived home with a big smile and a signed contract. He said I had found the perfect apartment. One of the managers from Bianchi Gelati had accompanied him that afternoon and had facilitated the process. The best thing about the location was that a well-known private school was right around the corner. We could enroll Lucie in the first grade and Marc could attend the preschool there.

We had a simple dinner with the children. Melon, sliced ham, salad and the cake I'd bought. It was a happy occasion. Françoise had completed the hemming of the tablecloth and the napkins, so the table was all dressed up. After I put the children to bed, we sat and talked about the new apartment.

Later in bed that night, Henri turned to me and asked me to take off my nightgown. Then he said, "You did a great job today. We've got a superior apartment in a good area. I'm proud of you." Then he was on top of me. It took all of two minutes: slam-bang, thank you ma'am. Then he turned on his side and was soon fast asleep.

Afterwards, I lay there feeling used and I asked myself, *Is this my reward?*

***

Henri took Friday off. He and his parents went down to spend the day in Verona. At first the children were disappointed when they saw the car drive away. But when I said we would go up the hill and invite Gabriella's children to play, they were thrilled. It was still early when we trudged up the hill. Gabriella had not left yet for the chicken farm. She agreed that her three could come spend the day with me.

The day flew by. Henri and his parents didn't return until late, having decided to dine in the city. The next day, Benoît and Françoise left for Paris right after breakfast. Henri left shortly thereafter. Apparently, he was urgently needed at the plant after having been absent one day. We were back to normal and I was glad to have my quiet life back. That afternoon, I walked over to the Perons' cottage. La Mama was there alone with her grandchildren. Adriana and Giuseppe would arrive in the evening.

In the late afternoon light, La Mama and I sat on the terrace and drank small glasses of Vino Santo. The boys played a game of bocce ball and the girls lined up the baby-dolls on a blanket in the shade. I felt calm and relaxed after the past week. I told La Mama about my apartment hunt and about the residence I found. She was impressed.

"It sounds like a lovely apartment and centrally located." Her eyes crinkled in the corners as she smiled at me.

"Henri is happy with the neighborhood because it's near a good school. His parents approve of it, too," I added.

"Well, that's important." She assiduously studied the folds in her apron.

I didn't know if she was being sarcastic or sincere. "There's a nice looking salumeria a block away," I added, the words tumbling out.

"Ah, the *Gastronomia e Salumeria Salvatore*. They have delicious cheeses and sausages. You could buy a whole meal there. The *arancini* are fabulous."

"Arancini?" I asked. It sounded like the word for oranges. I couldn't imagine buying oranges in a salumeria, which is like a deli.

"Arancini are rice balls stuffed with meat *ragù* or cheese or mushrooms." She pushed on the seat of her chair and slowly stood up. "I've got a leftover bowl of risotto from last night. Let's make some arancini. The children will love them."

In the kitchen we shaped the cold rice around a spoonful of cooled meat ragù and a small piece of mozzarella. Once all the balls were formed, we rolled them in beaten egg and breadcrumbs. Then we fried them. They looked like little mandarin oranges, so I'm sure that's where the name came from. As we cooked, I told La Mama about Françoise and Benoît.

"I never feel sufficient when Françoise is there. She makes me feel like a bumbling idiot." I told her about the tablecloth, the clean house, the excellent meals and the perfectly mannered children.

La Mama laughed as she rinsed her hands in the sink. Then she placed her hands on my shoulders and looked into my eyes, her deeply wrinkled face close to mine. "Dear Kate, your mother-in-law is a mature woman who has lived a long, rich life. She is a fading rose with experiences that have marked her. You are a young, green plant, with a tender bud ready to open. You have a great deal to learn. Your life is ahead of you. Listen and learn from your mother-in-law, but don't let her words suppress your spirit."

As we made our way home, with a bowl of arancini, I thought of what La Mama had said. It struck me that my insecurities came from within. Maybe I read criticism into Françoise's words that really wasn't there. Maybe she was just sharing her knowledge.

Chapter 15

As the fall approached, life calmed down again in Cerro. All the vacationers returned home. Around us the shutters were closed as though the cottages had gone to sleep. There were some warm days, but the nights were chilly up in the hills. We had our *bombola di gas,* but it only heated water. There was no central heating. Sometimes, after the kids were asleep, I would sit in the bathroom wrapped up in a blanket reading or writing. I would put my feet in the bidet and run the hot water. Beside me was a glass of wine.

***

We moved down to Verona in the fourth week of September. School was to start the first of October. We learned the shipping container with our household goods had arrived. We said goodbye to Gabriella and her family. I encouraged her to come down and visit us. After all, it was only a forty-five-minute drive, but I doubted I would see her. She was so busy with her chickens and eggs. I assured her we would come back up for weekend visits. La Mama and the Peron clan had already moved down to the city. As we pulled out of the driveway and drove down the lane, I felt nostalgic for the days we had spent in our little cottage. I had no idea that I would return there alone in the coming months, nor the range of emotions that homecoming would bring.

In that first week in Verona, while I unpacked, the children reacquainted themselves with their long-lost toys. The apartment was roomy and there was plenty of space to run around.

Since Italian apartments have no closets, appliances or kitchen cupboards, we needed to purchase everything. This was accomplished through cousins of cousins and friends of friends at the Bianchi ice cream plant. Henri chose a series of white, modern wardrobes for the bedrooms. Dark wood and stainless-steel cupboards were installed in the kitchen. A friendly army of workmen came through the door to put it all together. During that week, the washer, dryer and refrigerator arrived, but we still didn't have a stove.

That first week we had breakfast in the bar/café located on the ground floor of our apartment building. Signor Costa, the owner, settled us at a table in the back. Tall, slightly stooped with a greying beard and white hair, he looked like your favorite grandfather. Each morning, the kids had hot chocolate and I had a cappuccino. These were served with *brioches*. In France a brioche is a slightly sweet roll shaped like a muffin with a topknot. The brioches in Verona were shaped like croissants, filled with apricot jam and sprinkled with crunchy sugar. We were all addicted.

On Sunday the bar/café was closed. We were planning to go out and hunt down a restaurant. But at eight o'clock, there was a knock at our door. It was Signor Costa, carrying a large tray with pitchers of hot chocolate and caffè latte. Fresh rolls and brioches were nestled in a basket. He had come in to clean his establishment, which was his normal Sunday ritual, and had thought of us! He carried the tray into the kitchen and placed it on the table. I couldn't thank him enough.

Henri came into the kitchen, a frown on his face. "What's happening here?" He looked critically at Signor Costa, and I rushed to explain that this kind man had brought us breakfast. Henri didn't smile or shake Costa's hand. Frowning, he felt in his pockets and pulled out some *lira* notes.

Signor Costa looked affronted. He held up his hands and said, "No, no, signore. *Il piacere è tutto mio.*" (My pleasure.)

After Signor Costa left, Henri grabbed my elbow. "I don't like the fact that you are hanging out in some bar with that guy. I don't want you and the children to frequent such an establishment." Henri had that haughty, superior look in his eyes that I didn't like.

"I don't *hang out* in some bar, as you put it. With no stove, we had breakfast downstairs this week." I could feel my face flush with anger. "This man did a kind and thoughtful thing. You should be grateful." Then I turned away, my hands clenched.

The children were standing there watching us. Lucie was chewing on the end of her braid and Marc's lower lip was trembling. I smiled at them. "Come on, let's have breakfast. Look at those yummy brioches."

Henri took a cup of the caffè latte and escaped to the office where he was organizing his books. The children settled down and chattered as they sipped their hot chocolate.

***

That week, I enrolled the children in the school around the corner. It was a private girl's school called *Scuola Agli Angeli*—the school of the angels. They admitted only girls from first grade up, but the nursery school included boys. We enrolled Lucie in first grade and Marc in the nursery school. Then we shopped for the appropriate colored smock, school supplies and a backpack. In Italy, all children wore smocks over their clothes. It was explained to me that smocks protected the children's clothing and acted as a social equalizer. It didn't matter if you were wearing your sister's hand-me-downs or the latest children's fashion underneath the smock. At the School of the Angels, they wore white smocks, which meant they had to be washed often.

The school day started at 8 AM and ended at 1 PM. School was strictly reading, writing, math, science and history. Art, music and gym were not included in the curriculum. Community afternoon programs provided soccer practice and classes in the arts.

I dropped Lucie and Marc off at the school shortly before 8. Once the students had arrived, the door was locked and there was no admittance. At that time, there was a rash of kidnappings in Italy. Several of the students arrived in armored cars. Big, burly bodyguards ushered the children into the school, their guns drawn. Whether these abductions were instigated by the Mafia or other criminal elements was unclear. I found it off-putting and I hustled Timmy away as soon as the older children had disappeared through the door.

I met Lucie's teacher only briefly the first day. She was a short, compact woman with thick, carefully coiffed dark hair. She had a friendly smile but there was something inflexible about her. I imagined that her class was comfortable *and* well disciplined. Lucie wasn't particularly nervous that first day. She looked around at the other girls as potential new best friends. Her sparkling, wide-eyed expression usually invited friendship.

Marc, on the other hand, was frightened and grim. Lucie kept telling him school would be fun. There would be toys and games and other little boys. On the way to school, he clutched at my hand. At the door, I knelt down and hugged his skinny little body.

"Mommy will be back soon. This afternoon we'll go to the park. You can ride your bike."

Tearfully, he clutched at my skirt as I stood up. I was almost in tears myself. What to do? The other preschoolers were obediently following the white-smocked teacher. Then a young tousle-haired teacher's aide came over and asked Marc his name. She bent down and chattered away. There was something mesmerizing about her intensity. Marc stared into her eyes, tears slipping down his cheeks. He nodded and then his hand slipped from mine. The sweet little aide led him away. It was like magic. In the following weeks, Marc was thrilled to be off to school. He clambered up the steps and into the entryway, calling out to the other children. It was a relief to me that he was settling in.

After we dropped off the older children, Timmy and I would head to the café. In spite of Henri's admonitions, I treated myself to a cappuccino each day. Signor Costa greeted me, as did the other regulars. Timmy was everyone's favorite. He would wander around the café while I sipped my coffee. Businessmen in suits, shop girls, housewives and workmen alike, all were entranced by Timmy's happy disposition. He was a beautiful little boy with strawberry-blond hair and bright blue eyes.

Later, we headed upstairs. While I cleaned up the kitchen and made the beds, Timmy played. Then we went shopping. By the time I got home and made lunch, it was time to pick up the older children from school.

The good thing about this schedule was that Lucie and Marc came home starving. We ate our main meal then: meat, vegetables, pasta, yogurt and fruit. Afterwards, the boys took a nap and Lucie and I did her homework. In the first week, she had a poem to memorize for the following Friday. What a nightmare that first poem was! We both worked on it. There was a lot of crying and foot stamping, but eventually she got it down pat…and so did I. The memorization of poetry went on all year, but eventually she could sit down and master a poem by herself. I ask myself about the perceived necessity of rote memorization. It is no longer an essential part of education. But I wonder if it exercised a part of the brain and enhanced learning.

One of the first school readings that we translated together was about how to make wine: *Come si fa il vino*. Imagine teaching winemaking in an American first grade, there would be all sorts of parental histrionics. But in Verona, in the heart of Soave,

Valpolicella and Bardolino country, children needed to know about grapes and wine. Many of their parents and grandparents were involved in viticulture. That fall, we often saw a parade of horse-drawn wagons piled high with grapes heading down the street on their way to be crushed and made into wine.

Chapter 16

Our life in Verona began to take on a predictable rhythm. One morning, three weeks after we'd moved in, there was a crisp knock at the door: *rat-a-tat-tat*. We had just come up from the café. I was making a shopping list. Timmy was on his hands and knees, racing his Matchbox cars across the floor. Both boys loved the smooth marble surface because their cars sped unimpeded across it.

I opened the door to a tall, thin woman with sharp features and an angular body. "Signora, I'm Marina. Signor Colombo said you need help."

"I need help?" I repeated. Had I misunderstood?

Marina was wearing a well-cut, navy blue coat. Her dark hair was cut short and seemed to spring from her head. "*Sì*, signora. I will take good care of your house. Cleaning, ironing, washing. I'm very efficient."

For a moment I was speechless. Where had Signor Colombo got the idea that I needed help? As I was pondering all this, Marina stepped around me and into the foyer. She went into the living room and inspected the windows.

"Your windows need washing. And the floor…it's dusty and scratched." She continued to walk through the apartment, and I followed in her wake. On the kitchen table were the remnants of breakfast. Timmy's hot chocolate bowl was overturned. A stream of brown liquid had run across the table and pooled on the floor. Last night's dishes were piled in the kitchen sink, and dirty clothes were heaped on top of the washer in the laundry nook. Back in the bedroom wing, the children's beds were unmade. Clothes and toys were scattered across the floor. I felt embarrassed by the state of my housekeeping. In my defense, I would have attacked these chores sooner or later.

When we arrived back in the entryway, Marina crossed her arms and raised her eyebrows. Her eyes questioned mine. I felt cornered. Maybe I really did need help.

Timmy had followed us around, curious about this new lady who had taken over our house. In the hallway, Marina bent down and gave him a glorious smile. Timmy was charmed. He raised his chubby little arms and she swooped him up. They already were best buddies.

As it turned out, Marina was a godsend. She came three mornings a week, from eight-thirty to twelve-thirty. She always arrived in her neat coat and tailored dress. In the bathroom, she changed into a cotton housedress and felt slippers. She moved through the apartment like a tornado. Some days we worked together, other days I would take off to do the shopping or an errand. Timmy loved her. He followed her around, chatting unintelligibly in his version of Italian. Marina talked to herself as well, and they made a happy couple. I felt comfortable leaving him in her care when necessary. Under Marina's management, my windows shone, my floors gleamed, and Lucie's smocks were sparkling white and carefully ironed.

***

As before, Henri often came home late. He claimed Signor Bianchi and the plant managers needed to work on new products...or there were issues with the production...or the accounting system was under revision. It was always something, and I have to admit I didn't pay much attention. I didn't really understand the workings of the plant.

One night, Henri came home early, around nine o'clock. The children were asleep, and I was sitting at the kitchen table working on a story. When I heard the key turn in the lock, I felt elated. Since we'd moved down to the city, we rarely communicated except for the normal, daily back and forth. This would be a chance to talk without the kids around. We could have a glass of wine and catch up. All of this was going through my mind as I walked from the kitchen to the entryway. But our tête à tête wasn't to be. Henri was accompanied by a heavyset man in a brown overcoat whose back was turned to me. When he turned around, his eyes travelled over my body and he licked his lips. It was Francesco Ferrari. At that moment, he reminded me of a Komodo dragon with his thick body and heavily lidded eyes.

"Buona sera, signora." He smiled with those moist lips, but his eyes remained cold.

"Buona sera," I said, avoiding his gaze. Did Henri know of Francesco's clandestine visit in Cerro? I'd never said a thing and I doubt Francesco had.

"Kate, Francesco and I need to have a private talk away from the plant. We're going into the office. If you could bring in some glasses and that bottle of Armagnac, I would be most grateful."

"Of course. Would you like something to eat?" I said graciously.

"*Non, chérie,* just the Armagnac." Henri opened the frosted glass door into the office and ushered Ferrari into the room. Then he closed the door firmly behind him.

I felt irritated. *Chérie. Give me a break.* He never used terms of endearment. I retrieved the bottle of Armagnac from the pantry and found the only two snifters we owned. I rinsed and dried them and placed them on a black lacquered tray. Before entering the office, I paused, balancing the tray with one hand so I could open the door. As I stood there, I heard Francesco say in Italian, "We have to do it. We have no choice."

"But he killed someone," Henri said. "This could be dangerous for all of us."

I stood there, frozen by their words. Who in the world were they talking about?

They were ensconced in the den for an hour. When I heard Francesco leave, I came out to confront Henri. I wanted to know what or who they'd been speaking of.

"So, are you and Signor Ferrari great friends now?"

93

Henri sighed. "There were things we needed to discuss. No, we're not great friends." He headed for the bedroom.

I followed at his heels. "I don't like that man. He gives me the creeps."

Henri switched on the lights in the bedroom. "He's a bright guy. There are things I can learn from him."

"What kinds of things?"

"Kate, this is none of your business." He loosened his tie and took off his suit jacket.

I was not to be deterred. "When I brought you the brandy, I heard you say someone killed someone. What was that about?"

Henri swung around and looked at me hard. "I don't know what you mean. You must have misunderstood." He started toward the bathroom. Over his shoulder he said, "After all, your Italian is not that great."

Chapter 17

Each day at one o'clock, Timmy and I went around the corner to pick up Lucie and Marc from school. As we made our way home for lunch, the shops were closing for the afternoon. They would reopen at four. Movement on the street quieted down. We adopted a similar schedule. After lunch, I helped Lucie with her homework, while Timmy and Marc took a nap. Like our Veronese compatriots, at four o'clock, we reappeared. As long as it wasn't raining, we went to the *Giardini Reggio de Sole*—the Sunshine Gardens. The park was barely ten minutes away by stroller or tricycle.

The gardens were located along the old city walls. There were meandering paths, shaded park benches, soccer fields, and a café for refreshments. But the best part was the fenced-in playground with a guardian on duty. She watched who came in and out. Children were safe inside, watched over as they rode their bikes along the paths, played on the equipment or invented games among the trees.

The mothers and grandmothers would sit on benches or at the outdoor café drinking coffee and gossiping. In the first few weeks, I chased Timmy around in the playground. Then I met Giada. She had a little boy about Timmy's age and a little girl who was in school with Lucie. The girls had become fast friends.

Giada and I first met at a school meeting for first-grade parents. The gathering was held in an elegantly appointed room. About thirty mothers laughed and chatted until the principal entered. She was a no-nonsense matriarch, always dressed in sober dark suits, her hair pulled back into a tight bun. I immediately felt like sitting up straight and looking attentive. In the room, you could hear a pin drop. After a few welcoming words, the principal introduced a medical doctor to the group. The *Dottore* was there to talk to parents about good nutrition for their *bambini*. She had dark blond hair streaked with grey, blue-grey eyes and a slim build. She wore a white medical coat over her dress.

She smiled pleasantly and then launched into her presentation. Her message was that children needed to eat meat and vegetables before they were served pasta. Traditionally, Italians begin their noon meal with pasta and then move on to the meat, veggies and salad. The doctor pointed out that children filled their tummies with pasta and had no room for the rest of the meal, but nutritionally, they needed the vitamins and minerals provided by fruits and vegetables and some form of protein. She was met by silence. Then a few mothers asked questions about carrots over zucchini and polenta vs. pasta. I had a feeling that when these *mamme* got home, they would probably not change the natural order of a traditional meal. After all, they had been raised that way, and they were perfectly healthy.

As I glanced around the room, my eyes met Giada's. She was smiling and rolling her eyes. I returned the smile. As the group broke up, she came over to introduce herself. It turned out her little girl,

Francesca, was constantly talking about her American friend Lucie. We chatted for a moment and then made a date to meet at the park at four o'clock. That morning, I went home with a skip to my step. I had felt an immediate bond with Giada. Eventually, I learned that she felt as foreign in Verona as I did. She had been born in Milan and her parents, family and close friends lived there. Giada had a tall, slim body that looked good in anything she put on. Before meeting her husband, she'd done some modeling in Milano. She laughed easily and took life as it came.

Most days at the park, we chatted about the children. I appreciated the patience she showed when I tried heroically to make myself understood. We discussed appropriate bedtimes, recipes, fashion and everything else. I remember one day; I was bursting with indignation. I had gone to the post office to pay the utility bills, which needed to be paid in cash. The first month, I took all three children, which turned out to be a major disaster. People didn't just wait in line, they bunched, pushing and shoving to get to the front. I kept losing my position in the fray, because I would have to chase after one child or the other. I decided from then on, I would go alone. That day, I was met with another obstacle.

I explained to Giada as we sat on a park bench. "This morning I went to the bank to get cash to pay the utility bills."

She nodded in response. She was knitting a blue sweater for her son, with a complicated pattern, and she kept her eyes on her work

"The teller wouldn't hand over the money, because I didn't have my husband's permission in writing. What kind of country is this? A woman has no rights." I clenched my hands in frustration.

Giada laughed. "The man makes the money. It is his to disburse. The wife is chattel."

"That's not fair. In a marriage, the wife is pulling her share of the weight. Italy is living in the dark ages," I groused.

"So, what happened?" Her metal knitting needles clicked.

"They had to call Henri to get his permission, even though my name appears on the account."

"And did Henri approve?"

"Yes, but that's not the point. This is 1975."

Giada stopped knitting and patted my arm. "It's not worth getting in a snit," she said…or something equivalent in Italian.

***

Another day, when the children seemed happily occupied, we walked over to the *chiosco ristoro*. After ordering an espresso, we sat down at one of the little metal tables. My eyes were drawn to a red-haired woman who wore a colorful shawl. Several thick books were spread out before her. I later learned that these were astrology tomes. Near her feet, an aged white poodle lay curled up on a cushion. Two women had drawn their chairs up to the woman's table, one of the women was very pregnant. They watched silently as the clairvoyant pored over her books, turning pages and taking notes. Meanwhile, Giada was complaining about a reading assignment the girls had found difficult that day, but my attention was drawn to the anxious face of the woman with child.

After fifteen minutes or so, the fortune-teller looked up and addressed the women. Her face was a map of creases and crevasses, her deep-set eyes penetrating in their intensity. She began to speak with the voice of a Roman orator. All of us in close proximity and beyond learned that the stars and planets were positively aligned, and the pregnant woman would give birth to a healthy baby boy. Everyone applauded and the mama-to-be beamed with pleasure. Her friend gave her a hug.

The fortune-teller looked up and her eyes fell on me. I could feel them like daggers spinning to their target across the distance.

"Signora, I feel your special presence here today. Let me speak to you of the future."

"I don't know what you mean," I mumbled, looking around to make sure she was addressing me.

"You have a strong aura and many questions unanswered in your life," the woman said in a low, rumbling voice.

I shrugged and giggled, then looked over at Giada. Her eyes were crinkled in amusement. "Go ahead, do it."

"How much does it cost?" I asked.

The astrologer mentioned a small amount. Giada urged me on. It would be a lark. I shrugged and nodded in agreement. The woman asked me the place and date of my birth. Then she got to work. She opened one book and her finger moved quickly down the page. Then she went to another volume, rifling through the pages. I nervously chatted with Giada, but both of us kept glancing over at the fortune-teller. After several minutes, the woman looked up and asked to see my hand. I reached across the table and she took my hand in hers, turning it over and studying my palm. Her hands were warm. She traced the lines in my palm with a knobby finger. For some reason, I was feeling breathless and flushed.

After a minute or so, the woman looked up. There was fire in her eyes. Like the oracle at Delphi, she announced to all within earshot, "Signora, I see that you will have a long life." She paused and looked back down at my hand. "I wanted to study your palm to check if the prognostications in my astrology books were correct."

I'll admit I was fascinated. It's human nature to want to believe in your horoscope in the newspaper, and here was a bona fide fortune-teller.

"But there will be tragedy in your life: the death of someone close to you." She pursed her lips.

"Who? Do you know who?" I asked. I was trembling.

"No. Someone who is a major figure in your life."

That could be one of the children. Or Henri. I began to think I didn't want to hear any more of this nonsense. I tried to pull my hand away, but she held it tight.

"I am not finished." She looked deeply into my eyes. "Standing in the wings is the great love of your life. This person will bring great joy, abundant happiness...but also deep sorrow."

"And I don't know this person now?"

"No, but they're nearby...very nearby."

I'd had enough. I pulled my hand away and reached into my purse for some lira notes that I tossed on the table. Then I stormed off towards the playground to gather up my children and head for the safety and security of home.

Chapter 18

That night and for days to come, I relived those predictions. As I watched the children eat their minestrone that night, I couldn't stop thinking about what the fortune-teller had said. Would one of my precious children die? I looked lovingly at each one. Was it darling Timmy who was making a valiant effort to get the soup from his spoon into his mouth, half of it dribbling down his dimpled chin? Was it sweet Marc? He was spreading butter meticulously on his bread, the tip of his tongue between his lips. Or adorable Lucie? She was humming to herself as she nibbled on a piece of cheese, her mind elsewhere.

In bed that night, I lay awake. Henri had come home late and I'd been asleep when he arrived. Now, in the early morning he was sprawled out beside me snoring softly. Would he die suddenly, and the children and I would be left stranded in Italy?

Sometimes I allowed myself to think about the great love that awaited me. I felt slightly guilty. After all, I was a happily married woman, wasn't I? My great love should be Henri...*was* Henri. In my mind's eye, I went through the men I'd met recently. The grumpy fruit and vegetable man? The jovial owner of the salumeria? Signor Costa at the cafe downstairs? Or the doorman, Signor

Colombo? Definitely not. Then I felt silly even contemplating such foolishness.

***

It takes about an hour and a half to drive from Verona to Venice. The two cities are both in the Veneto Province. In late October, Giada and I made a trip to Venice with the kids. There was no school that day, due to some revered saint. I have photographs of Timmy toddling after the pigeons on Piazza San Marco and Marc chasing Lucie and Francesca over a stone arched bridge. We rode the *vaporetto* (water taxi) and went out to the Island of Murano to see the glass blowers. In the afternoon we went to the Lido to play on the beach. The children took off their shoes and socks and ran in and out of the water. It was a wonderful day.

Not long afterwards, Henri came home to tell me we were invited to go to Venice for dinner with Signor Bianchi, and two other couples.

"Who are the other couples?" I asked.

"Francesco Ferrari and his wife, Giulia. You know her. We met them last summer at the Perons' house."

I grimaced. I never wanted to see Francesco again.

Henri chose to ignore my expression. "Then there's a man visiting from Rome. He's in town with his wife." Henri eyed me critically. "You need to look your best. I want to be proud of you."

"Proud of me? More likely you're worried I'll embarrass you. Is that it?" I pushed a wayward strand of hair behind my ear. I was wearing a dirty apron and felt at a disadvantage.

"Come on, Kate. You need to fix yourself up. Maybe get a haircut? What do you have to wear? I'll give you money for a dress."

I sighed. "I'll think of something. I *will* make you proud."

***

For the big dinner, I wore a dress Giada lent me. It was a deep-red knit and it fit me like a glove. We were both tall, although I had more curves.

"Oh, you look lovely. It's perfect on you," Giada said.

I twirled around in front of her full-length mirror. Lucie and Francesca were watching. "You look beautiful, Mommy," Lucie said, and giggled at Francesca.

Giada smiled. "I've got the perfect necklace for you to wear. What about shoes?"

That afternoon, Giada gave me a lesson on how to apply make-up; after all, she'd had that brief stint as a model in Milano. As she showed me how to apply eyeliner, she frowned. "What coat do you have to wear?"

Giada had only seen me in my dark blue cloth coat. "You know, the blue coat," I said.

"I think you need a mink coat. I'll lend you mine."

"A mink coat?" I sputtered.

She opened one of the doors on her wall of armoires and pulled out a three-quarter length mink coat. The two little girls ran over to pet the coat as if it were a furry dog. I had never even tried one on and it seemed unnecessary in the Verona climate. I mean, I can see wearing a mink coat back in Chicago where the winters were sub-

104

zero. But as it turned out, Bianchi's wife was wearing a full-length mink along with an abundance of diamonds. And in the chilly and damp November air, I was glad to snuggle in the warmth of that coat.

Signor Bianchi's driver drove us in the company's van. We set off in the late afternoon. The men talked about soccer and the women discussed shopping in Rome. I was an ignoramus where soccer was concerned, and I'd never been to Rome. As we sped along, I gazed out the window, feeling alone and invisible. No one expected me to join in. When Giulia did turn to me, she spoke loudly and slowly. Apparently, I was expected to be mentally deficient.

"Francesco tells me you are a famous writer?"

"I did write a book several years ago that had some success," I responded, speaking slowly, partly to mock her.

"Are you writing a book now?" Signora Bianchi asked.

"No, it's difficult to find the time with small children. Sometimes, I do write little stories for the children."

"How charming." Signora Bianchi smiled vaguely. She had clearly lost interest and turned to the lady from Rome to discuss one of the latest movies, *Grazie...Nonna (Thanks, Grandma)*. I'd seen publicity posters plastered on walls around town. The film looked pretty racy. The posters depicted a partially clad woman with her rump in the air. I hadn't wanted the children to catch a glimpse of that sensuous image.

We were dropped off at Piazzale Roma and took a vaporetto to the Piazza San Marco. After an aperitivo at Caffè Florian, we set off for a *passeggiata* and to do some shopping before dinner. A leisurely passeggiata is essential to Italian life. Giulia and Signora Bianchi walked slowly arm in arm, chatting, their heads close together. The man and woman from Rome walked together and Signor Bianchi and his two lieutenants, Henri and Francesco, were in lockstep. I trailed behind, enjoying the shop windows and observing the people we passed. I often made up background stories for interesting individuals I observed. That handsome man in the well-cut suit had a beautiful wife at home who was a famous artist. When he got home, they would eat pasta alfredo, gazing into each other's eyes, and then tumble into bed to make mad, passionate love. The tall, skinny man with the short, chubby wife both wore anxious expressions. I imagined they were on their way to the hospital where their dear little girl was dying from leukemia. After her death, they would never be happy again.

We wandered down small passageways and over stone bridges. Signora Bianchi stopped at several jewelry shops. We ladies accompanied her. She bought a delicate gold bracelet with sparkling amethyst stones. Later, the signora from Rome stopped at a *librerie* that specialized in rare books. She was looking for a first edition of an Italian classic. It was a gift for her mother, as I recall.

Our destination for dinner was in the neighborhood of the old fish market. Eventually, we arrived. The maître d'hôtel led us down some stairs to a lower level, with elegantly rustic stone walls, where

106

we were ushered to a long table. Several other tables were occupied. Across the room a group of men were just sitting down. Lively conversation echoed in the low-ceilinged room.

Signor Bianchi asked the waiter where the kitchen was. Then he got up and made a beeline toward it. Signora Bianchi shrugged off her coat and looked heavenward. "Giancarlo always consults with the cook about what is fresh in the kitchen. Often he tells the man what he wants to eat and how to prepare it."

We all laughed, somewhat obediently. Giancarlo wielded a lot of power in his small world.

I don't remember the entire menu. We started with *sarde in saòr*, sweet and sour sardines, followed by spaghetti with squid ink. It was a seafood dinner ordered by our host. The atmosphere was upbeat and the conversation brisk. I was seated between the man from Rome and Francesco. They talked across me. Several times, I felt Francesco's hand on my thigh. I tried to brush it off and then jabbed him with my elbow. When my neighbor on the other side realized what was happening, he frowned. After that, Francesco left me alone.

Across the table, Giulia and Signora Bianchi discussed favorite comic books. I recognized the titles because I'd seen women reading them that summer. The picture books were geared to adults and seemed to involve sordid love stories. We didn't have that sort of literature in the U.S. at that time.

We ate a leisurely dinner, taking time with each course and drinking quite a lot of wine. The restaurant emptied out except for the group of men across the room. One of them raised his voice in song and the others joined in. They were singing in German. When they'd finished, our group applauded, and we sent a pitcher of wine to their table. Everyone laughed. Then our group began to sing an Italian song. Henri seemed to know some of the words. I hummed along. When we'd finished, the German speakers applauded and sent us a pitcher of wine. As the evening progressed, the atmosphere became more raucous. We sang, clapped our hands and shared more wine. The women got up to dance. We danced together; we danced with Francesco and Signor Bianchi; we danced with the German fellows. The feeling was wild pandemonium. Henri would have none of it. He sat back in his chair, arms crossed, surveying the scene. I remember twirling around in my red dress. He eyed me with barely concealed distaste and anger. I was making a spectacle of myself, but I didn't care.

Then all of a sudden Francesco stood on a chair, raised his arm in a Nazi salute and said, "Heil Hitler." His harsh voice carried across the room. And then there was total silence. We were frozen in place. Some of the German-speakers mumbled, "But we are not Germans. We are Austrians." The delightful evening had turned into a train wreck.

On the walk back to the car along darkened passageways and over arched bridges, we stumbled along. I trailed behind the others. I had taken off my high heels, something the Italian ladies would never have done. Just as I lost sight of the others around the corner of a building, I felt hands grab me and pull me into a dark alcove.

Then I was slammed up against the rough stone wall behind me. It was Francesco. He pressed his body hard against me. I was pinned like a flailing butterfly. His mouth found mine and his thick tongue slid through my open lips, like a slick snake. I gagged and tried to push him off. Then I felt his hand push up under my skirt and press against my crotch. I felt powerless and frightened. I dropped the shoes I was holding, pulled my hands up and pushed at his chest, to no avail. I clamped down hard on his tongue. He groaned and loosened his grip. I tasted blood in my mouth. Then, from around the corner, I heard Henri's voice.

"Kate, *où es-tu*? Kate?"

"I'm here," I managed to answer, my voice a muffled sob.

Francesco stepped back and stumbled on the uneven pavement. Then he staggered away in the opposite direction.

Henri appeared and grabbed my arm roughly. "Kate, you've made a fool of yourself…drinking and dancing like some tart." He was very angry.

I leaned into him and began to cry, but he pushed me away. "Stand up and stop crying. We're keeping the others waiting." He looked down at my bare feet. "For God's sake, put on your shoes."

I reached down and found my high heels. With one hand braced against the wall, I slipped them on. Then Henri put his arm through mine and pulled me along.

Chapter 19

The next day I felt rotten. Along with a massive hangover, my feet hurt, and my arms were bruised. I had asked Marina to babysit and she had let the children stay up late. That morning they were grumpy and feisty. Marc and Lucie were teasing Timmy.

"You're a baby, baby, baby," they sang, while Timmy screeched. His voice throbbed in my head. Henri didn't deign to say a word to me. I got the cold shoulder Sunday and all that week. I didn't tell him about Francesco and how frightened I had been. I'm sure he would have thought it was my fault, that I had brought on the attack with my wanton dancing and drunken behavior. Maybe he was right. I had drunk way too much, something I normally didn't do.

When I met Giada at the park Monday afternoon, I told her about the evening and the attack.

"I was an idiot, drinking too much and dancing provocatively," I said.

"Come on, Kate. Even if you were crazy drunk, that man had no right to assault you."

"Maybe I should tell Henri. Maybe he would tell Bianchi and Francesco would be fired."

Giada laughed derisively. "*Questa è l'Italia.* This is Italy. It's a man's world. Men have their rights and their desires."

"And women?"

"We're possessions. Men want to show us off, possess us; but they're in charge." The skin around her mouth had tightened and turned white from anger. I wondered about her relationship with her husband. I'd never met him, and she had never suggested a get-together with spouses.

When I look back on this conversation, I remember it wasn't until after WWII that Italian women were given the right to vote. In addition, gender equality became the law in Italy about the time Giada and I were having this conversation. A little later, in 1978, abortion laws were liberalized. We were right on the cusp of the changes.

***

At the beginning of November, Bianchi provided Henri with a company car. A Fiat sedan, it was perfect for him to drive back and forth to the plant. I didn't understand at the time that the car was another perk that tethered Henri to Bianchi's wants and desires.

I was thrilled to have our Volkswagen at my disposal. I could drive to the supermarket and load up on groceries. It made life much easier. In the afternoons, I took the children on outings to visit other parks. There was the *Giardino Giusti* with its intricate labyrinth, where the children ran around giggling as they tried one path after another, trying to find the way out. Another time, I invited Giada to accompany us. We went to the *Parco delle Cascate*. The children scampered up the slopes, along the many paths and under the

111

waterfalls. I wished I'd had the independence a car brings when we were living in the cottage in Cerro.

***

Once in a while Giada and I would take an hour or two in the morning and stroll down Via Mazzini, Verona's pedestrian shopping street. We looked in the shops and stopped for coffee. Marina was happy to babysit Timmy and I was glad for some time off. Giada loved jewelry and lingerie. She claimed her husband didn't complain when she bought a necklace or bracelet within reason. As for the lingerie, I gathered that he wanted her to wear silky, lacy undergarments. I wore stodgy cotton briefs and Warner bras. I told myself they were a lot cheaper and infinitely more practical. And Henri rarely saw me in my underwear anyway.

On one such adventure, we entered a small boutique specializing in beautifully made lingerie. Giada picked out a black bra and miniscule panties. While she discussed the workmanship with the shop girl, I wandered around the boutique. In a glass case, I glimpsed a soft peach-colored set of bra and panties. They were sheer and lacy with a floral motif. I stared down at them. It would be fun to wear something so lovely.

"What are you looking at?" Giada asked, glancing over at me.

"I love this set here…the color and the style. They're beautiful," I said wistfully.

"Buy them. Surprise your husband. He'll want to swoop you up and carry you to bed." Giada laughed.

I blushed and looked away. Henri would probably be shocked and disapprove.

"Try on the bra. It needs to fit perfectly," the shop girl said. They both were looking at me with critical eyes.

"You'll feel so special when you're wearing them. You need something beautiful," Giada said, encouraging me. The shop girl came over and inspected my breasts, reaching over and feeling their weight. Then she opened a drawer and pulled out a peachy bra and handed it to me. The material was wonderfully silky.

"Go on," Giada said. "Try it on."

Feeling foolish, I went into the changing room. The carpet and walls were covered with rosy velvet. The lighting was muted. I took off my coat, sweater, blouse and cotton bra and placed them on a small period chair. Then I slipped on the peachy bra and fastened it. The full-length mirror reflected the room and my slim figure. I turned this way and that, studying my reflection. I giggled to myself. Did I look like some harlot in a bordello? No, the color and fit were sexy, but also sweetly angelic.

Giada poked her head through the curtains. She eyed me critically. "Fantastic. It fits perfectly."

"I don't know…" I said.

"Believe me, when you're wearing lovely underwear, you feel special. It will make a rainy day seem sunny."

After dithering for another few minutes, with Giada pestering me, I decided to buy the bra and the panties. I walked home feeling deliciously wicked.

Chapter 20

That fall we were invited several times to Signor Moretti's family's farmhouse for Sunday lunch. There was a barnyard with farm animals that delighted the children and plenty of hay to jump in. The stone farmhouse was ancient. There was one main room with a large, open fireplace in which you could probably roast a pig. In the middle of the room was a long dining table, grooved and indented from years and years of use. Usually twenty people or more attended these family gatherings. Children ran in and out while the women stirred the polenta or risotto. Several men manned the fireplace where meat and slices of cold polenta were roasted. Everyone brought a dish. Usually there was a selection of antipasti, vegetables, salads, cheese, fruit and desserts. All of this was watered with quantities of good wine. It seemed everyone had a cousin with a vineyard to provide a special bottle. All of them were unmarked and dark green.

We enjoyed polenta in two forms, grilled or as a creamy purée. Mr. Moretti's brother-in-law owned a mill that produced polenta flour and he would bring the latest batch to be prepared on the spot. It had to be constantly stirred. The women took turns. For northern Italians, polenta was as basic as bread.

In early November we received an invitation for lunch, the weekend of All-Saints Day. Traditionally this is a somber occasion as one remembers the dearly departed. People visit cemeteries and decorate graves. The meal that day should be frugal and austere, in remembrance of the dead. On this occasion there was the usual grilled polenta and plenty of wine, but maybe not the best wine since it was All-Saints Day. Twenty-five or thirty people were gathered around the ancient table. I remember two dishes. One was an onion sauce on whole wheat pasta. The sliced onions were cooked very slowly in a large quantity of olive oil for a couple of hours. The resulting sauce was absolutely delicious.

The second dish was a large platter of steaming bones. This was late autumn and they'd killed the fatted pig and cut pork chops and made sausages. The remaining bones were boiled in a flavorful broth and sprinkled with coarse salt. At this meal, we helped ourselves to a big bone and scraped the bits of meat off. It was rustic and tasty. Lucie dug in, holding a large rib in both hands. Marc was horrified, his eyes enormous when he saw the bones. He grabbed a slice of crispy polenta and left the table. He was blessed or cursed with too vivid an imagination.

After the meal, I wandered outside to check on the children. Lucie and Timmy were playing with some black and grey kittens, teasing them with stalks of hay. Both kids were entranced. Lucie was a good little babysitter and I could count on her to watch her little brother. Marc was kicking a soccer ball with two other kids. I walked across the farmyard towards the arched entryway made of rough-hewed stone. It had been constructed centuries earlier. As I approached the wall, I heard Henri's voice.

"Kate tells me it's cold in the cottage. She went up with the children."

Who was he talking to? It was true. One weekend when Henri was on a trip to Torino, I had driven up to Cerro with the children. I had planned to spend Saturday night in the cottage. Bundled in their coats and hats, the children had played outside in the driveway in the pale sunshine. But inside the cottage it had felt like a refrigerator. The cement block walls seemed to vibrate with cold air. I turned on the oven and cooked a pot of spaghetti for lunch with some tomato sauce I'd brought up. Steam vapor covered the windows. We sat on the wooden chairs in our coats and slurped the pasta. After another hour of playing outside, I closed up the cottage and we went back home to Verona.

I recognized Signor Moretti's voice answering. "It's not winterized. You'll have to wait till spring now."

"Kate has expressed a desire to go up there and write. You know, she's an author. She says she needs some peace and quiet."

"She can't write at home?" He sounded a little skeptical.

I was feeling skeptical as well. What was Henri up to?

"No, she needs to get away from home and the noisy children. We thought we would bring up some space heaters, if you don't mind?"

"As long as she's careful. We don't want a fire." As they moved away, I heard Moretti say, "But I don't think they will be very effective."

I turned away and walked back towards the farmhouse. I couldn't imagine what Henri was suggesting, or why. When had I expressed a need to get away and write? Although as I approached the doorway, it struck me that a few days alone would be nice. But that would never happen. I had three little children and a household to run.

Later, as we drove back to Verona, Marc and Timmy fell asleep in the back seat. Lucie was humming to herself and gazing dreamily out the window. I turned to Henri and said in a low voice, "I heard you talking to Signor Moretti."

"Oh?"

"Yes, you were talking about my need to write."

He said nothing. His mouth was set in a hard line and he was gripping the steering wheel.

"You said I needed to get away and go up to the cottage to write. When did I ever say that?"

He glanced over at me. His dark eyes were obscured in the early evening light. "I can't explain," he said hoarsely. Then he quickly looked back at the road, just in time. I could hear the tires screeching as the pebbles along the shoulder shot out behind us. I clutched the door handle and gasped in fear that we would plunge down the side of the mountain.

"Shut up. You're not helping," he barked.

Chapter 21

A few weeks later, Henri arrived home early. The children rushed to the entryway and jumped for joy. It wasn't often he was home for supper with them.

"Papa look at what I drew at school," Marc said. He held up a piece of paper with blotches of color.

"Very nice, Marc." Henri was distracted and didn't bother to look at the artwork. Marc looked up at him hopefully, seeking a sign of approval. But Henri turned away. In a swift movement, Marc tore up his picture and then he turned around and punched Timmy in the stomach. Timmy began to scream, and Marc ran to his room. I picked Timmy up and pulled him close as he sobbed.

"What is wrong with that boy, Kate? You need to take him in hand. He's turning into a monster and he's only five." Henri was lugging in a cardboard box. He placed it on the floor by the door. Then he went out in the hall again and brought in a second box.

I was seething. How could he be so insensitive to his own son? Why couldn't he give him the attention and approval Marc so craved? "Your son was showing you a picture he was proud of and you couldn't give him the time of day. What's wrong with him...is his father," I hissed.

Then I turned away and headed for the kitchen, where I was cooking a pot of *pasta e fagioli* for supper. Why hadn't I seen this side of Henri back in those days in Paris when we had first met? I'd been oblivious to his self-absorption. It was true that love is blind.

Later, after the children had had their baths, we sat around the kitchen table and ate the soup, bread, cheese and pears. Henri poured me a glass of red wine and I took a long sip.

"Tell me about your day, dear?" I said, half mockingly.

"Same as always," he responded. Then, looking around the table, he said, "What did you do today, children?"

"Same as always," Lucie mimicked, and Marc giggled.

***

After the children were in bed, I went into the living room. Henri was seated on the sofa with a glass of Armagnac. His arms were crossed, and he was frowning at a painting of a Paris street scene that hung over a small chest across the room. I loved that painting. It had a whimsical, magical quality. Henri thought it trite. But to me it represented that romantic Parisian year when we'd met.

He'd brought in the bottle of crème de cassis. I rarely drank hard liquor, but I loved the berry-sweet taste of that brandy. He poured some into a small cut crystal glass. I sat down next to him, but he moved ever so slightly away. What was he about? I was on edge, but I decided to remain silent. I pulled my legs up under me and smoothed my skirt. Then I took a small sip of the elixir.

"Kate, I need to talk to you about something."

I raised my eyebrows and said dryly, "I imagined you did. You never come home early."

Henri looked annoyed. "Remember, Gelati Bianchi sells ice cream in cafés and bars all over Italy." He looked at me. I nodded.

"Well, some of these cafés are owned by the Mafia. Giancarlo has a relationship with some of these *capos*."

I knew a capo was someone in a senior position in a mafia organization. It made sense that Giancarlo would do business with some top guy. But why was Henri telling me this? I took another sip of the liquor and huddled into the corner of the sofa.

"Are you listening?" he asked.

"Yes, I'm listening." I yawned and took another sip of the fruity deliciousness.

"A month ago, the son of one of these capos killed a member of a rival Mafia family. He shot him in a bar fight."

"This sounds like some black-and-white Italian movie. I can see the dark smoke-filled interior of the bar and two short, hefty Mafia guys with cigarettes hanging from their lips. They argue, gesturing with their hands, then…" I pointed my finger. "Bang bang…"

Henri interrupted me, his voice tense. "Kate, this isn't some imaginary film. This is real. This man killed another man and he was whisked away before the *carabinieri* arrived. This occurred down below Naples. The Mafia gang drove him all the way up to Verona, to the Gelati Bianchi plant. Giancarlo agreed to hide the man until it all blows over."

I sat up. "Until it all blows over? Wow! This is a killer and you're hiding him at the plant? Isn't that illegal? Couldn't you all get in trouble?" I shook my head in disbelief.

"Well…" Henri glanced at me and then down into his glass. He had reddened slightly.

"Well…what?" I could feel there was something he wasn't telling me.

"Well…he's not at the plant now." He gulped down the rest of his brandy. "He's at the cottage in Cerro."

"Our cottage?"

"Yes."

"Why?" I sat up and put my feet on the floor, then placed the delicate glass on the table.

"Someone was sniffing around the plant. Giancarlo was afraid the guy would be discovered. So, he had him moved out hidden in an ice cream truck." Henri still wasn't looking at me.

"Well, it's too cold up there in the mountains for us, so I guess it doesn't matter except now you'll be liable. Henri, you should have refused." I was angry. What hold did Giancarlo have over Henri? Whatever Giancarlo wanted; Giancarlo got. It made me sick.

"You could go to jail for aiding and abetting a criminal. Why didn't you tell Giancarlo 'no'?"

"I felt I needed to help out. There was no other place he could go, no other solution," Henri said.

I stood up to clear the glasses off the table. Henri grabbed my wrist. "Sit down. There's more."

I sighed and sat down obediently.

He took a deep breath. "We need you to take some provisions up to this man. His name is Andrea. He seems nice enough."

"What?" I exploded. "You want me to carry stuff up to a killer. You want me to participate in this criminal act?" I pulled my arm away and headed to the kitchen. Henri followed me.

"No one will know. You can just tell people you need time alone to write."

"Time to write?" I banged the glasses on the table. The little crystal aperitif glass broke at the stem. I felt tears welling up in my eyes; tears of anger or desperation. I turned to look at him. "Do you realize what you're asking me to do?"

"Kate, it's no big deal. I'll put the boxes of foodstuffs in your car. In the morning, you will drive up there. Drop off the boxes. Spend a couple of hours and then drive home." He was speaking so matter-of-factly, it enraged me.

"What about Timmy? Do I introduce him to this murderer?" I knew my face must be red and blotchy. That happened when I got emotional.

"You can leave Timothée with Marina. It would only be for a few hours."

I was shaking. "This is crazy. You are crazy to ask this of me. Why doesn't Giancarlo ask his wife, or that Giulia. Why me?"

"Come on, Kate. It's our cottage. You have an excellent cover. You're a writer and you need time to write. It's a perfect alibi."

"Alibi? That will be my defense when they drag me to jail." Tears were running down my cheeks.

Henri tried to put his arms around me, but I pushed him away. "Don't touch me. Don't pretend you care about me." I turned my back and went to the sink and began washing the dinner dishes. Henri stood right behind me.

"Will you do this tomorrow? Please? It's important to me. I'll talk to Giancarlo about another solution," he pleaded in French.

I didn't turn around. I let the scalding hot water run over my hands.

"Please, Kate." His voice was rough with emotion.

I nodded. "Just this once," I said.

Once we were in bed and Henri was asleep, I got up and took a blanket from the armoire. In the living room, I lay down on the sofa and curled up under the blanket. Henri was a wimp, afraid to stand up to Giancarlo. I felt a mixture of fear and disgust. How could he let this small-town Napoleon rule his life? Or was Giancarlo holding something over Henri? That gave me pause. Was there something Henri hadn't told me?

Eventually I returned to bed and fell into a troubled sleep.

Chapter 22

In the morning, Verona was socked in with heavy fog. As I buttoned my blouse, I looked out the window. The lights from the street below were barely visible. We wouldn't be seeing the sun that day. I woke the children and went into the kitchen to prepare breakfast. At the door, I noticed the two cardboard boxes from yesterday were gone. Henri had left early, scurrying out before I awoke. He had undoubtedly carried them down and deposited them in the car.

After breakfast, Timmy and I walked Lucie and Marc to school. When I got back, Marina arrived and began cleaning up in the kitchen. I fed her the lie Henri had proposed. She knew I was an author, right? I needed some time to get away and write.

Marina looked up, a sponge in her hand, "Signora, why don't you go into the office and shut the door. I'll take care of Timmy. He likes to follow me around."

"I need to concentrate. It's not possible for me here." I gestured vaguely around the kitchen.

She raised an eyebrow. "Where can you go?"

"Somewhere quiet." I had decided not to tell her I was driving all the way to Cerro. She would think I was nuts.

Back in the bedroom, I pulled on wool pants, two sweaters and the furry snow boots I had brought from Chicago. In the hallway, I found my winter coat, gloves and a knitted cap. If I was going to sit in the cottage for an hour, I needed to dress warmly. Along with my purse, I had a satchel with a couple of writing tablets and some sharp pencils. Maybe I would actually write while I was there. I yelled goodbye to Marina and snuck out before she could see me leave.

I drove carefully through town. The traffic moved slowly in the thick fog. The traffic lights were misty blurs. Out of town, I drove slowly, searching for the sign indicating the route to Cerro. I knew it was the SP6 road. I clutched the steering wheel, trying to peer through the mist. Right before the turn-off, I spotted a wooden picnic table at the side of the road. I knew where I was. In the summer months, an old man had a watermelon stand at that spot. He had hooked up a bamboo pipe that brought freezing water from a mountain stream into a large barrel containing bobbing watermelons. People pulled up and bought a slice of icy watermelon and ate it there at the picnic table.

I turned left and started the ascent to Cerro. Ahead, I saw the taillights of a truck. I sped up so I could follow the slow-moving vehicle up the mountain. We went back and forth up the steep incline, slowing at the hairpin turns. I was perspiring with fear as I tried to peer through the gloom. Hopefully, the driver of the truck could see where he was going, or he would send us both over the edge and into nothingness. As I drove, I debated with myself. Would I be safe with this stranger? What if he shot at me? What if he raped me? But Henri and Giancarlo knew I would be alone with this man. *They must think he's not a danger.*

After what seemed like hours, we made another turn and straightened out, and then *bam*, we came out of the fog. Blue sky and bright sunshine momentarily blinded me. I glanced behind me through the rearview mirror. It was as though I were coming out of a fluffy, grey soup. I had arrived in Cerro. Moments later, I turned right off the highway and up towards the cottage.

A light dusting of snow lay on the ground. I turned left and approached the cottage gate. The house looked secretive with the blinds covering the windows. I got out of the car to open the gates. Then I drove into the courtyard and maneuvered the vehicle around, so it was facing the gate. If I had to make a quick escape, I could jump in the car and barrel out into the lane. I sat for a minute clutching the steering wheel, perspiring and shivering. Finally, I got out of the car and opened the rear door. Both boxes were there, jampacked and heavy. I couldn't carry them up the metal stairs to the door, so I took three bottles of wine and a can of tomatoes out of one box. Then I picked it up, crossed the courtyard and started up the stairs. Each step rang in my ears.

At the door, I pulled out the key and fit it into the lock. At first it didn't turn, but then I remembered I needed to lift the handle slightly. The key turned and the door opened. It was dark inside except for horizontal stripes across the floor from the sun coming through the slats of the blinds. I reached around and felt for the light switch. The blazing brightness from the chandelier over the dining table momentarily blinded me. I placed the box on the table and then looked toward the little hallway into the bedrooms. That's when I spotted the glint of a gun barrel. A shadow moved slowly out from the master bedroom, gun at the ready.

I raised my hands and shouted, "*Sparami allora*. Go ahead and shoot me." I spoke in Italian and English, rage bubbling up inside me. This guy had some nerve. I was bringing him sustenance and he was acting like some shoot-'em-up cowboy. "You should be happy I'm here," I snarled at him. I didn't care if he understood English or not.

He raised his hands, the gun towards the ceiling. "*Mi scusi, signora*. I'm sorry." He said the second half in pretty good English.

I would have none of it. All the anger I felt towards Henri and Giancarlo Bianchi welled up inside of me. I glared at him and then marched out the door to fetch the rest of the provisions. After three trips, I went back to the car one more time to retrieve my satchel. When I came back, I placed the bag on the table and then I went to the blinds and yanked them open. I couldn't stand being in the dark. He was in the kitchen putting away the groceries. There was pasta, rice, cheeses, salami, eggs, and coffee along with wine and olive oil. Someone had also thought of a flashlight and batteries. I saw him rip open a plastic bag wrapped around a loaf of bread. He tore off a piece and stuffed it into his mouth. *What a pig,* I thought.

"Signora, thank you. I am very grateful for the food. I have not eaten for two days." He pulled off another piece of bread and made

127

an effort to eat it more slowly. I turned away, not wanting to look at him. He filled me with such anger.

I went into the main room, sat down at the head of the table, and pulled out a pad of paper and a pencil. Only then did I notice how cold the room was. The walls seemed to vibrate with Arctic cold. Even with my extra layer of clothes, I was freezing. I got up and went into the hallway. I planned to grab a blanket from the children's beds, but the bedclothes were gone. Across the hall, I could see a mountain of blankets covering the master bed. I turned away. It was unsettling to see my bed taken over by this murderer.

I sat back down, shivering. Maybe I should leave, but I couldn't yet. I needed to maintain the charade. If anyone saw me come, if anyone asked questions, they needed to think I was in here writing.

"Are you cold? You aren't warmly dressed," the murderer said.

I didn't want to answer him, but I nodded. He went into the bedroom, came back with a heavy blanket, and handed it to me. I took it without comment and wrapped myself up. He went back into the bedroom and came out with a couple of electric heaters. He plugged them in on each side of the room. I continued to look down at my pad of paper. Why should I be grateful to him?

He went into the kitchen. I heard the rustle of paper, then the sound of coffee beans raining into the grinder. With the whir of the machine, the aroma spilled into the room. He filled the base of the espresso coffee pot and set it on the stove. I never looked back, but I recognized the sounds. I stared down at the empty sheet in front of me. What could I write? My mind was empty, drained, curled in on itself. I willed myself to not turn around. I heard the water bubbling up through the grounds and the smell of espresso circled the air.

"Signora, would you like coffee?"

I nodded.

"How many sugars?"

Without turning around, I held up two fingers.

Minutes later he brought me a small cup and placed it on the table. I didn't thank him. Why should I? He owed me. I sipped the hot brew. It was sweet and delicious.

He pulled a chair over to the window and sat down, basking in the sunlight. He sighed. "I have missed the sunlight. At the plant, I was in a dark closet. Up here, I cannot open the blinds. I am starved for light."

He didn't turn around and I didn't answer.

Chapter 23

I sat staring at the empty page. I had to write something. My mind was still blank. I glanced over at the guy's back. It was difficult to deduce the shape of his body. He was wearing several sweaters and a heavy jacket. Dark curls snaked out from under a woolen knit cap. He had seemed tall when I'd entered the cottage, taller than me, maybe six feet. A thick, black beard covered his face. I hadn't seen his eyes. It had been too dark.

He stretched his arms over his head and made animal sounds of contentment. He resembled a big black bear in the pool of sunlight. I felt guilty, a covert voyeur. My face felt warm. I quickly turned back to the empty page.

He cleared his throat. "My name is Andrea." He paused, as if waiting for me to respond. I didn't answer. He certainly didn't need to know my name.

"I want to tell you about what happened. I'm not a murderer. You shouldn't be afraid."

"I'm writing. Don't bother me," I growled.

I picked up the pencil and carefully printed the date in the right-hand corner. Then I began to write about the trip up the mountain that morning. I took my time picking just the right adjectives, trying to depict my fear, the fog and my anger. As I wrote, I lost myself in my recollections. It wasn't until he stood up, scraping the chair on the tile, that I emerged. I looked at my watch. It was almost noon. I would need to fly if I wanted to get to the school in time to pick up the children. Shrugging out of the blanket, I stuffed the tablet and pencil into my satchel and stood up.

Without looking at him, I pushed past and roughly pulled the metal blinds closed. *There, no more sunlight*, I thought. Then I picked up my bag and walked to the door.

"Signora?"

I didn't turn around but pushed open the door.

"Signora? Could you bring me some books, a newspaper, a magazine...something to read?"

I shrugged. I wasn't really planning on coming back. Henri could do it. I slammed the door shut and hurried down the stairs.

The fog had dissipated, and the trip down the mountain took no time at all. I pulled up in front of the school, just in time. Inside, Lucie and Marc were coming down the hallway following their teachers. They looked like ducklings following their mother. I saw Giada across the foyer, but I avoided her gaze. I was worried she would question me about my morning, and I knew my face would be like an open book. Lucie's teacher beckoned me over. We exchanged pleasantries while the foyer emptied out.

"Signora, I would like to talk to you a moment about Lucie." She smiled down at my daughter and patted her on the head. Lucie smiled up at her and then skipped off.

"Is there a problem?" I asked.

"Lucie is learning Italian quickly, but sometimes she seems distracted." The teacher frowned.

"Is she disturbing the class?" I felt a tightness in my chest. I glanced around the large, high-ceilinged foyer. Most of the children and their parents had cleared out. Lucie was chasing Marc around the wide-open space.

The *maestra* responded, "No, she doesn't bother the other children, but there are times during the morning when she gazes into space and isn't paying attention to the lesson."

"Oh, I know what you mean. Lucie has been like this her entire life. She loses herself in daydreams." My words came bumbling out. I glanced nervously across the room. The children were laughing hysterically. Their voices reverberated between the marble floors and the high ceilings.

"Signora, perhaps you could talk to her about the importance of paying attention," she said, concern in her voice.

"Yes, yes, I will," I said, distractedly. Across the room I saw Marc skim around a low marble-topped table. Lucie raced up behind him and fell forward on the edge. A second later there was a horrendous explosion as the marble tabletop crashed to the floor. Lucie screamed as she fell face-down into the shards of stone. Marc stood frozen, his eyes round in shock. I rushed forward to help my daughter up. Luckily her face was fine, but a marble chip had scraped her hand and it was bleeding profusely.

From the entrance to the administrative wing, the school principal and her secretary came racing into the room. In typical Italian style, they screamed bloody murder, shaking their hands in the air. Lucie's face was buried in my coat and she was crying uncontrollably. I kept apologizing. Marc ran outside to get away from the clamor. After a few minutes, the principal calmed down and inspected the damage.

"We will pay for the table or buy a new one. Whatever you want," I tried to say. "I'm so sorry. My children were out of control. It's my fault." I dabbed at Lucie's hand with a tissue.

The principal surveyed the floor, then looked up at me. Her mouth twitched. "I hated that table and it was most inappropriate in a school entryway." She began to laugh and so did the secretary. The free-form piece of marble had been balanced on a three-legged base, which could easily be tipped over by exerting pressure on one side. It was an accident waiting to happen.

"Don't worry, signora. Signor Barbieri gave us that table and because of the funds he provided for the new auditorium, I had to accept it. His cousin had designed it." She shrugged in a gesture of *che sera, sera.* (Whatever will be, will be.)

Seemingly by magic, a clean-up crew arrived as we headed for the door. Outside, Marc was huddled by one of the pillars that graced the entrance to the Scuola Agli Angeli. My children had definitely not been angels that morning and were appropriately subdued during the short walk home.

It was one-thirty when we arrived at the apartment. Marina was upset. She usually left before one o'clock in order to pick up her daughter from the local public school. Then she prepared lunch for her husband, who came home every day. I kept apologizing as she pulled on her coat and wrapped a wool scarf around her neck. "This cannot happen again. If you don't come home on time, I will quit." Before slamming the door, she scoffed, "You should stay home to write your *capolavoro* (masterpiece)."

By the time the children had eaten their lunch, the fog had rolled back in, making a trip to the park impossible. I put Timmy down for a nap, but he kept climbing out of bed. Lucie was grumpy and didn't want to work on her math lesson. The afternoon dragged on forever. Timmy and Marc raced their miniature cars up and down the hallway and Lucie screamed at them about the noise. Then Marc hit Timmy and they tussled on the carpet. I herded them all into the kitchen and covered the table with newspaper. I brought out the paint boxes, paper and glasses of water to clean the brushes. This activity didn't last long. Lucie and Marc made fun of Timmy's scribbles and he overturned a water glass. I screamed at all three of them. Then I banished each one to a different room to cool down.

I was glad when five o'clock came around. Bath time was relatively calm and soon all three were in their pajamas, smelling sweet. Supper was uneventful. By eight o'clock, they were in bed. I took a prosciutto panini into the living room with a glass of wine. I had to admit to myself that part of the reason the children had been impossible was because I'd been on edge since early morning. They had sensed my unease. I don't know whether I was angrier at Henri or myself. I felt I had been taken advantage of...but I had let it happen. He shouldn't put me in the position of harboring a criminal and I should not let him force me into it.

I took only a few bites of my sandwich. It seemed dry and tasteless. I pushed it away and picked up the glass of wine. At the window, I pulled back the curtain. Below, I could see the hazy beams of cars in the murky gloom. The usual sounds were muffled by the fog. I felt insulated as though wrapped in cotton. Without thinking, I gulped down the wine and went back into the kitchen to refill my glass. Then I went into the study and sat down on the floor, placing the glass beside me. Three shelving units contained our small library. Henri's First and Second World War history books filled the top shelves in perfect order. Underneath were heavy tomes from his graduate studies. The last two shelves held my well-read books. My fingers ran across the spines of my old friends. I had several books on writing and then an eclectic selection of novels, mysteries and poetry. I pulled out Agatha Christie's *Murder on The Orient Express*, Hemingway's *A Farewell to Arms* and a tattered leather-bound book of Emily Dickinson's poetry. It had belonged to my mother. I leafed through the pages.

There is another sky
Ever serene and fair
And there is another sunshine,
Though it be darkness there...

I finished my wine, reading through my favorite poems. In the pantry, I put the three books in a plastic bag. Then I went to bed.

Henri came home late. I was vaguely aware when he slipped into bed like a masked thief. He reached over and pulled up my nightgown. His breath on my neck was thick with fumes of grappa and wine. When he entered me, I held my eyes tightly shut. I'd become aroused, but behind my flickering eyelids, I saw the amorphous shape of another man.

Chapter 24

In the morning Henri came into the kitchen while I was heating milk for the children's hot chocolate. I didn't look up when he entered the room.

"Did it go well?" he asked.

"Did what go well?"

"You know what I mean. The delivery..." He spoke in measured tones as he poured himself a cup of coffee.

I turned around and glared at him. "I did it and he didn't kill me...this time, anyway."

Marc came in then, still wearing his pajamas. "Who didn't kill you, Mommy?" I saw a flash of fear cross his face.

"Nobody, sweetheart. I was telling a joke." I bent down to give him a hug, but he squirmed away. I looked up at Henri. "It was a joke, right, Papa?"

"Yes, a silly joke." Henri said. His forehead creased and he faked a smile. But Marc wasn't looking at him.

"Go get dressed for school, sweetheart. Breakfast isn't quite ready," I said.

Reluctantly, he walked to the door. He looked back at me frowning. His antennae had spotted a lie.

***

That morning, I had a date with Giada, her friend Anna, and Anna's sister-in-law. We were going to the *Mercato Generale*. Anna was a pediatrician and the mother of two little girls who were younger than Lucie and Francesca. Anna had a matter-of-fact way about her. She bustled when she walked. A smooth cap of dark hair framed her shrewd, grey eyes. Her smile was quick and genuine. Anna's sister-in-law was a pretty, quiet woman that I don't remember very well. She was definitely overshadowed by Anna's verve for life.

The four of us met in the café in my building. Signor Costa served us cappuccinos and sweet brioches. As we sipped our coffees, Anna made a list of the vegetables and fruit we would look for at the market.

In the 1970s, Verona was the point of convergence of the agricultural industry in northern Italy. Fruits and vegetables arrived from warmer climes. After high-level bartering by European grocery chains, the produce was loaded onto trains destined for northern cities: Paris, Berlin, Stockholm, etc. That morning we were going to the Mercato Generale to buy commercial-sized boxes of ultra-fresh produce, to be divvied up among the four of us. Anna's cousin worked at the market and had procured a day-pass.

Again, that morning, thick fog held the city hostage. Remembering the drive up the mountains the day before, I shivered involuntarily. Giada looked over at me and frowned. "Are you all right?"

"Yes, fine. I'm fine."

"By the way, what happened yesterday? I waited for you outside school and you never came out. You looked pretty frazzled when you arrived. I wondered if something was wrong."

"Oh, I had to talk to Lucie's teacher. Everything is fine." I turned towards the window, in case my face revealed too much. I wasn't good at dissembling. I could feel Giada's gaze.

We left the café and loaded into Anna's car. She drove carefully, following the taillight of the car in front of us. Fifteen minutes later we arrived at the Mercato. At the gate she handed over the permit, which was closely examined by a chubby guy in a green uniform. After much discussion with another guard who was doing a crossword puzzle, we were permitted to enter the parking area.

We bumped over railway tracks and parked the car on the side of the warehouse by an industrial-sized scale. The building was enormous, like an airplane hangar. At the entrance we obtained a flat-bed cart. Shopping was tedious; locating the produce we desired and the exact box that met with Anna's approval took much of the morning. She was a great cook and knew exactly what she wanted.

Screeching forklifts rolled up and down the wide passageways, driven by operators in blue overalls. We piled boxes of golden carrots, mushrooms, cippolini onions and crates of dark green spinach, baby artichokes and pears onto our flat-bed. It was freezing in the hangar. Up near the roof, wisps of fog crept into the warehouse.

We arrived at the citrus aisle and saw a vertiginous stack of boxes of mandarin oranges, piled up to the roof. Anna walked over and inspected the boxes. She decided the fifth crate from the bottom was by far the best. There were ten or so crates piled on top of it. But she was convinced she had found the best box. Giada and I looked at each other and groaned. Anna's sister-in-law shrugged in acquiescence. She knew Anna better than we did.

Meanwhile, Anna marched over to a forklift zipping by and waved her arms. The driver stopped and she convinced him to help us out. With the forklift, he moved the palettes of boxes to uncover the perfect one. Anna thanked him while Giada and I stood back, embarrassed.

After paying at the gate, we rolled our flatbed cart out to the parking lot. We headed to the industrial-sized scale, where we weighed each box and divided up the fruits and vegetables in portions. Anna even insisted we weigh each individual portion, so they were certifiably equal. It was a dirty business, but I remember a lot of laughter. By the time we finished, rays of sunshine had pierced the fog.

Chapter 25   2019

I must have dozed off. I wake up with a start, wondering where I am. The steward smiles down at me and asks if I would like a glass of water. I nod and smile up at him. He hands me a cup and a small napkin. I know it's important to keep hydrated on long flights. Lucie is still asleep beside me. She'll probably sleep for much of the trip. She really needs the rest.

I glance across the aisle. Tim is in the aisle seat, his head bent over a sketch pad. In his hand is an artist's graphite pencil. He's drawing at a remarkable speed, his lower lip protruding in concentration. Gone are the chubby cheeks of his childhood. His profile exhibits a strong nose, hollowed cheeks and full lips. He's become a handsome man, tall and slim-hipped. He has an aesthetic appeal that stands him in good stead in his profession. Tim is the owner and designer of a small fashion house. He has the knack to predict where fashion is going. His designs are considered avant-garde by the young fashionistas who favor his line of clothes. He has several small boutiques in New York, Paris, Tokyo and Milan.

Tim's partner, Pierre, is a Parisian who works in museums around the world. An exhibitions designer, he's sought after by big galleries and museums in major cities. Tim and Pierre maintain an apartment in New York and one in Paris. Somehow, they manage to coordinate their busy lives, so they can spend time together each month. At one point, Tim talked about adopting children, but they both came to the realization that their frenetic lives couldn't include the needs of a child.

Pierre is short and dark with thick features and a balding head. He and Tim are total opposites physically, but they're on the same wavelength intellectually and spiritually. They both live for art, design, line, color and beauty. They live relatively cheaply except for the purchase of valuable works of art. The walls of their New York apartment are covered with their beloved paintings and drawings.

After our visit to Verona, Tim is off to Florence to spend a week with Pierre, who just finished a big show at the Art Institute of Chicago. It was one of the Impressionists...maybe Monet or Renoir...one of those soft, warm, colorful painters. I can't remember what Tim said.

I learned Tim was gay when he was a sophomore in high school. He didn't tell me, Marc did. One afternoon, I was at my desk in my study, my hands flying on the computer. I was writing a short story that would later be published in the New Yorker. *Beside me was a cup of tea growing cold and two molasses cookies.*

Marc came into the room. "Mom, I need to talk to you."

Internally, I groaned, but since it was a rarity that my sons took me into their confidence, I turned and faced him, giving him my full attention.

Marc shut the door behind him and perched on the side chair, then stood and walked to the window. With his back to me, he said, "Mom, Tim is gay."

"What? Say that again." Mechanically, I picked up the teacup and took a good swallow.

I looked at Marc's broad back. He was tall, sturdy and played football. I think they called his position a linebacker. At that moment, he was rigid and radiated discomfort. He turned around and looked directly into my eyes. "I'm sure he's gay and I don't want him to get hurt. I mean, right now, it's all right. He's a sophomore and nobody seems to realize...but he could have a rough time next year...and I won't be here. I'll be in college." There were tears in his eyes.

I sat back, at a loss for words. Tim? Gay? He was the happiest, most carefree of my children. He seemed to bump through life like a happy-go-lucky bouncing ball. Friends came over after school and hung out in the kitchen and the basement. He didn't seem like a tortured kid, hiding his sexual orientation. I gulped more tea.

"How do you know?" I asked.

"Oh, come on, Mom. It's so obvious. He doesn't really like girls."

"What do you mean? Oodles of girls come over here every afternoon. Right now, we have the entire 'Hello, Dolly' gang eating my brownies. Those girls are Tim's best friends."

"That's just it. Those girls like Tim as a friend, period. I mean, he's like one of the girls himself."

143

I didn't know what to think about all this. I shook my head and leaned back in my chair, then scanned the cozy room. One wall was lined with shelving and stuffed with books, mementos and pictures of the kids. My cluttered desk faced the window with a view of our tree-filled backyard. When I needed a break, I could look out at busy squirrels and flittering birds. An overstuffed chair and ottoman sat in one corner. I curled up there to read manuscripts. This room was my workspace and my haven.

I rubbed my temples with my palms. This revelation was a surprise, but maybe not totally. Maybe subconsciously, I had realized Tim was different from his brother. Whereas Marc was a jock, Tim was in love with the world of theatre. He did sets and costumes with Mrs. Rosenkranz. As I think back, I realize he was already on the way to his current profession. But until that moment I hadn't equated his love of costume and design to being gay.

Marc was insistent. "Being gay is really hard in high school. Lots of kids might tease him. Bully him, even."

"Did you talk to him about this? Maybe he's the one you should talk to...find out what his feelings are. You guys are so close."

I don't remember how we ended our conversation, but things came to a head several days later. It was almost eleven at night. I was in the kitchen rinsing my wine glass. Tim came in, slamming the door behind him, and started up the stairs. I flew out of the kitchen and called up to him.

"Hey, Tim. You're awfully late. I thought practice finished at 9:30?"

No answer. I heard the door to his bedroom slam shut. But before that, I thought I heard a sob. I went up the stairs and knocked gently on his door.

"Honey. Is there something wrong?"

No answer. I was sure I could hear him crying. I waited a few seconds and then I pushed open the door. He was sprawled across his bed, his face buried in his pillow. His shoulders shook with sobs.

I went over and sat on the edge of his bed. "Talk to me, Tim. Maybe I can help."

"Mom. Just leave me alone. I need to be alone," he mumbled between sniffles.

"Sometimes, talking helps," I said.

He turned over and looked at me. His face was red and blotchy, and his blond hair stood in spikes. "Nothing will help. Nothing. Leave me alone." Then he flopped back around, turning his face towards the wall. I patted his back and then left the room, shutting the door behind me.

A short while later, I lay in bed, tossing and turning. Was Marc, right? Had something happened at play rehearsal? What else could be wrong? I knew teenagers were plagued by peer pressure, fears about grades, college...all sorts of things. It must have been two in the morning when I felt a hand on my arm. I was instantly awake.

"Mom. You're right. I need to talk to you," Tim whispered.

I sat up and patted the empty spot beside me. Then I waited. But Tim didn't sit next to me. He sat on the far edge of the bed.

"Tonight, Mr. Robertson asked me to stay late after rehearsal." He took a jagged breath. "We were in the back, in his little office." I heard a sharper intake of breath and a sob. Then he whispered, "He came on to me."

"What do you mean?"

"Well, he kissed me and stuff."

I stiffened, shocked and horrified. Mr. Robertson was everyone's favorite teacher. He had been the theatre director for several years. He was young and vibrant. I held him in the highest regard. How could this have happened?

"Oh, Tim. Oh, honey." I reached out to him. But he remained rigid, his shoulders inflexible in my embrace. "I'll call the school tomorrow. We'll get to the bottom of this. Robertson will be out on his ear."

"Don't do that, Mom. It was probably my fault. I've been spending a lot of time with him."

"That's ridiculous. It's not your fault. You're a kid. He's an adult. He is one hundred percent responsible for his actions." I was seething.

Tim fell back on the mattress and curved his body into a fetal position. "You don't get it, Mom. He didn't do anything bad. I mean, it wasn't sex or anything."

I groaned. "Kissing you is bad. That's abuse."

"But Mom, you're not getting the point." His voice was raw and pained.

"What do you mean?"

He swallowed another sob. "The point is, I liked it. I liked kissing him. I wanted him to kiss me. I know he shouldn't have, being my teacher and all..." He took a big breath. "You see, Mom. I'm gay." And then he began to cry in earnest. And I was able to gather him into my arms.

When I called the school in the morning to arrange a meeting with the principal, the secretary asked what it was about. I said I wanted to discuss Mr. Robertson. She responded, "Oh, you already heard the news?"

"What news?"

"He gave his resignation last night. He quit and the school is in a real bind, what with 'Hello Dolly' being scheduled for next weekend."

Chapter 26

The following Wednesday was another foggy day. The night before, Henri had come home early with two more bags of supplies. He and I had barely spoken that evening. I could feel him tiptoeing around me. He even offered to do the dishes after supper, which was a first. I didn't think he knew how to do the dishes.

That morning before heading to the car, I added two copies of the *Corriere della Sera* newspaper to the books I had put aside the previous week. In addition, I added several mandarin oranges from our shopping trip. I don't know why I went out of my way to provide reading material, when I was still seething at Henri and what I was being forced to do. Before leaving, I pulled on another sweater and another pair of wool pants. Underneath, I was wearing long underwear that I'd bought the previous day. Marina was scrubbing the tub as I headed out. She didn't look up when I said goodbye, but mumbled that I had better be home on time.

The fog quickly dissipated as I made my way up the mountain road. As I came around the bend approaching Cerro, the sun blinded me. Again, I drove into the parking area below the cottage and maneuvered the vehicle so I could make a quick getaway. I pulled on my blue knit cap and a ski jacket before getting out of the car. I didn't want to freeze in there. As I walked up the stairs, I was swearing under my breath. At the door, I fumbled with the key before managing to push the door open. Inside, I placed the grocery bags on the kitchen table, glancing towards the bedroom door where the guy had appeared the last time. No one was there, but as I turned to open the blinds, I became aware of a looming presence behind me. I spun around, gripped by fear. He was there, gun in hand. I gave a screech and he dropped the gun. It clattered across the stone floor.

"My God, you could have killed me. That gun could have gone off when you dropped it," I screamed.

"Scusa, signora. I'm sorry. I live in fear that someone is coming to get me." He bent over to retrieve the gun.

Adrenalin was pumping through my veins. "Maybe they should. I don't know why I should protect a killer. Maybe I'll fetch the carabinieri and get them to arrest you."

"*Non sono un assassino*. I'm not a killer. It was my brother," he yelled back. He was shaking with emotion in response to my outburst.

I shook my head in disbelief. "Right. Blame your brother. That's a pretty flimsy excuse."

We were barely six inches apart and going head to head. Somewhere in my subconscious, I saw this man that I had failed to look at properly the first time I was there. He was a few inches taller than me, maybe six foot. Between the dark, wavy hair that fell to his shoulders, his scraggly heavy beard and the multiple layers of clothing, he resembled a scruffy caveman. His eyes were chocolate pools with glints of gold. They were intense with emotion as he pleaded with me for understanding.

I stepped back; my hands clenched in fists. For whatever reason, I was no longer afraid of this man, but I was angry…angry with him…angry with Henri…angry with Bianchi…angry with myself because I was such a chump. Why in the hell was I in this position? I turned away from this *non-assassino* and went back outside. I stomped down the stairs to the car and fetched the bag with the books, the bag of mandarin oranges and my satchel. Then I tromped back up the stairs.

Inside, he was unpacking the groceries and putting them away. There were toiletries this time, including soap, shampoo and a toothbrush, which he put in the bathroom. I flung the two additional plastic bags on the table without saying anything. When he came back into the main room, I gestured to the bags. He came over and pulled out the books and the oranges. Then he looked over at me. His face lit up. Tears glimmered in his expressive eyes and he smiled an almost childish smile. "Thank you, Signora. This is so kind of you."

I looked down at his long fingers that caressed the cover of the poetry book…*my* poetry book. I felt myself blush and looked away.

"Well, you said you wanted reading material. Now you have a nice variety." I pulled out my notebook and a couple of pencils. Then I sat down to write. I was determined not to look at or talk to this man. I would stay the required two hours and then I would drive home.

"I'll make you a coffee," he said. His voice held a gentle note.

I nodded as I picked up a pencil and opened the notebook. Reading what I had written the previous week, I was amazed at the anger and turbulence reflected in my words. But it was good. It was intense and real. Maybe this experience was what I needed to kickstart my writing.

An espresso appeared by my side. "You didn't tell me your name last time. I am Andrea Mongelli." He paused. "You are the wife of Henri, the French man, but you don't seem French."

"You don't need to know my name or anything about me," I blurted out. I picked up the coffee and sipped. "Now please don't talk to me. I need to write."

He moved off. From the corner of my eye, I saw him pick up one of the mandarin oranges. They looked like balls of gold in the sunlight. He peeled off the skin and the room filled with a sweet, citrusy perfume.

"This is my favorite fruit. They are a special gift from you?" he asked.

I didn't answer.

"Thank you." He sat down facing the window. He quietly ate the fruit, apparently relishing the warmth of the sun.

I began to write about our trip to the market. For a few minutes, I lost myself as I covered the page with flowing sentences. When I paused to find a word, I glanced over at Andrea. He looked over his shoulder and smiled at me. His teeth were white, and his eyes danced. Quickly, I looked down at the page filled with my scribblings. I laced my fingers together and closed my eyes.

After another few moments, he broke the silence. "It's true. I did not kill anyone. I need to tell you about it."

I didn't look up, but I nodded imperceptibly.

"We were in the bar, Massimo and me, with some other men. Massimo is my brother. An argument broke out with some enemies of my family. It was a heated argument." His English was good, but with a strong accent. I sensed he had been practicing this explanation. "One man pulled out a gun. Massimo shot the enemy before he could shoot at us. Then he put the gun in my hand and ran out the back door. Everyone was looking at me. They thought I had killed this *testa calda,* this crazy hot head. I stood there staring at the gun. Antonio, one of our *soldati*, grabbed my arm and led me out the back. A car was there. We drove north towards Rome. We stopped once and Antonio called my father. In Rome we met a *consigliere* and changed cars. It had been decided that I should hide in Verona at the Bianchi plant."

I studied my fingers laced tight in my lap.

"I speak the truth. I would never kill a man," he declared. He was breathing heavily. I looked up. His eyes pleaded with mine. We were communicating soul to soul. I nodded ever so slightly.

After what seemed like an eternity, I looked back down at my hands. Then I whispered, "My name is Katherine…Kate."

"Kate…Catarina," he murmured.

Abruptly, I stood up. I shoved my pencils and the notebook into my satchel, then pushed my chair back and stumbled to the door, down the stairs and into my car. Above, I heard the shutters bang shut. I shivered as I headed out the driveway, down the mountain and home to Verona.

Chapter 27

I arrived home with time to spare. As Marina buttoned her coat, she told me Timmy was asleep on the sofa and that she had prepared lunch. Before leaving, she smiled at me wryly. "Did you write many pages today, signora?"

"Yes, it went well," I said, and smiled brightly. I wondered if she could tell how nervous I was.

After she left, I went into the bedroom and stripped off several layers of heavy clothes. From the living room I heard Timmy's little voice: "Mommy, Mommy." Quickly I pulled on a wool skirt, a blouse and a sweater.

He was sprawled across the cushions. His face was damp and rosy. He smiled up at me sleepily. I picked him up and felt his warmth against my chest. I kissed the top of his sweet-smelling head and he snuggled against me.

"I love you, pumpkin," I said.

He giggled in response.

I carried him into the kitchen. Marina had indeed gotten lunch on the way. There was a pot of tomato sauce on the stove and she had cooked a veal roast in the heavy-bottomed Dutch oven. It was perfumed with sprigs of rosemary, garlic and white wine, and smelled incredibly delicious when I lifted the cover. I set the lid back down and left the kitchen, then quickly dressed Timmy in his coat and hat. Then we went around the block to the School of the Angels to pick up Lucie and Marc.

Since Timmy had already taken a nap and we were blessed with sunshine, I decided to leave for the park right after lunch. I worried that the fog would roll back in and we would be stuck in the house for another long afternoon. We went down to the parking garage under the building and got out the bicycles for Marc and Lucie. Timmy usually rode in the stroller or toddled along beside me.

The sidewalk along Corso Porta Nuova was very wide and Marc and Lucie liked to race along as fast as they could. The shopkeepers along the route tsk-tsked and shook their heads at these unruly American children. The kids were dressed in jeans and their colorful Sears winter jackets that I'd purchased stateside. Well-mannered Italian children walked sedately beside their parents and wore tailored wool coats and pants. Marc and Lucie careened ahead of me as I pushed Timmy along. He was clapping his hands as he watched them go. Up ahead, I saw Giada come out of her apartment building. *Oh good, we can have a nice chat while the kids play*, I thought. But that was not to be.

Marc was ahead of Lucie, barreling along. He must have spotted Giada and wasn't looking where he was going. Just before reaching her building, he hit an uneven spot in the sidewalk. He went sailing over the handlebars of his little green bike and onto the stone sidewalk. I began to run. I could feel my heart pounding. Giada was there first and was crouched over him when I arrived.

"He's unconscious," she said, looking up at me.

Marc lay flat on his stomach, his head turned to the side. Blood was pouring from a cut on his head. His face was white, and I could see the fine, blue veins on his eyelids. I yelled at him, "Marc, Marc. Wake up. Talk to me." But he didn't respond. He really was out cold. I looked at Giada. I felt frozen and wasn't thinking clearly. "What should I do?"

"You need to take him to the hospital, right now. I'll take the other two children."

I looked at her, bewildered. Then I bent down and picked Marc up in my arms.

Giada waved down a taxi and bundled me into the back. She told the driver to get us to *Pronto Soccorso,* fast. What seemed like an eternity later, we arrived at the hospital and I rushed in, carrying my little boy, who was still unresponsive. No one was sitting at the grey metal desk in the cavernous, white-tiled room. Along one wall were wooden benches. One elderly gentleman sat there clutching a cane. Along the other wall, two white-coated men were smoking, deep in conversation.

"My little boy is hurt. We need help," I said.

The old man looked at me and shrugged. One of the white-coated orderlies glanced over and picked a piece of tobacco from his lip. Then he continued his conversation with his colleague.

"Is there a nurse or a doctor I can talk to?" I said, loudly.

At that moment, the door at the far side of the room swung open and a woman strode out, carrying some files. She sat down at the

156

metal desk, put on her spectacles that were hanging around her neck on a cord, and began looking at a file. I went over and stood in front of her.

"My little boy is hurt. He needs to see a doctor."

The woman barely looked up. "Please sit over there, Signora. We'll get to you soon."

Frightened and annoyed, I snapped, "Isn't this the emergency room? He needs to be seen now."

The woman frowned. "Please sit down. We'll get to you soon."

I couldn't believe this. Here was Marc out cold, his head covered with blood, and she tells me to sit down. Seething with anger, I did sit down, pulling Marc against me. I looked across the room at the two disinterested smokers. Above them on the wall was a sign, *Vietato Fumare:* No Smoking. I noticed their white coats were dirty and spattered with blood. Everyone's indifference to my son's state was infuriating. I was about to start yelling and screaming when Marc began to vomit. I held him as he emptied his stomach on the grimy white-tiled floor. It spattered on my coat and my shoes. But I held him close.

Now we got some action. The woman called someone on the phone. Moments later, a gurney appeared through the swinging doors, pushed by a tall, emaciated orderly. He picked Marc up and wheeled him into the inner sanctum of the emergency room. I followed along. Inside, we were taken into a curtain-draped cubicle. A nurse appeared and took Marc's vitals and cleaned him up. She draped an adult-sized hospital gown over his small frame, then

157

wrapped his soiled clothes in a piece of paper and handed them to me. Next she washed the wound on his head, which thankfully wasn't a deep cut. Marc's eyes were open now, but he was clearly disoriented. I sat next to him, holding his hand and murmuring words of love and encouragement.

Chapter 28

"Where am I, Mommy?"

"You're in the hospital. You fell off your bike. Do you remember that?"

He looked at me with wide, frightened eyes. He began to shake his head *no,* but quickly stopped and his eyes glazed over. The motion must have hurt. We waited a while and then a very young doctor appeared. He looked at Marc's pupils, moved his arms and legs. Studied his head injury. Then he asked Marc some basic questions: his name, how old he was, what happened. Marc responded in a tiny voice, in English and Italian. The doctor disappeared and we waited some more. Then he came back and said Marc had suffered a concussion, and he should stay in the hospital for twenty-four hours for observation. Then he left to see about a bed.

I wanted to call Henri, but no one appeared in our cubicle. The doctor had said to keep Marc awake for a while. This proved difficult because my little boy kept dozing off, so I kept talking and urging him awake. The hours crawled by. I had no sense of what time it was; no window to look through to tell me if it was still afternoon or evening.

Finally, an orderly appeared and rolled us down a long dark hall, up an elevator and then down another hall. Occupied beds lined one side of the hallway. We pulled up beside an empty bed, and the orderly and a nurse picked Marc up and placed him on the mattress. The nurse told me I needed to stay with him in case he rolled out of bed. The top of the mattress was several feet off the ground. I looked down at the hard marble floor. Indeed, it would be dangerous if he fell off.

"Aren't we going into one of the hospital rooms?" I asked.

"Signora, the rooms are full. We have to keep some patients in the hall."

I looked up and down the clogged hallway. It seemed as though every patient had a retinue of family around their beds. I heard talking, laughing and crying from the various groups huddled around their sick loved one. A window at the end of the hall showed darkness outside. How long had we been here?

"Will someone be coming to check on my son?"

"Eventually, yes. But we are very busy, as you can see, and we're understaffed."

"I need to call my husband. Could you please stand here with my son while I go call?"

She huffed. "I'm very busy, Signora."

"I'm sure you are, but I have no one else. I need to call my husband and tell him what happened and where we are.

The nurse screwed up her face, but grudgingly agreed to stay with Marc for a couple of minutes. She pointed down the hall to the public phone. I had the number of the Bianchi plant in my purse in a little notebook. A woman was on the phone when I got there, talking and crying. She kept sniffling and wiping her nose on the back of her hand. She turned once towards me and I indicated that I needed to use the phone. She turned her back to me and kept on with her lament. After a few minutes, I tapped her on the back. She turned around and glared at me. I must have looked pretty desperate because finally she hung up and flounced off.

The phone rang at the plant several times. Eventually, a male voice responded.

"Hello, this is Mrs. Joubert. I would like to talk to Mr. Joubert."

"I am sorry, signora. Signor Joubert left already with Signor Bianchi and Signor Ferrari."

Left? "Do you know where they went?"

"I'm sorry. I do not...oh, wait."

I heard some mumbling and then another voice came on the phone. "Signora, this is Giuseppe Peron. Can I help you."

"*Buonasera*, Giuseppe. I'm at the hospital with Marc. He fell off his bike and has a concussion. I need to find Henri." I sounded desperate, on the edge of tears. It was eight o'clock, and I was exhausted from worry and tension.

"I'm sorry, Kate. He is not here, and we don't know where he went. I will call Adriana. She will come to you."

The thought of Adriana with her bustling, practical efficiency filled me with joy. "Oh, would you? It wouldn't be too much of an imposition?"

"No, of course not. We are your friends. Don't worry. She'll be there soon."

I hung up and went back to Marc. The nurse said sarcastically, "You were gone long enough." Then, she rushed off. I did feel sorry for her. I don't know how she could manage to take care of so many people. It was like a circus up and down the hallway and in the rooms. Some friends or family members were drinking wine, eating salami panini and chomping on apples. I wondered if there were visiting hours or if everyone spent the night there with their sick loved one.

Marc drifted in and out of sleep. With all the noise and revelry, it wasn't much of a problem keeping him awake. When Adriana arrived, I burst into tears and fell into her arms. She patted me on the back and crooned reassuring words. Then she bent over the bed and smoothed Marc's hair off his forehead. She looked into his eyes. His pupils were no longer dilated.

Adriana stood up and pushed a wayward lock of curly hair out of her eyes. She glanced up and down the hallway. I caught her look of disapproval. "This place is a circus. Why aren't you in a room?"

"The rooms are full. We need to be in the hallway."

"This isn't acceptable. How will your little *bambino* rest with all this noise and movement?" She turned and caressed Marc's cheek. His frightened eyes looked between Adriana and me. "*Non ti preoccupare. Sono sicura che tutto andrà bene* (Don't worry, I'm sure everything will be all right)," Adriana said to reassure Marc and me.

I nodded in agreement, although I didn't feel as positive as she did.

"I'm going to go down the hall and check with the nurse." She bustled down the hall with purpose and fire in her eyes. After a long time and lots of shouting, she reappeared. "I've told her we want Marc to be evaluated and we would like her to call a doctor. He should be here soon."

We settled down on the end of Marc's bed. Adriana entertained me with stories about the people she worked with. I half listened, but my mind wandered. Where was Henri? How would I get through this night? Should I make the children walk their bikes on the sidewalk? Was I responsible for this fall? Undoubtedly Henri would blame me. I needed to call Giada, but I didn't have her number.

There was a pause in Adriana's narrative. She was looking at me questioningly. I blushed. "Oh, I'm sorry. My mind wandered."

"I wondered why you were up at the cottage yesterday," she asked. I must have turned bright red. Her eyes widened; her eyebrows raised in inquiry.

"Well…" I was trying to think of an appropriate answer. Then I remembered. "I've been up there writing."

"Writing?" She frowned.

"Yes, you know I'm a published author. It's difficult for me to concentrate at home, so I've gone up there to take advantage of the quiet."

She looked incredulous. "Aren't you freezing? That cottage doesn't have central heating or even a fireplace."

"I've got an electric heater and I wear lots of clothes."

"Mama told me she'd seen your car. She's staying at our cottage with Chiara and Antonio. They've both been sick, and we thought it would be good for them to get some fresh mountain air and to get out of the smog."

I nodded vigorously. "Yes, the fog has been terrible. It must be bad for the lungs."

She studied me. "So, what are you writing?"

I looked down at my hand, clutching the light cotton blanket. I searched my tired brain for a feasible answer. "It's a love story about an American and an Italian," I blurted out.

"A love story...I would never be able to write something like that...or any fiction, for that matter. I can barely write a letter." She laughed and I joined her...maybe a little too heartily.

"You should stop by and see Mama. You could have lunch."

"Oh, no. I have to get home for the children. I really need this time to write, so I can't waste a minute. The time there is very precious. I can't be disturbed." I didn't want La Mama to show up at the cottage when I was there.

Adriana raised her eyebrows and eyed me curiously.

A little voice interrupted us. "Mommy, I'm hungry. Can I have some dinner?"

Adriana looked at her watch. It was eleven PM. It had been an hour since she'd spoken to the nurse.

"Kate, I think you should take Marc home. No one is taking care of him here. It's noisy and unsanitary. If he has problems at home, you can go around the corner to Dr. Petrini."

I knew Dr. Petrini. I had been to his office in the fall when Timmy had an earache. It was true, his office was around the corner from our apartment building.

As it turned out, I signed a form taking full responsibility for Marc's health and recovery and absolved the hospital of any responsibility. Adriana drove us home. No one was there. I gave Marc some soup and called Giada. She told me Lucie and Timmy were fast asleep and all was well. I tucked Marc in and fell into bed.

Chapter 29

Henri must have come home after midnight. I didn't hear a thing. I was dead asleep after that horrendous day. We both slept until seven-thirty. I awoke with a start and hurried in to make sure Marc was all right. When I looked in his room, his head popped up off the pillow and he smiled at me…that wonderful, sweet, ingenuous smile.

"How do you feel, sweetheart?" I asked.

He frowned and seemed to consider his response. "I'm hungry, really hungry. Can I have pancakes?"

"Of course, you can. How about your head? How does it feel?"

He reached up and gingerly touched the top of his head. "It hurts a little when I touch it."

"Do you feel dizzy or weird?"

"No, I just feel hungry."

"Good. I'm going to make you a big stack of pancakes."

Later, while he was eating, Giada called. She said she would take the girls to school and drop off Timmy afterwards. As I hung up, Henri came into the room.

"Where are Lucie and Timmy? What have you done with them?" His tone was aggressive.

Did he think I'd given them away to a dope peddler? "Where were you last night?" I responded, equally aggressive.

"I had dinner with Bianchi and some important clients." He was straightening the knot of his tie.

"While you were with your important clients, I was at the hospital with your son. He had a bad fall off his bike and suffered a concussion. I took him there to have him checked out. Giada kindly took Lucie and Timmy to her house."

Henri bent down to look at Marc. "He looks all right. Maybe you overreacted."

"I didn't overreact. He was unconscious and the cut on his head was bleeding like crazy."

"How did he fall? Weren't you watching him?"

"He and Lucie were racing down the sidewalk and Marc didn't look where he was going. His bike hit an uneven patch in the pavement, and he sailed over the handlebars."

Marc watched us, his head swiveling back and forth like at a tennis match. His normally pale face had turned white.

"You should make them walk their bikes to the park." Henri walked over to the coffee pot and poured himself a cup. Then he sat down and looked distastefully at the plate of half-eaten pancakes swimming in syrup. He disapproved of that quintessential American breakfast. Marc asked to be excused.

"Of course, honey. But don't you want to finish your pancakes?"

"No, Mommy. I've had enough."

167

"If your mother prepared these awful pancakes for you, you should at least finish them. It's wasteful," Henri said.

I gestured to Marc. "Go get dressed."

He scuttled out of the room, obviously eager to escape the stress and tension.

***

When Giada brought Timmy home, I invited her in for coffee, but she was in a hurry. We agreed she would come back with her children to decorate Christmas cookies that afternoon. For Giada, this was a novel idea. Christmas cookies were not an Italian tradition. Giada wasn't quite sure what I was talking about, but she agreed to come over at three-thirty.

I had decided to keep Marc home from preschool that day. I tried unsuccessfully to encourage the boys to play quietly. It seemed to me Marc shouldn't get over-excited and start running around. Heaven forbid he should fall again on the hard marble floors. To this end, I pulled out the card table I'd used back in the States to play bridge with friends. We set it up on the carpet in the living room and covered it with blankets. The boys played all morning in their fort. While they were shooting at Indians, I mixed up two batches of a favorite sugar cookie recipe. Then I rolled out the dough and cut out Christmas trees, stars, reindeer, etc. After I'd baked several batches of perfect cookies, I called the boys in, and they played with the dough and cut out some less-than-perfect cookies.

At three-thirty, Giada arrived with Francesca and Umberto. Umberto was an adorable brown-eyed, chubby cherub. He and

Timmy were nearly the same age and played well together. Francesca was long-limbed like her mother with pretty, delicate features and a sweet personality to match. I settled all five children around the kitchen table. In our move from Chicago, I had included not only the Christmas-cookie cutters, but also several little bottles of sprinkles, cinnamon candies and tiny candy silver balls. Before Giada arrived, I had prepared little bowls of colored icing.

While the children got to work decorating cookies, Giada and I took cups of tea into the living room. We settled on the sofa.

"The children were marvelous, last night. They ate supper, had baths and went to sleep. No one cried or fussed," Giada said.

"I can't thank you enough. I don't know what I would have done without you." I told her about my experiences at the hospital and about Adriana's arrival.

"So, you walked right out of the hospital, just like that?" Giada shook her head in amazement and laughed.

"There was no point in staying there. Nobody was taking care of us and finding a doctor seemed impossible."

She gestured towards the kitchen. "Marc looks fine now."

I sighed. "Yes, thank God. Henri told me I overreacted and shouldn't have rushed off to the hospital."

"I don't know how you could have done otherwise. He was unconscious, and all that blood…" She rolled her eyes. "You did the right thing."

After that, we talked of various things. I told Giada I had started writing again. She knew I'd published a couple of books in the past.

"When do you write? With the children it must be hard to concentrate."

I picked at a loose button on my cardigan. I was debating what to tell Giada. "I go up to Cerro to write…one morning a week."

"You go all the way up there? Why?"

"It's very quiet and I can concentrate." I avoided her gaze.

"Couldn't you get Marina to take Timmy out and just write at home?"

I turned away from her to place my teacup on the side table. "No, I need her to clean and I need to get away from here, from my everyday life."

I could feel Giada's eyes on me. I turned and smiled at her. "Hey, I think we need to supervise the children. It's getting noisy in the kitchen."

The kids were having a great time. We sat down with them and decorated a few cookies ourselves.

Chapter 30

It was pouring when I set off for Cerro the following week. Henri had brought home a small bag of supplies. I added some fresh fruit and vegetables since Andrea was probably tired of pasta and tomato sauce. I noted that I had begun to think of him by his name, rather than as *the killer*.

The trip up was slow going. I found myself behind a tentative driver who practically stopped at each hairpin curve due to poor visibility. In Cerro, the rain had turned into light snow. Clouds in the overcast sky hung low on the horizon, and a brisk wind buffeted the cypress trees when I turned into the lane. The mountains had disappeared behind nature's dark curtain. Andrea would not be able to enjoy the sunshine today.

At the cottage, I pulled the bag of provisions and my satchel out of the car. Then I scurried up the steps to the door of the cottage. Before I could get my key out, the door was pulled open. Andrea stood there, grinning. He reached out and took the bag from my hand and stepped back so I could enter. I stomped the snow off my feet and Andrea shut the door against the cold wind. I had only glanced at him, but I saw he had shaved and was smooth cheeked. He looked a little less like a caveman. His face was partially covered by his dark, wavy hair and the knitted woolen cap he'd pulled low on his forehead, but I could see angular features with strong cheekbones.

I brushed the snow off my shoulders, but I didn't take off my coat. In spite of the fact that both heaters were installed in the main room, it didn't feel warm. The wind whistled in under the doors. Nonetheless, I pulled open the blinds. We both needed light.

"Coffee, signora...Kate?" he asked.

"Yes, please. That would be nice."

I pulled out a small plate of Christmas cookies from the bag I'd prepared the previous evening. I uncovered them and held the plate out to him. "The children and I made these."

His eyes lit up. "The cookies of Christmas. Thank you, *grazie, grazie mille*. I've been thinking about *Natale*. It is very soon."

"Yes, in about ten days. We're going to Paris to be with my in-laws." It registered with me that we were having a conversation. I had promised myself I would never talk to this man and here we were discussing Christmas.

"We will have the cookies with the espresso." He turned away to prepare the coffee in the kitchen. I sat down in my usual seat and pulled out my notebook and a couple of sharpened pencils. I turned the pages until I came to my stopping point the previous week. Neatly, I printed the date and began to record the weather, as I had the preceding week. Then I began to write about Marc's accident. When Andrea brought my little cup of espresso, I had mentally transported myself to the Corso Porta Nuova and Marc's body on the pavement.

172

"What are you writing about?" he asked.

I took a sip of the coffee, and then I sat back and crossed my arms and began to tell him about Marc's accident. At first, I avoided eye contact, but when he responded with sympathetic words, I found myself looking into his eyes. They were pools of concern and empathy. He was shocked at the state of the hospital and the lack of care, but he laughed when I told him how we'd whisked Marc away. He had a deep laugh.

I ran out of words and fell silent. Suddenly, I felt exposed, as though I had given away too much of myself. This was my enemy and I was treating him like a friend.

"Well, I better get to work," I said brusquely.

Andrea picked up a cookie, a Christmas tree I had painted with green icing and carefully decorated with silver balls. "This is too beautiful to eat." He picked up another, a yellow star, and took a bite. "*Delizioso!*"

I didn't respond but picked up my pencil and began to write. He respected my need for silence and went over to the window to look out at the softly falling snow. I glanced up at his back. It was hard to tell what he looked like under all those clothes. I didn't know if he was soft and flabby or hard and muscular. The same could be said for me. We resembled two hippopotami or two woolly polar bears. I giggled softly. At that moment Andrea turned around, his eyes questioning. I told him what I was thinking, and he smiled back.

I put down my pencil and crossed my arms. "So, I've been wondering where you learned English? And I've been wondering why you agreed to take the blame for the shooting? Why would you let your brother off scot-free?"

He turned his chair around with his back to the window. "I learned English in New York."

"New York?" I was flabbergasted.

"Well, Brooklyn. I lived there with my uncle and aunt."

"When?"

"In the nineteen-sixties. I was studying finance and accounting at NYU."

I took a moment to digest this piece of information. "So, you know a lot about America?"

"A very small amount. I was only there for four years."

"Do you have a degree from NYU?"

"Yes. I am the accountant for the family. I manage the money for my father, who is the *capo*, the boss. He sent me to New York to learn good accounting procedures." He grimaced. "But what I do is not necessarily legal."

I lean forward. "So, you work for your father's Mafia family and manage the books. But then, why did they decide you should take the blame for the shooting? Don't they need you?"

"No, they don't really need me. They really need my brother." Andrea got up and began to circle the room. "Massimo is my father's assistant, shall we say. He helps run the business. He is the strong man and keeps everyone in line. I am what you call a pencil-pusher." He continued to walk around the table.

"So, you love numbers and mathematics? That's why you have that job?"

He twisted his head to look at me. "No, I love literature and reading. But it was decided I was the intellectual one and I should learn accounting." His jaw tightened. "I had no choice in the matter."

When I left, he gave me a list of items he needed. He was running out of batteries for his flashlight. He needed more reading material and more detergent to wash his underwear.

Chapter 31

That Saturday night there was a company Christmas party at a well-known restaurant. Henri seemed to think it was important that I be dressed to the nines. He took me shopping that afternoon while Marina watched the children. I had promised to pay her a king's ransom to watch them both in the afternoon and at night. She brought her eleven-year-old daughter over and Lucie was thrilled to have a big girl to play with.

Henri and I went to a small boutique on Via Mazzini. He chose a muted-green straight skirt with a kick-pleat in the back. The background of the silk blouse was cream-colored with violet flowers and green leaves. A silk knitted lace sweater completed the outfit, along with some dark green pumps. Henri had never shopped with me before and I felt like a model he'd hired to show off the clothes. The whole outfit was very expensive. The shop girl kept saying I looked *molto elegante*. When we got outside, I gave Henri a big hug and we kissed.

"Thank you so much for giving me this outfit. It's very generous of you."

That night before going out, I twisted my hair into a French chignon and put on my gold earrings and pearls.

Lucie came in as I was finishing up my make-up. "Mommy, you look beautiful."

I bent down and gave her a hug. "Thank you, sweetheart."

***

We arrived at the restaurant a little late. Henri was in a twit, but I don't think the others cared one way or the other. They were all seated around a large table drinking wine and chatting. Signor Bianchi was in the kitchen giving orders to the chef. Only two seats were available. I was seated between Francesco Ferrari and an unfamiliar gentleman.

He introduced himself as Avvocato Ricci. Apparently, he was the company lawyer. I had heard Henri mention his name before but had never met him. The *avvocato* was short, with greying hair and sharp grey eyes. His wife, sitting next to Giuseppe, was willowy with dyed-black hair and a smug expression. She was dripping with diamonds and wore a garnet-colored dress.

Unfortunately, I also had to acknowledged Francesco, who was on my left. I shook his hand quickly without any eye contact. I would have done anything not to be in his vicinity. Henri took a seat between Adriana and Giulia Ferrari. I smiled at Adriana, who looked elegant in a simple black dress.

As I sat down, the waiter came over and filled my glass with champagne. Francesco leaned close to me and whispered in my ear. "How have you been? I think of you often." I could feel his hot breath on my neck. He was way too close. I didn't respond but turned to Avvocato Ricci.

177

We began a discussion about cities and natural wonders in the United States. Ricci's son, Renaldo, was studying architecture at the University of Illinois. The lawyer and his wife had visited Champaign that fall. Their trip had included several days in New York and Chicago. He had been surprised at how beautiful Chicago was along Lake Michigan's shore.

At some point, Bianchi returned after determining the menu. I remember we had a tri-color pasta course and a delicious affogato for dessert with meringue cookies. Avvocato Ricci continued to discuss his admiration for the natural wonders of the States. The summer before, he and Renaldo had made a trip out to the Grand Canyon. They had ridden mules down to the bottom of the canyon and spent the night at the Phantom Ranch. That night they went outside and lay down on their backs on a bridge and looked up at the star-studded sky. From that vantage point, deep down in the canyon, they had had a spectacular view of the constellations, undisturbed by city lights. I've often thought of this experience when I've looked up at the sky on a starry night.

Several times during our enjoyable discussion, I felt Francesco's hand on my thigh. Each time, I pushed it off. The last time, I tried to jab my fingernails into his hand. I never looked at him. I was aware that Adriana, seated on his left, was making a valiant effort to engage him in conversation.

Across the table, Henri was in deep discussion with Francesco's wife, Giulia. Their heads were almost touching. As usual, she had on a tight-fitting outfit. Her peroxide blond hair was piled in a complicated arrangement on top of her head. She wore heavy make-up, kohl-rimmed eyes and blood-red lipstick. I found myself looking at her with distaste. I truly disliked that couple.

At some point, Ricci asked me about my writing. "I understand that you're an author and have written an English best-seller."

"That's true, I wrote a successful book when I was nineteen. But I haven't been writing much lately, with three children."

"You undoubtedly need peace and quiet to practice your art."

What was he getting at? Did he know about my trips up to Cerro? I looked at him, trying to register his interest in my writing. Then I glanced over at Giancarlo Bianchi, who was eavesdropping on our conversation. He smiled at me knowingly.

At the end of the evening, as we were getting our coats, Bianchi said to me, "You look lovely tonight, signora. That's a beautiful outfit." He gave me the once-over from head to toe. Then he handed me an envelope. "*Buon Natale, grazie.*"

When Henri and I were in the car, I opened the envelope. Inside was a packet of lire notes. I counted the money and figured the amount with the current exchange rate. Bianchi had given me about $1,000. I was angry. I felt as if he'd paid me off like a prostitute. I turned to Henri, shaking the money at him. "Is this for taking care of your company killer?"

"He knows you resent going up there. He's showing his appreciation. You should be grateful."

"Grateful? The whole thing makes me feel dirty." Then I thought about the clothes that Henri had insisted on buying. "Did Giancarlo pay for the outfit I wore tonight? Was that his idea?"

Although it was dark in the car, I sensed Henri's discomfort.

"I should have known you would never go shopping with me. It was totally out of character. You're just Bianchi's pimp."

Chapter 32   2019

The stewardess brings us a continental breakfast. We will be landing in an hour. Although it's the middle of the night at home, dawn is breaking in Italy. The coffee actually is quite good. I eat a few bites of the croissant and swallow a few spoonsful of yogurt. I'm really not that hungry. I glance over at Marc, who has the window seat next to Tim. They're laughing about something and eating every morsel of their breakfast.

Marc is a handsome man. He's maintained his youthful physique through consistent exercise. I know he never misses a day at the gym. Not like many athletes, who turn into mush as they get older. A shock of hair falls over his forehead as he bends forward to sip his coffee. He still has pale skin, set off by his dark, straight hair and swallow-tail eyebrows. Although his life is totally different from that of his brothers, he enjoys their company. Gone is the tentative, insecure boy of his childhood. When his father died, he came into his own. I could see him grow in self-confidence. He became his own man. No longer did he have to satisfy Henri.

Marc attended Brown as an undergraduate and Yale law school. He met his wife, Mary Jane, at Yale. They started out as study partners and moved on to marriage. They live in the San Francisco area. Both of them work as tech lawyers. I'm told they're transactional lawyers, which means they're not litigators. They work for different firms and deal with patents, IPs and...okay, I'm out of my depth here. Those are just some terms I hear bandied about.

They have a beautiful home that must be worth millions and three adorable children: Robert, 16, Rachel, 14, and William, 12. When Robert was born, Mary Jane was working on a big case. Two hours after Robert's birth, she was hard at work, her hospital bed covered with files and she was on the phone. When I entered the hospital room, she waved at me and then went back to work. Marc and I sat in the corner and cuddled and cooed over the baby. A day later, when they brought Robert home, I babysat for a couple of weeks. Mary Jane couldn't or wouldn't take any extra time off and Marc was working half-days. It became obvious before I left that they needed to hire a nanny. Marc found a site online that featured nannies and caregivers. He did some research and then he and I interviewed several candidates. None of the women seemed quite right: too old, too young, too rigid, too lax. Just when we were feeling desperate, Fate stepped in and introduced Anna. She's a small, tidy woman with a friendly, open face and a heart of gold. For years now, she's been raising the three kids. She's a stickler for homework, unyielding for appropriate bedtimes, and a genius at preparing healthy meals. Marc provided her with a minivan, and she drives the kids to all their activities.

Robert and William both play soccer and basketball. Rachel is a marvel on the clarinet and has won several local music awards. In addition, she plays volleyball and participates in tournaments all over the country. I attended one in New York last year.

Sometimes, I wonder what glue holds Marc and Mary Jane together. They seem to lead parallel lives: separate but equal. They probably have dinner together only once a week and yet they seem happy.

When I told Marc about my trip to Verona, he asked if he could come along. He thought it was important to be there for me when I received the Verona Literary award. I was touched. I'd been on my own for so many years, doing readings and book signings all over the country. Sharing the moment with family would be special indeed. Marc called the other kids and encouraged them to come along, too. So here we are on our memory tour. I'm excited and a little unsettled.

Chapter 33

Henri and I didn't say much to each other on Sunday. I had put the envelope with the thousand dollars in lira notes in the bottom of my satchel under the removable lining. It would be safe enough there until I decided what to do with it. Perhaps I would return the money along with a terse note to Giancarlo Bianchi, or maybe I'd go out and buy myself something outrageous.

That day, we were invited up to the Morettis' farmhouse for a Christmas get-together. I didn't feel like going and making polite conversation, but I knew the kids were looking forward to the day. They always had fun playing with the other children in the farmyard. After mass, we got into the car and drove through town. Weak sun rays broke through the fog.

When we arrived, there was a lot of commotion. Alberto, Signor Moretti's brother-in-law, was upset. His son-in-law had lost his job several months earlier and couldn't find anything. Alberto was worried for his daughter and their two-month-old baby. Unfortunately, the son-in-law, Vicente, was born in Chile and didn't have a work permit. Apparently, he was a good mechanic, but times were rough. Alberto's wife was crying while her daughter sat holding the baby and looking distraught.

"What will become of my granddaughter. She will have no food, no clothes. Life will be impossible for them." The grandma was ready to pull her hair out. The other women in the room were trying to calm her down.

Henri stood near the fireplace, warming his hands and talking quietly to Moretti. I joined the women and took my turn at stirring the polenta.

Alberto's wife kept crying. "My real worry is that they will leave. Vicente will take my grandchild across the sea to Chile. I'll never see her again." She reached over to gather the baby into her arms. The child began to wail.

Then Signor Moretti came over and patted Vicente on the back. "Tell me, would you like to work at Bianchi's ice cream plant? Henri says he thinks there might be an opening."

Vicente was a skinny young man with a pockmarked face. "Yes, yes, I would be most grateful," he said. Tears glimmered in his soulful brown eyes. Then he threw himself at Henri and gave him a bear hug. Henri drew back in shock and disdain.

Vicente's wife began to laugh as she squeezed the baby to her breast. Then the grandma came over and hugged Henri, crying for joy. I smiled at Henri's discomfort as he tried to extricate himself from her grasp.

Alberto came around the table and joined in the chaos. "We will never forget this. You have saved our family." He wiped his sweaty forehead. He was visibly relieved. I could imagine life at home must have been hell those last few weeks, with these two melodramatic women and morose son-in-law.

After the emotional tsunami had passed, we enjoyed a copious meal and drank way too much wine. At the end of the feast, several Christmas *panettones* were sliced and watered with bottles of *spumante*. Singing and laughter followed. Henri was treated like a king, or maybe more like a savior by all the Moretti family. The children ran in and out, grabbing a panini, some roasted polenta or a piece of cake. It was a joyful, raucous celebration.

On the way home, Henri and I reinstituted our mutual silence. The children didn't seem to notice. The two younger ones fell asleep and Lucie sang to herself.

Monday morning, when I came back from taking the children to school, there was a gift box by our door. It contained bags of polenta flour, wine, chocolates and a couple of panettones. This was the beginning of Alberto's thanks for saving his family's sanity. As the year went by, I often found gift boxes containing more polenta, or wine, or boxes of perfect pears or peaches. Alberto was indeed eternally grateful.

Chapter 34

The next Wednesday, the air was cold and crisp as I drove up into the hills. With bright sunshine and good visibility, it was a quick trip. At the cottage, I swung open the gates and drove into the courtyard. I didn't bother to angle the car for a quick getaway. I guess I had begun to trust my friendly, neighborhood assassin. I carried two plastic bags up the stairs. Andrea was at the door to let me in. He grabbed the bags from my hands, and I went back down for my satchel and another bag containing two wrapped gifts. Once inside, I pulled open the blinds. We could see the snow-covered mountains in the distance. I rubbed my hands together. It was very cold, even though Andrea had brought both heaters into the room.

He carried the provisions into the kitchen and began to unpack. He tore off a piece of bread and opened a paper-wrapped piece of Taleggio cheese. With a knife he cut off a slice and stuffed it into the bread. "Please excuse me, I am so hungry."

"Yes, make yourself a sandwich," I said. "Shall I make coffee?"

"I can do it," he said.

"No, you eat. I'll prepare the coffee." I set about grinding the beans as he circled the table munching his panini. That was how he got exercise, walking around and around.

Later, we sipped the espresso. He sat in the sunshine and I tried to write, but my muse had deserted me. After recording the date and the weather, I tapped the pencil on the table, trying to think what to write about. My mind was blank. I looked over at Andrea's back. He was peeling a mandarin orange.

"Do you mind if I sit in the sun for a while?" I asked.

He turned and smiled. His eyes were bright with pleasure. "Of course not. Please come sit with me."

I pulled my chair over to the window and sat down. I closed my eyes and let the sun warm my face. We sat in compatible silence.

Eventually, Andrea said, "You told me about your little boy, Marc. Do you have other children?"

"Yes, I do. Lucie is seven. She's a darling girl with a winsome way about her."

"Winsome?"

"Charming or endearing. Marc has brown eyes and almost black hair. Lucie is blond and blue-eyed."

"Like her mother," he said.

I opened my eyes and saw Andrea studying me intently. I felt myself blush, and looked down at my empty cup. "My baby is Timmy. He's almost three and he's blond, too." I tripped over my words. Then I closed my eyes again and told Andrea about Lucie and school and Timmy's antics. At one point, I asked if I was boring him, but he said no.

"Mothers can talk about their children forever, you know," I said.

"Children are a mother's joy."

188

"Yes, their joy and their sorrow."

Silence fell. He sighed. I wondered what he was thinking.

"Remember, we're going to Paris for Christmas. We leave on Friday," I said.

"Ah…"

"But I will be back next Wednesday." I turned to him. "You will not starve."

His eyes twinkled. "I will already be looking forward to next Wednesday when you leave today."

I blushed and stood up. I took his cup and mine to the kitchen and began to rinse them. "Did you see I brought you a panettone and a bottle of prosecco. I thought you could celebrate, although it will be a lonely one." I turned to look at him. Our eyes linked across the chilly room.

"No, I want to celebrate right now with you. Please drink a glass of prosecco with me." He stood, came into the kitchen and rummaged in the bags, then pulled out the bottle.

"I don't know. It's only eleven in the morning…kind of early for alcohol." I placed the cups in the drying rack. I noticed how clean and neat he kept this tiny kitchen. Of course, he had nothing else to do but wash dishes and organize boxes of pasta.

"Please, drink a small glass with me," he insisted.

"Well, okay. Just a small one."

He set two of the heavy juice glasses on the counter. Then he twisted the cork off the prosecco bottle. It made a gentle pop. He poured the wine into the glasses, a full one for me as well as for

189

himself. "Drink as much as you want." He smiled at me. His teeth were white, his lips full and soft. His eyes glimmered with specks of gold.

We clinked glasses. "To Kate, my savior," he said.

I looked down into the bubbly liquid, feeling somehow embarrassed. I had so hated the idea of coming here, and yet to this man, I represented his sole contact with the outside world.

"Let's drink to a swift resolution to your predicament, so you can go home to your family," I said.

"Ah yes, my family." He frowned, drank down the prosecco, and poured himself another.

We went and sat back down in the sunshine, which offered a bit of warmth. Then I remembered the gifts. "Andrea." It was the first time I'd used his name.

He turned to look at me. Our eyes locked. I smiled in confusion. Then I said, "There are two presents for you. You should open them now, while we're celebrating."

I got up, pulled out the two wrapped gifts, and handed them to him. I watched as he unwrapped the larger one. It was a clock radio I'd owned in college. I'd had the Italian plug spliced on so he could plug it in up here in the cottage.

"A radio." His voice radiated pleasure. "*Grazie, grazie mille.*"

"Plug it in. Let's see how many stations you'll get up here."

Andrea went over to the sideboard, placed the radio on the bare surface and plugged it in. At first, we heard some scratchy voices. It sounded like a news program. He kept turning the knob. He found another talk show that was clearer. He continued fiddling, and suddenly, Debussy poured into the room. The music rippled through the air, clear as a bell. We looked at each other and smiled.

"I love Debussy," I said.

"As do I. My mother was a musician. She loved Debussy, also. I can see her at the pianoforte, her fingers racing up and down the keys." Sadness played around his eyes, and he gazed out the window.

I nodded and made my voice cheery. "Come open the other gift," I said, and handed him the smaller package.

Carefully, he unwrapped it. Inside was a copy of my first book, *Kindred Kindness*. He looked at the cover and then up at me. "This is your book. I knew you were an author." He ran a finger across the title and across my name. "Katherine Goodall. That's your name before you married."

"Yes, my maiden name."

"Ah…maiden name," he repeated. "Thank you, Katherine Goodall."

We sat back down in the sunshine. Andrea held the book against his chest. We drank the prosecco and listened to Debussy. The music was like the bubbles in our glasses, it flowed and gurgled around us.

Chapter 35

Clickety-click, clickety-clack. Henri had gotten tickets on the night train to Paris. We had couchettes in the overnight coach. The children found this very exciting, to sleep all together in our cozy compartment. An elderly gentleman had opened the door as we were settling in. When he saw the three children, he slid the door shut and disappeared. Undoubtedly, he had found another compartment. Normally, a couchette contained six seats by day. At night cots dropped down from the walls and formed six bunks.

I had packed sandwiches, fruit, juice and cookies. As we ate our picnic, the train sped across northern Italy towards France. After our meal, the children ran up and down the corridor outside our compartment and we played Go Fish. When it was time for bed, they giggled for a while and then fell into a deep sleep to the clickety-clack of the train wheels.

Henri and I had each taken a bottom bunk. He lay down and I crept over and lay down next to him.

"Really, Kate. This bunk is too narrow for the two of us." I heard irritation in his tone.

I chose to ignore it. "I know. I just came over to snuggle for a minute and say hello." I paused. "We don't talk much these days."

"You are often angry. You don't want to talk with me." He sounded petulant.

"Sometimes that's true. I've been resentful because of my involvement with your assassin."

I felt him shrug. "I've learned the fellow didn't actually kill the man in the bar. He's taking the rap for his brother."

"I know, I learned that as well." I sighed.

"So, you're talking to him?" Henri turned on his side to look at me.

"Yes, we've talked a bit…mainly, he knows to leave me alone."

Henri smirked. I could see his face in the semi-darkness. "Talking to you is like patting a porcupine."

"Huh." I decided not to share my conversations with Andrea. I got up and moved over to my own bunk. So much for a cuddle.

It was seven AM when we arrived in Paris at the Gare de Bercy. Benoît was there on the platform when the train pulled into the station. He hugged the children and shook Henri's hand. It was cold and rainy outside, so we hurried to the Peugeot. Henri sat in front with Benoît and the children and I squeezed into the back, Timmy on my lap.

Henri's parents lived in the sixteenth *arrondissement* in a roomy third-floor apartment. There were four bedrooms, a study, a living room, dining room, kitchen and pantry. A wide corridor ran down between the rooms, which were lined up on each side. French windows looked out on tree-lined streets, and from the dining room the Eiffel Tower was visible. The apartment was furnished with Louis XV-style fauteuils, ornate chests and Persian rugs.

Parking was always an issue, but today Benoît found a spot right in front of the building. As we entered the foyer, the concierge, Madame Dupont, came rushing out to welcome us. She'd known Henri since he was a boy. She greeted him with a hug and clamored over the children.

"How beautiful the children are. This one looks just like his Papa. Oh, and the little one...what is his name? He is a little blond angel. The girl, she will be a looker..." She could probably have gone on for a half hour. I smiled and let her words wash over us. I knew being on the right side of the concierge was very important. She serves as doorman, postmistress and informer. It's always wise to be in her good graces.

We took the lift up to the third floor. Henri dug out his key, but before he could put it in the lock, the door opened. Pauline stood in the gap, beaming at us all. She was the cook, cleaner, laundress, babysitter...*une femme à tout faire.* She'd been with the Joubert family forever. She hugged me, then crouched down and gathered the children into her arms. They automatically moved into her embrace. She had that wonderful sweetness children intuitively respond to.

"How are my little poppets? I've got a surprise for you." From her pocket she pulled out three candies wrapped in shiny blue paper.

As the children were about to unwrap them, Françoise came down the hall. "What are you doing, Pauline? No candies for the

194

children. You mustn't spoil them." She bent and hugged each child, and carefully removed the sweets from their small grasps. They didn't complain. Pauline turned and hurried into the kitchen.

Françoise stood up and hugged Henri for a long time. Then she patted me on the back. "Come now, let's have breakfast."

The dining room was large, with French windows that opened onto a small balcony. The oval table was set with cups for café au lait or hot chocolate. There were baskets of croissants and thickly sliced baguette. Two glass jars contained homemade apricot and plum jam. A block of fresh creamery butter sat on a porcelain dish. We all sat down and enjoyed this simple but delicious repast.

Lucie talked excitedly about the train ride and sleeping on the topmost bunk. Marc told them how fast the train went and demonstrated by racing around the table. Timmy clapped his hands and giggled. Françoise and Benoît looked on as adoring grandparents. I felt smug. I must not be such a bad mother, after all.

Due to the drenching rain, we spent most of that day inside. The children played house in the small room reserved for storing laundry and ironing. Later, Françoise set up a plastic set of bowling pins and balls. This provided some entertainment, with lots of running up and down the long hallway. Henri was gone much of the day with colleagues from the Paris office. Benoît was buried in his study.

That night was Christmas Eve. The grownups were going to midnight mass. Pauline would babysit while we were gone. I nearly fell asleep during the long service, surrounded by spicy incense and interminable chants. I shivered as we walked back to the apartment in the cold, crisp air. Rather than a proper *révellion*, which is a full meal with luxury items like caviar, oysters and champagne followed by a *Bûche de Noël*, Françoise had prepared a creamy lobster bisque for the four of us. The plan was to have a feast the following day with all the family. I was too tired to eat much at one AM, but I managed to finish my soup. Henri and his parents were wide awake, talking and laughing. I excused myself and went to bed.

Later, I was roused from a deep sleep when Henri slipped into bed. His hands moved over me, cupping my breasts, sliding over my stomach and down between my legs. Then he moved on top of me, his mouth on mine, his tongue probing. He entered me, moving fast and hard. In my semi-conscious state, I tried to push him away, but he was too heavy and too drunk. When he rolled off of me, I moved to the edge of the bed, as far away from him as I could get.

Chapter 36

Christmas Day passed in a whirlwind. Lucie and Marc had been worried about Santa Claus. How would he find them, here in Paris? Would he leave any gifts? I had assured them Santa would leave gifts for them in Verona around the little tree I had managed to find. Before we left the apartment for Paris, Henri stayed downstairs with the children while I ran back upstairs, pulled gifts from the pantry where I'd hidden them, and placed them under the tree. They would be waiting when we got back.

Christmas morning, I heard the children whispering in the bedroom they shared next to ours. Henri lay on his back, snoring. I crept out of the room and into the kids' room. I helped them find their slippers and then we went down the hall to the dining room. I told them to shush because Françoise and Benoît were still asleep after a late night. The table was set for breakfast, but beside each child's place were a couple of wrapped gifts.

Lucie's eyes lit up. "Mommy look, Santa Claus found us here." She and the boys were jumping around with excitement.

"I think these are some Christmas gifts from Bonnemaman and Bonpapa. Maybe we should wait and open them when they get up."

"Please, can't we open them now? It's Christmas. We're supposed to open presents when we get up," Marc whined.

"How about you each open one gift now?" I said.

At that, Marc and Lucie began to rip the paper off one gift and I helped Timmy with the bow on his chosen box. After he managed to pull off the paper, he found a cuddly rabbit. His eyes lit up and he hugged the rabbit to his chest. "Mommy, this is a friend for Lolly." Lolly was Timmy's favorite teddy bear. He had insisted on bringing Lolly along on the train.

"What will you call him?" I asked.

"Mr. Rabbit," he said, caressing his new friend's long silky ears.

Looking awestruck, Lucie held out a beautiful new doll dressed in a gorgeous period costume like a miniature Marie Antoinette. This was a doll she would need to take good care of…not like the naked Barbie dolls I found under her bed or dripping wet in the bathtub.

Marc opened a miniature mechanical train set complete with train tracks. I wondered how we were going to get all these gifts back home. But I was amazed at Françoise's generosity and clever choice of gifts.

With all the racket, Pauline came into the dining room bearing pitchers of hot chocolate, coffee and hot milk. "*Joyeux Noël, mes enfants*," she sang out.

I prompted the children to respond, "Joyeux Noël, Pauline."

She pulled some caramels from her pocket and handed them out. Françoise was not there to chastise her, and I didn't care. After all, this was Christmas.

While the children played with their toys and nibbled disinterestedly on croissants, Pauline talked to me about everything she had to do that day. For her it was definitely not a day of rest. She was already hard at work preparing the luncheon for twelve.

"Now, I really do love working here. This is my family. I've been working here for thirty years. Madame hired me when I was sixteen and Jean-Pierre was just a baby. But I get tired and at the end of the day, my feet hurt."

"Why don't you sit down and have some coffee?" I suggested.

Pauline looked shocked. *"Jamais, Madame Katherine."* Never would she think of sitting down at the dining room table.

"Is there something I could do to help you today? I could peel potatoes or set the table," I suggested.

"Oh, Madame Françoise would not like you to be in the kitchen. That wouldn't do." She shook her head emphatically. "You must tend to your children."

At that moment the dining room door flew open and Françoise bustled into the room. "Pauline, don't you have something to do in the kitchen?" she said.

Pauline turned red, ducked her head and scurried out of the room.

***

At twelve-thirty, Henri's brother Jean-Pierre arrived for lunch with his wife and daughters. Remember the perfect girls, Martine and Laure? They were dressed in matching grey-wool jumpers over Peter Pan collared blouses embroidered with pink roses. Pink ribbons circled the ends of their neat, tight braids. They were pretty

199

girls with dark eyes and nearly black hair, like Henri and his brother. Jean-Pierre's wife, Claude, wore an elegant cashmere dress, Hermès silk scarf and loops of pearls. Her light brown hair was carefully coiffed. They were an attractive family.

Lucie was jumping up and down, thrilled to see these big girls. Her eyes shone with adoration. "Mommy, I want braids, too. Can you braid my hair now?"

I turned to Martine, the elder of the two, and asked if she could braid Lucie's hair. She nodded, smiling shyly, and off the children went.

We sat down in the living room for an apéritif. Jean-Pierre was a good conversationalist and had a low-key sense of humor. He entertained us with stories about the foibles of government officials. He had attended Polytechnique and had a position in the Ministry of Finance. I could feel Claude's gaze, checking me out. I was wearing my favorite blue knit dress that matched my eyes, and a simple string of pearls my parents had given me upon graduation from college. Was I presentable? Probably not by Parisian standards.

We were waiting for Marie-Claire, Henri's sister, to appear. Françoise kept looking at her watch. Finally, she said we would go in to lunch."

"One can never count on Marie-Claire. She is never on time," she scoffed, and rang a silver bell to alert Paulette. Then we moved into the dining room. We had finished the mushroom and sweetbread *vol-au-vent* when Marie-Claire came rushing in.

"*Désolé, Maman.*" She gave no explanation for her tardiness.

Françoise's eyes were sending poison darts, but she said nothing.

Marie-Claire sat down between Benoît and Lucie. She hugged her father briefly and kissed Lucie. Marie-Claire was quite plain. Although she resembled her mother, she just missed being pretty. Her nose was a little longer, her lips a little thinner, her complexion a little pastier. Her bland personality lacked her mother's spark. I sometimes thought this was because she had been put down her entire life by her demanding mother.

When Pauline brought in the roast beef au jus and potato gratin, we were discussing the Catholic Church. Françoise and Benoît were disappointed in changes that had been made in the 1960s. Primarily, they didn't approve of the use of French in the mass. They wanted to return to Latin.

"But Maman, most people don't know enough Latin to understand what is being said," Jean-Pierre said.

"There are many missals with a French translation on one side of the page for the ignorant. Latin is the true language of the church." Françoise put some potatoes on Marc's plate and passed it on.

Benoît shook his head. "That wasn't always the case. The use of Latin began in the fourth century with the split of the Roman Empire after Emperor Theodosius in 395. Before that, Greek was the language of the church."

Henri rolled his eyes and grinned at his brother. They were used to their dad's ability to pull up precise dates for just about every important or unimportant moment in history.

"Well, maybe we should go back to Greek, Maman," Henri said, shaking his head. He served himself a slice of beef and spooned on some of the jus.

"Well, I approve of Lefebvre. In spite of everything he will continue to say a mass in Latin, no matter what the pope says." Françoise picked up her fork and held it aloft before plunging it into the meat.

I had heard about Lefebvre. He was an archbishop who had formed a group of priests who rejected the new requirements of the Catholic Church. I rarely took part in any of these arguments. I wasn't born Catholic and I didn't have strong religious convictions. But in Henri's family the state of the Catholic Church was a favorite subject of conversation.

I watched Lucie, who was watching the big girls. Martine and Laure were already masters of the fork and knife. They held their meat just so with their forks and expertly cut a small piece before putting it into their mouths...and they chewed with their mouths shut. Now Lucie was trying to copy their movements.

As I was watching all this, Claude said to me, "Tell us about your life in Verona."

I was about to answer, when Henri said, "It's going exceptionally well. We've made some friends and the children are enrolled in an excellent Italian school."

"What about Katherine, is she enjoying Verona?" Marie-Claire's gaze zeroed in on me.

Again, before I could answer, Henri said, "She is very helpful to me with my business."

"What do you mean?" Françoise asked.

Everyone was looking at me expectantly. Why had Henri said that? Should I tell them I was helping to harbor a criminal? I must have looked nonplussed. Then I blurted out, "I entertain the wives of his colleagues."

"That's an excellent idea. You must help your husband in his career. Behind every successful man is a strong wife," Françoise said.

Claude was eyeing me with suspicion. She must have found my explanation questionable. She also didn't want her mother-in-law to place me above her. For Claude, we were in constant competition. After all, she was the perfect mother and wife.

Just then Timmy began to cry. "Marc is making faces at me," he wailed. Marc was across the table and he probably was making faces. This meal was way too long for little children and Timmy was missing his nap. I got up with him in my arms and apologized as we left the room.

In the back bedroom, I lay down with Timmy while he fell asleep. He clutched his new bunny and his beloved teddy bear to his chest. My mind wandered and I thought of Andrea, who was alone in the freezing cottage. The strains of Debussy whirled in my head and I whispered, "Merry Christmas, Andrea."

Chapter 37

We took a night train back to Verona and arrived in the early morning. When we got home, we celebrated Christmas again. The children tore into the gifts Santa had left with unadulterated joy. I made pancakes for breakfast with homemade maple syrup and crispy prosciutto. While the children played, I unpacked our suitcases and started a load of wash. Henri stayed home from the plant and puttered in his office.

Since it was a sunny day, after lunch we drove to the Giardino Giusti and went for a walk. The children screeched as they made their way through the labyrinth. Henri had brought his camera, and he photographed the children peeking out of grey stone grottos and seated in the gnarled branches of the ancient trees.

That night I made spaghetti alla carbonara, a favorite of the whole family. It was a happy time. Once the children were in bed, Henri and I sat on the sofa and drank wine. I was feeling mellow. I pulled up my legs and settled back into the sofa pillows.

"We had a good visit in Paris. Your parents are doing well," I said pleasantly.

Henri nodded. "Yes, I just wish Marie-Claire was more attentive."

"What do you mean?"

"Maman says she never visits, and she never calls."

"Your mother puts her down constantly. She's terrifically critical. Why would Marie-Claire want to subject herself to that? I feel sorry for her."

"Come now, Kate. That's what mothers are supposed to do. They're supposed to mold their children so that they become proper members of society."

I was flabbergasted. "Mold their children? No way. Maybe guide them, but not mold them as though they were little plastic figurines."

"Maybe that was a poor choice of words…" He turned to look at me. "By the way…our children need to be taken in hand."

I felt attacked. "What do you mean?"

"They were running around the apartment like Indians and Timmy ruined the Christmas luncheon with his crying. You left the table and didn't come back until dessert." Henri's face contorted into an angry grimace.

"These are ridiculous complaints. Timmy needed his nap. I took him back so he wouldn't disturb the meal." Now, I was steaming.

"Even today, you let the children run wild. That's why…"

"That's why what?"

"Well, that's probably why Marc fell that day. He wasn't walking his bike on the sidewalk like Italian kids do."

For a moment I was speechless. Then I said, "Maybe you should stick around more and help raise your children. You're never here. Therefore, you have no right to criticize." I got up and left the room. Why did our nice day have to end like this?

***

Tuesday was gloomy and rainy. Henri left early, and the children slept late. I sat at the kitchen table and drank my coffee, pondering my marriage. When I fell in love with Henri, I thought our cultural differences would melt away. But they seemed to be growing larger, like a burgeoning fungus. Americans raised their children in a very different way than the French. We saw childhood as a time of exploration and growth. In my mind, children should be children...not mini adults. Rather than applying strict discipline, I wanted to give them the tools of self-discipline so they could succeed in life. The French were strict disciplinarians, and yes, Henri was right. Parents wanted to mold their children into quiet, submissive grown-ups when they were only three years old. At the same time, I was questioning myself, wondering if I was really such a great mother. Was I too laissez-faire and not enough of a drill sergeant?

I could hear the boys giggling in their room. I needed to think about breakfast and the rest of the day. The children were on vacation for the entire week. Maybe Giada's kids could come over in the afternoon? Then I could ask her to babysit mine the following day. I needed to take provisions up to Andrea, and I couldn't leave all three kids with Marina. She would have a conniption.

Later, I called Giada. "Ciao, Giada, how was your Christmas holiday?"

"It was the same as always. My parents wanted us to stay at their house and spend every minute with them. Meanwhile, my in-laws made a scene when we left to drive across town. The whole thing was quite stressful. I'm actually glad to be back home. How about you?"

"It was fine, although Henri was upset about the children and their behavior. He and I have very different ideas about child-raising."

Giada didn't respond and I changed the subject. "*Ascolta*, listen. I have some errands I need to run tomorrow. I'm wondering if I could bring the children over tomorrow afternoon. In exchange, your children could come over here today and you would have the afternoon off."

"I would love to have your children over, but tomorrow won't work. Could I watch them on Thursday instead? What were you planning?"

What choice did I have? Andrea would have to wait an extra day. I hoped he had enough pasta to tide him over. I fumbled for an answer. "Oh, dry cleaning, grocery shopping…a bunch of stuff. So yes, Thursday would be fine."

"No problem, my kids need entertainment. Maybe we could all go to the movies on Friday afternoon. What do you think?"

"Sounds good. Bring the kids over after lunch," I said.

"Wonderful, see you then."

***

The afternoon passed quickly. The girls played dolls in Lucie's room with the door closed. The boys set up the train track on the parquet floor in their room and constructed a train station with

207

Legos. I made some chocolate chip cookies for tea and then I went into the study to choose some books to take up to Cerro on Thursday. I chose a couple of thick James Michener books, *Hawaii* and *The Source*, which would provide hours of reading along with Hemingway's *A Moveable Feast*. Tucked in among the larger volumes was a leather-bound copy of *The Prophet*. I opened it at random and came upon the chapter on pleasure:

Speak to us of Pleasure.

And he answered saying:

Pleasure is a freedom-song,

But it is not freedom.

It is the blossoming of your desires,

But it is not their fruit.

It is a depth calling unto a height,

But it is not the deep nor the high.

It is the caged taking wings,

But it is not space encompassed.

Ay, in very truth, pleasure is a freedom-song.

Chapter 38

Thursday morning, I woke up with a sore throat. I gargled with saltwater and took a Vitamin C tablet, praying my sore throat wouldn't morph into a giant cold. The children woke up on the wrong side of the bed and were jabbing each other when they came into the kitchen. Marc and Lucie began by fighting over a blue bowl for their hot chocolate. I had five breakfast bowls: one blue, two red, and two yellow. Timmy had broken the other blue bowl several weeks earlier. I have to admit I wasn't very patient with them that morning.

Later, while I was trying to put the kitchen in order and catch up on the laundry, the boys argued over some Fischer-Price action figures and ended up throwing them around the room. I marched in and separated them, Timmy in my room and Marc in the boys' bedroom. During all this drama, Marina hummed as she washed windows.

At eleven o'clock, Henri called. He was bringing someone home for dinner.

"Not today. I'm going up to Cerro this afternoon. Remember, I couldn't go yesterday."

"Could you go tomorrow?" he said.

He knew perfectly well why I was making the trip, yet now he expected me to cancel it on a moment's notice? "No, there's no one to take care of the children. Giada is going to help me out this afternoon."

"Please, Kate. You need to be more flexible. I rarely bring anyone to the house."

"More flexible? That's a low blow. Besides, I've got nothing special for dinner." I was feeling overwhelmed. When would I prepare this meal for our mystery guest?

"I know you'll manage. We'll be there at eight." Then he hung up.

I was steaming mad. I peeked into the bedrooms. Lucie was reading a picture book. Marc was constructing Lego towers and Timmy had fallen asleep. I apologized to Marina and told her I had to run out to the store. Grudgingly, she said okay. I rushed to the salumeria and bought the makings of an antipasto platter. I would follow that up with a mushroom risotto, salad, cheese and fruit. There were still some cookies. I could pull all that together when I got back from Cerro.

By the time I dropped off the children with Giada, it was raining buckets. With the bad weather, it took a while to get up the mountain. I was behind a long line of cars. People were probably heading up to the mountains to ski.

By now my throat was killing me and all I wanted to do was crawl into bed. How could Henri expect me to deliver food to his Mafia friend and then prepare a fancy dinner? What a nerve! And who was coming for dinner? It better not be Francesco Ferrari. I couldn't bear the thought.

When I arrived at the cottage, it was pouring cats and dogs. I didn't have an umbrella. Between the car and the house, I would get drenched. I slipped on the top step of the staircase and landed on my knee on the hard metal tread. At the door, I couldn't find the key in my purse. I stood there rummaging in my bag as the rain soaked me. I had forgotten to wear a hat, and the icy water ran down into my collar. I knocked on the door. Seconds later, it was flung open. Andrea stood there, his eyes wild and accusatory.

"Where were you yesterday? I waited all day," he yelled over the pounding rain.

"Can I come in? I'm getting drenched out here." I pushed past him into the cottage.

"Where were you?" he repeated.

I stepped over to the table and dumped the two bags I'd brought up. "I couldn't come yesterday. Remember, I have three children, and they're on vacation right now. I couldn't get away," I yelled back. The rain was thudding on the roof like a herd of elephants.

"I thought you might have stayed in Paris. I thought you might have forgotten me." There was desperation in his voice.

"I didn't forget. I couldn't come." I turned and went back downstairs for the fresh bread and vegetables I'd bought that morning. When I came back upstairs, he was still agitated.

"I have to be able to count on you," he complained.

211

This made me really angry. "Count on me? I don't owe you anything. It's from the goodness of my heart that I'm here. You are a Mafia goon who kills people, runs prostitution rings, commits robberies and fraud," I sputtered. "You and your family make me sick."

"I don't do any of that. I was born into this family. I had no choice."

We stood very close together, almost nose to nose.

"In life, there are always choices. You could have walked away from your family." My voice rose. "You're a coward." I handed him the last bag and turned to leave.

He looked stricken. "Don't leave. I'm sorry. This last week has been especially difficult. Please don't go."

I pulled the door open. The rain hit me straight on. "I'm actually paid to bring you food. But I'm not your nanny. I don't have to babysit you or entertain you."

I slammed the door behind me and raced down the stairs. All the way down the mountain, I sizzled with self-righteous anger.

Chapter 39

I'd barely gotten the kids to bed when Henri arrived home with Alonzo Monteverde and Francesco Ferrari. Alonzo was tall and thin, wiry like a rangy coyote. Untamed black hair sprouted from his head. Big white teeth showed between full lips and a wild, overgrown beard. He was repellent and arresting, an unsettling combination. He came over to me and performed a deep bow, swooshing his red beret like one of the three musketeers. Then he held my hand a little too long. His was moist and cold. Who was this guy?

I soon learned Signor Monteverde was a painter. I couldn't help laughing at that. Not only did he have a beret, but he wore a patterned scarf around his neck. He was a pantomime of a bohemian.

"Signora, how wonderful of you to invite me to your home!" He bent down and kissed my hand. His lips felt moist, like a garden slug.

I rescued my hand. "You are most welcome. Please come in."

Henri took their coats, while I showed the two men into the living room. Once they were seated, I hurried off to the kitchen, hoping to escape, but that was not to be.

"Let's keep your little wife company while she cooks," Alonzo said. He got up and came into the kitchen, followed by Francesco.

Henri looked perturbed as Alonzo sat down at Marc's spot and pushed away the dirty soup bowl. I had yet to clear the table after the children's supper. I hurried to pick up the dishes and put them in the sink. Meanwhile, Henri brought out a couple of bottles of red wine and some glasses. He poured while I wiped the table. It looked as though they were all determined to sit there in the kitchen.

"Come sit with us, signora." Alonzo patted a chair.

"I've got to get dinner ready." I smiled over my shoulder while I organized the antipasto platter, with salami, prosciutto, roasted peppers, olives, and so on.

The men began talking about a mutual acquaintance. I gathered it was someone they met at a café or restaurant. Alonzo had an accent I didn't recognize, and it was difficult to understand everything he said.

"*Che idiota* (what an idiot)," Francesco said. "He would believe anything." They all laughed uproariously.

I placed the platter on the table and then provided everyone with a plate and silverware. I sliced some bread and put that in a basket. As I bent over, Alonzo snaked his arm around my waist and pulled me down to the empty seat. "Join us, signora."

I extricated myself. "I'll join you later, when I've got the risotto done."

Henri seemed oblivious to this guy and his behavior. If anything, he seemed awe-struck at entertaining an actual artist in his house.

The men continued to talk, laugh and drink while I cooked the mushrooms in butter and oil and stirred in the rice. I put the cheese

214

I had bought on a platter and arranged apples, oranges and pears in a bowl. This would be a simple meal.

I served the risotto in soup bowls and the men dug in. Alonzo shoveled food in his mouth as though he had not eaten for days. He helped himself to a large slice of gorgonzola and placed it on top of his rice, stirring it in. Then he guzzled more wine. Francesco wasn't much better. He had slathered cheese on some bread and was stuffing it into his mouth. I glanced over at Henri, but he didn't seem to care about our guests' table manners. He was eating with gusto himself.

I can't remember what they talked about. Their voices seemed muffled and the words rolled over me in an unintelligible wave. Their laughter and what little I understood of their conversation seemed vulgar and full of innuendo. Where had Henri met this guy Alonzo? Why had he brought him here?

The truth was, I kept thinking about Andrea; up there in Cerro, all alone in the cold. I felt incredibly guilty for having spoken to him the way I did. In my heart, I knew he wasn't a Mafia monster. Why had I run off? Of course, he depended on me...not only for food, but also for companionship. I thought about his loneliness. How could he stand it?

When I began to clear the dishes, Henri pulled me over and said, "What do you think? Wouldn't you love it?"

I looked at him vacantly. "Love what?"

"To have your portrait painted. Alonzo would like to paint you."

I looked at Alonzo, Francesco and Henri, who were staring up at me. "I don't know. I'd never thought of doing that." My voice was scratchy, as if my sore throat had shut it down. "I probably don't have the time for a sitting." I definitely didn't want to be alone with this man while he painted my picture. I shivered at the thought.

"Signora, you are a beautiful woman. I want to paint you…I must paint you," Alonzo gushed.

"I don't know." I bent over to pick up another dish. I could feel myself blushing.

"Come on, Kate. We could hang it over the sofa." Henri had a self-satisfied smile on his lips. He liked having his wife called "a beautiful woman." He took it personally.

I placed the dishes in the sink and went back for more.

"Come sit with us, signora," Francesco said.

"I'm sorry, gentlemen, but I've had a long day and I've got a bad sore throat. I'm going to bed," I whispered.

***

I don't know what time the men left. I had taken some cold medication and was out like a light. In the morning I went into the kitchen and found a mess. Henri hadn't bothered to put away the leftover food. Empty wine bottles, a bottle of Armagnac, glasses and silverware littered the table. The sink was piled high with dishes and the clean-up seemed like a monumental task. I made coffee before getting to work. Luckily, the children were still asleep.

216

When I'd finished putting the last dish in the dishwasher, Timmy and Marc appeared. I whispered a good morning and they both started to laugh.

"Mommy, why are you whispering?" Marc giggled.

"My voice disappeared."

"Mommy's voice disappeared," Timmy mimicked in a whisper Apparently, this was incredibly funny. They spent the rest of their time at the table whispering and giggling to each other. Then Lucie came in, followed by Henri. He looked terrible.

"What time did you come to bed?" I whispered.

"It must have been two o'clock or later." He served himself coffee and sat down, his head propped in his hand. "Oh, I feel terrible."

"It looks like you kept on drinking after I went to sleep. You should drink lots of water and take a couple of aspirin."

He groaned and sipped more coffee. Then he looked up at me. "Why did you go to bed so early when we had guests?" As usual lately, he was turning his bad humor on me.

"Because I felt lousy. I've got a bad cold and I lost my voice." As if that wasn't obvious.

The kids started giggling again. "Mommy, where did you lose your voice?" Lucie asked. They seemed unaware of the tension in the air.

I stayed focused on Henri. "I found that painter a noxious presence. I really don't want to be alone with him in some atelier."

217

"He's coming here on Sunday afternoon. I'll take care of the kids."

He never took care of the kids. "Why are you so insistent on this portrait?"

"He's pretty famous. We're lucky he wants to paint you and he's giving me a bargain."

I sighed. As long as I wouldn't be alone with the guy, I could go along with it. After all, did I really have a choice?

As it turned out, Alonzo Monteverde arrived at two on Sunday. But he didn't bring paints, a palette or a canvas. He came with two cameras. I'd put on make-up in part to cover my red nose. I'd been blowing it non-stop. I'd spent some time arranging my hair in a French twist and I wore my pearl earrings and my blue dress. If I had to do this, I might as well look decent.

Henri went into the kitchen with the children. He would entertain them with some homemade playdough I'd mixed the previous day.

I felt nervous. Alonzo was all business, very different from his persona of Thursday night. He had me sit on a straight-backed dining room chair. Then he photographed me from different angles. He didn't say much except *look up, look down, smile, think of a happy moment, stare out the window,* etc. At one point, he came over and undid my chignon. Then he arranged my hair over my shoulder. His fingers caressed my cheek. I pulled back involuntarily.

"Don't be afraid, signora," he said, a sly smile on his lips. "I won't hurt you."

I couldn't help smiling back. I was embarrassed. "Let me catch that," he said.

After many more shots with both cameras, he was finally finished. Henri came out of the kitchen and thanked Alonzo over and over.

"I'll begin by painting from these pictures," Alonzo explained. "When I decide on the best pose, I will need to arrange some sittings."

"That will be marvelous," Henri gushed. "We're at your disposal."

I think I rolled my eyes. Henri was blatantly charmed by this bohemian con artist.

Chapter 40

The following Wednesday, I felt a lot better. Along with the bags of items Henri brought home, I shopped for some good bread and fresh fruits and vegetables. It was a beautiful, crisp morning. I made good time driving up the mountain.

At the cottage, I parked and began the trek up the stairs. I felt nervous about seeing Andrea after my behavior the previous week and planned on apologizing. As I reached the terrace, the door opened and Andrea was there, his eyes wild and regretful. I probably looked the same. I lowered my gaze and handed him the bags. Then I went down for my satchel and the bread. When I came back up, he was already opening the shutters to let in the bright sunlight. Under the dazzling rays, he looked tired. There were smudges under his lovely gold-flecked eyes.

"I'm so sorry," I began.

He started apologizing at the same time. "*Mi dispiace di essere egoista.*"

"No, it was my fault. I was angry about a lot of things and I was getting sick."

"No, I had no right to say those things to you." He paused. "I should be more grateful."

"I'm sorry," I said again.

We stood there in the blinding sunlight and our eyes locked, and then he stepped closer and I was in his arms. I don't know how it happened. He bent down and kissed my lips. His were soft and warm, and I lost myself in that kiss. It went on and on. It was as though all the previous weeks had been a preamble to this moment. I kissed him back. I wanted this embrace to last forever.

Then he stepped back and began to apologize again. "Mi dispiace…I've been wanting to kiss you since the first day you came here. I shouldn't have done that."

I stepped over and placed my hand against his cheek. "I'm glad you kissed me," I said. We were melting in each other's gaze.

Andrea took my hand and kissed my palm. I felt a stirring in my soul. Then he pulled me in again and we lost ourselves in another kiss. When we came up for air, he gestured to the bedroom. I nodded. He took my hand and pulled me to the back hall. It was freezing in there because the two heaters were in the front room, but we didn't care. We were on fire. I pulled off my coat and a couple of sweaters until I was down to my long underwear. He did the same and then we were in bed together under a mountain of covers.

We kissed for a long time, our hands exploring each other's bodies. I didn't think of Henri or of my children or of what I was doing. I only wanted to feel, to touch, to explore. Then we removed the rest of our clothes and Andrea was on top of me and we were moving like a well-rehearsed duet. I moaned with desire and he matched my rhythm. Then he was inside me, charging ahead, bringing me along and then filling me with an explosion of pleasure.

I screamed with joy, with ecstasy, with amazement. I had never felt like this before. It was magical. It was beautiful.

Then Andrea was kissing me again. I felt tears on my cheeks, and he licked them away. I smiled and licked his lips. He started to move off of me, but I placed my hands on his hips and held him there. I didn't want this to be over.

"Shall I apologize again?" he asked.

"No apology necessary," I murmured.

He covered my mouth with his and I groaned again.

Chapter 41

When I left the cottage, after that first encounter, I felt euphoric, complete and fulfilled. By the time I got down to the streets of Verona, I was awash in a sea of guilt. There and then, I swore I would never do that again. In those two hours I had become a wayward woman, a whore, a prostitute…I called myself every possible despicable name. What had I done? I'd never even looked at another man since I'd married Henri. How could I have been so easily won over? Where was my moral compass?

***

That afternoon, I met Giada at the park. After the children ran off, we sat down at the café kiosk. I had been in my euphoric state on the way there. After we had our coffee, Giada looked at me, frowning.

"What happened to you? You look different…happier than I've seen you lately."

I shrugged and looked down at my coffee. I couldn't help smiling.

She grinned. "Did Henri come home for lunch?"

I blushed. She had come incredibly close to the truth. "No, no, I just feel good today with the sunshine. And my cold is just about gone."

Giada narrowed her eyes and cocked her head. I don't think she believed me.

The rest of the afternoon, I nodded and smiled as she recounted her New Year's Eve spent with her in-laws. They'd had the traditional cotechino sausage and lentils to bring prosperity. During the meal her mother-in-law had continued her ongoing criticism of Giada and her husband didn't defend her. Instead, he would nod his head and avoid Giada's gaze. Her father-in-law was a nice enough guy, but he wouldn't put his wife in her place. At some point, Giada had responded in kind. There had been a yelling match and the in-laws left. Afterward, Giada's husband had upbraided her for not respecting his mother.

As Giada talked, my mind wandered again and again to that morning. I felt euphoric and despicable in turn.

***

Henri came home late that night. The next morning, he took his time getting ready for work. I felt guilty and was sure he could see the scarlet letter emblazoned on my chest. But he didn't even look at me when he walked into the kitchen.

"Alonzo called and asked me if you could come to his studio…" He poured his coffee and avoided my eyes.

I gripped the back of a kitchen chair. "The answer is no. I don't trust that man. He's a womanizer."

"Come on, Kate, do you think he would drag you to bed when he has a relationship with me? *C'est ridicule.*"

"I do. I do not want to be alone with him." This seemed ironic in light of what I'd been up to the previous day. "He'll have to come here and set up his easel in the kitchen."

Henri turned and smirked. "You have a high regard for your sexual attraction. Let's face it, Kate, with your American Puritan manner, you put off European men."

I could not believe we were having this conversation and that he would describe me in that way. Until recently, Henri had been the reserved one in our relationship. I smiled grimly. Perversely, what he'd said seemed to validate my dissolute behavior.

***

In the weeks ahead, my life became an emotional roller coaster. I went from euphoria, to guilt, to rationalization. Alone in bed at night, I would relive every caress, every kiss. In the morning, in broad daylight, I would chastise myself for my weak, immoral behavior. Later, when my two oldest were at school and I was making lunch or doing the dishes, I would say to myself, *Kate, you've been an excellent wife to Henri. But he's never here. Let's face it. He's probably out whoring with Bianchi and Ferrari every night. You're lonely. You have a right to some happiness.*

But I had a hard time convincing myself. My mother would have told me I was lying to myself and selling myself short. *You're better than that, Kate. Don't do something you'll regret the rest of your life.*

Chapter 42

The following Wednesday morning, I took a bath and washed my hair before anyone else was awake. I shaved my legs and sprayed on a light flowery eau-de-cologne. Through these ministrations, I repeated to myself that I would tell Andrea we could only be friends. We would have coffee, talk a bit and then I would write. I needed to take advantage of those rare moments and move ahead with a new book.

I was feverishly happy as I bustled the children off to school and handed Timmy over to Marina. I left early for Cerro, but I had to stop for gas. The attendant took forever. I kept looking at my watch and then at my reflection in the rearview mirror. When I arrived at the cottage, I grabbed the grocery bags and raced from the car, up the stairs. They were icy and I nearly fell. Andrea must have been standing by the door. He pulled it open and his face was ablaze with pleasure. His lovely eyes glistened and his smile glowed.

I had to be strong. Once inside, I turned away and walked stiffly into the kitchen and placed the bags on the counter. With my back to him, I said, "I need to work on a book while I'm here. I can't let anything happen like last week." I gulped for air and turned around to face him.

Andrea was smiling. "Then, my love, where is your satchel?"

I realized in my haste to get out the door at home, I'd forgotten the satchel with my writing materials. I felt my cheeks redden in embarrassment. Andrea lifted my chin with his long fingers and bent down to kiss me ever so gently. My heart was pounding; he had called me his love. As we kissed, he pulled off my woolen cap and my hair came cascading down. His hands combed through my freshly washed tresses. "You smell delicious…like a bunch of wild flowers."

I was swooning and barely registered what he said.

"Come, my little wildflower…come…"

The bed was neatly made, and the two heaters provided some warmth in the small room. Again, we ripped off our clothes. I was down to my underwear when he took me in his arms. He kissed my neck, my shoulders and cupped my breasts. I shivered, but not from the cold.

We spent the next two hours in bed under the covers, making love and sharing vignettes about the past week. I told him how I had felt euphoric and exhilarated when I thought of him. Then how guilty I felt, and then in the next minute how I wanted him passionately.

He told me he had spent the week thinking only of me, going over everything I'd said; how I looked; how my body felt under his caress; how I moved; how I responded. Here, I buried my face in the crook of his neck from embarrassment. In response, his hands began to move over me, and I rose up to meet him, giving and receiving exquisite pleasure. I wanted that morning to never end.

My old clock radio told me when it was eleven forty-five and time to get ready to leave. Our clothes littered the floor. They were icy cold as I pulled each item on. We shared a long embrace at the door and then I was in the car on my way down to Verona, to my family, to my life.

Chapter 43   2019

Lucie wakes up when they pass out the breakfast tray, but she only wants some coffee.

"Hey, Mom," she says after checking her phone. "I can't believe I slept all this time. I should have been strategizing for the meeting next week. I wasted six hours sleeping."

I scoff gently. "You didn't waste time. If you slept, it's because you needed it. You drive yourself to exhaustion."

Lucie stretches her arms over her head and yawns. "When do we arrive?" she asks, just as her hands are grabbed from behind. Then a face appears between the seats. Lucie giggles, something she rarely does. But Drew has that effect on her.

"Stop manhandling me, you monster," she says and turns to grin at him.

"Hey, sis, how's your Italian these days? Are you going to be our translator?"

"Almost non-existent. Maybe it'll come back after we're there for a while. Anyway, Mom speaks pretty good Italian, don't you?" She glances at me.

"I'll manage, I think."

Drew never lived in Italy. He was born after we returned to the states. When Marc called him and proposed the trip, Drew had declined at first. Obviously, he had no memories to relive. Even Tim barely remembered his time there. He'd been so young. But Lucie had convinced Drew to come along. "It'll be special to be just the five of us, without spouses or children...like old times."

Of course, I felt the same way. I had not been alone with just my four children for years. It was a different dynamic when we were a cozy five-some. Before they went off to college and eventually got married, we had been a tight group.

Drew is a veterinarian and lives in a small town in Iowa. His wife Jenny is a large-animal vet, whereas he deals with dogs, cats and the occasional hamster. He has an engaging smile and twinkly eyes. When you're in Drew's orbit, you feel special. He has a great bedside manner, much appreciated by his four-legged patients, but more importantly by their owners.

In short, Drew is an animal whisperer. In contrast, Jenny exudes competence and assuredness, but has no charisma. I suppose you don't need a great bedside manner while attending to cows and pigs.

Their marriage seems happy. They have two children, Cammie and Connor. They've never employed nannies or babysitters. The children just come along to work with them. Both kids have spent plenty of time in trucks, barns and pastures with Jenny. Drew's office is next door to their house and the kids are always in and out. Beatrice, Drew's assistant, is an honorary grandmother.

Along with his veterinary clinic, Drew has a media presence. He'd begun with a series of YouTube videos on animal care. He filmed these episodes with either Cammie or Connor when they were little, and he developed quite a following because of the variety of animals and his cute kids. Compared to other homespun videos on the internet, his were sleek and superbly filmed by Jake, a local teenager. The kid had a real talent, and is out in California now, studying cinema at USC. After establishing a following, Drew moved on to produce a podcast where he told amusing stories about animals and gave advice and even interjected some poetry. It all sounds kind of quirky, but Drew has a sizeable following. I think it has to do with his personality...he exudes genuine kindness and a subtle sense of humor.

When Drew was a baby, Lucie had been a wonderful little babysitter. The two of them connected on a special level. As adults, they're still on the same wavelength. They laugh at the same jokes and view the world in a similar way; they're both out to help people and animals.

"How are you doing back there?" I ask Drew. "Did you sleep?"

"I did...fabulous dreams about Lucie and..."

"Ha ha...must have been a nightmare." Lucie is twisting her hair into a topknot. "So, Mom, what are we going to do when we arrive?"

"Someone from the prize committee will be at the airport to greet us. They've organized transport to the hotel."

"What's the name of the hotel again?" Drew asks.

"Hotel Gabbia D'Oro. It's a five-star hotel."

"Gabbia D'Oro," he repeats, trying to pronounce the unfamiliar Italian.

"Cage of gold," I say.

Chapter 44

The following days and weeks were a blur in my mind, interrupted by a series of cut-glass images. Sometimes I felt as though I transcended my life and looked down at it from above, like a heavenly voyeur. Other times I was mired in anguish and guilt. At those times, it felt as though I couldn't pull myself out of the mud.

Nevertheless, each week before I left for the mountains, I bathed, slathered on body lotion and sprayed myself with cologne. I had become a shameless Jezebel. One Wednesday morning, I remembered the lingerie I had bought with Giada months before. The lacy bra and panties, still wrapped in tissue paper, were in the bottom drawer of my bureau, under some summer shirts. When I put on the silky garments, I felt incredibly sexy and desirable. My reflection in the long mirror behind the door of the armoire showed a tall woman with full breasts and gently curved hips. I had slimmed down in the last few weeks from stress and unbridled joy. Much of the time, I wasn't even hungry.

At the cottage, I told Andrea to sit on the bed and then I disrobed in the bathroom. I had planned on parading around the bedroom in all my lascivious glory, but when the time came, I hesitated, standing partially hidden at the doorway.

Andrea saw my embarrassment and encouraged me gently "*Viene, qui uccellino.*" (Come here, little bird.) *Uccellino* was a pet name he had for me. I came around the corner and into the room, my face and body glowing with embarrassment and anticipation.

"*Quanto sei bella!*" (How beautiful you are.)

That day, our lovemaking was slow and tender. We took time with each gesture, each caress, to bring mutual pleasure.

***

When we were lying in each other's arms, warm and satiated, we would talk. Andrea told me about his childhood. His mother had died when he was quite young. Apparently, Andrea favored her in looks and personality. When he was a child, his father would say, "Get away. I can't stand to look at you. You remind me of your mother."

Andrea was raised by his *Nonna*, his grandmother, a hard, spare woman who wasn't prone to hugs or kisses. She seemed purposely oblivious to the family's illegal business dealings and the crime associated with it. They lived in a house in the hills. Nonna cooked, washed and took care of their chickens and goats. She rarely disciplined Andrea. This was left up to his brother, Massimo. When Andrea was eight, he followed Massimo and his friends up into the hills. The big boys were hunting and trapping small game. Before they left, Massimo told Andrea he couldn't come with them. But Andrea snuck along behind, thinking he was well-hidden behind scrub bush and rocks.

At one point, following the boys up an almost sheer façade, he got stuck on a ledge above a precipice. He was too small to reach up to the ledge above. He began to cry and called out to Massimo. Of course, Massimo had known Andrea was following them. He looked over the cliff from above and shouted down, "It serves you right. I told you not to follow me. You can just sit there until I decide to help you."

Andrea had spent the night on that ledge in fear of falling off and plunging down the mountainside. After that, he always did what his brother said.

I told Andrea about my childhood in the Chicago suburbs. I described summers at the beach on Lake Michigan, family picnics and chasing fireflies in the early evening. Buried under the covers, I told him about snow blizzards, ice skating and building snowmen with my sister. I told him about trips to museums: The Art Institute and The Museum of Science and Industry.

In this recounting of my childhood memories, I realized how fortunate I'd been with a lovely, warm family and rich cultural experiences. I thought of Andrea in his rustic farmhouse with no running water and the simple village life. We were worlds apart and yet, on some level, we were the same. I felt closer to Andrea than anyone else in my life. Our hearts and minds were in perfect synch.

Really, you're thinking. *How could you possibly say that? You knew this man for only a few months and yet you claim to have been closer to him than anyone else...ever? It sounds like an affair, pure and simple. Sexual attraction, undoubtedly, but a sustainable relationship of love and trust? No way.*

Chapter 45

Henri never asked me about my trips up to Cerro. I think he avoided the subject because he didn't want to be attacked by my wrath and indignation. He seemed oblivious to my highs and lows. Of course, he'd never been good at reading people, mostly because he was self-absorbed.

Before long, I learned there was more to his lack of interest in me or the kids. One evening in February, Anna invited me to a play. She included Giada as well. One of her patients had given her tickets to a comedy that was in town. I wondered if I would be able to follow an intricate plot in Italian or get the jokes. Humor requires a high-level knowledge of a language and a deep understanding of culture. At least the action would give me a clue as to what was going on.

We had dinner first in a small restaurant located in a narrow alleyway in the pedestrian shopping area. We ate pasta alla puttanesca, prawns and tartufi di gelato for dessert, and we shared a bottle of wine. During dinner we discussed Coppola's film *Il Padrino,* The Godfather in English.

"I don't like how he depicts Italians…like we're all lowlifes," Anna said, tapping her knife on the white tablecloth.

"Come on. This is fiction…" Giada said, looking up. She frowned as she swirled the wine in her glass. "…though the Mafia does exist, and they are lowlifes."

"Yes, but the world will watch this movie and have a negative impression of all Italians. It's unfair," Anna said.

"Americans know the Mafia doesn't represent all Italians," I protested.

"The problem is, it was the Italians from the south who moved to America and brought the Mafia with them," Giada said.

I had heard this argument before. Some Italians living in the north complained about the south. They felt southerners were a drain on the economy, uneducated, and the source of crime. The truth was that most industry and agriculture thrived in the north of Italy. Milano and Torino had factories, the fashion industry, and were business and financial hubs with robust economies. The Po Valley provided rice and vegetables, as did Tuscany. The Veneto region was rich in wine and grain. By contrast, the land in the south was arid and rocky, making it more difficult to grow crops, and it was harder to find jobs. So, in the last century, many southern Italians had moved to the Americas.

Without thinking, I said, "Well, not all members of the Mafia are bad…I mean, what about their wives or their children…or their accountants."

"Accountants?" Giada said, and burst out laughing. Anna started laughing too, and I joined in for fear they would question the source of my ridiculous statement.

We left the restaurant, walked down the alley and into a piazza. We crossed the open area and went down another narrow street on our way to the theatre. Giada and Anna were walking slightly ahead, and I trailed behind. At the corner, I glanced in the illuminated window of a small trattoria. The others walked on, while I remained frozen in place. Inside, at a table for two, I saw Henri. He was with Giulia Ferrari. They were leaning across the table toward each other, as though pulled by an invisible string. They were holding hands and gazing into each other's eyes.

In spite of my transgressions with Andrea, I was shocked and hurt by what I saw. My eyes filled with tears and I stood transfixed. Up ahead, Giada and Anna had turned around and were beckoning to me to hurry up.

"*Cosa fai*? What are you doing?" Giada asked.

I didn't want her to come back and see what I saw. Quickly, I pulled out a handkerchief. "I've got something in my eye. I don't want to ruin my mascara." I dabbed at my tears as I hurried toward them.

***

As it turned out, I didn't need to worry about my comprehension of the play. I couldn't concentrate on the action. My mind kept straying to what I'd seen. It made me look squarely at my marriage. I'd been blind, or purposely deceiving myself. This wasn't the first affair Henri had perpetrated. No. There had been others. Even in Chicago, he had been gone nights without explanation. I remembered trips with colleagues over weekends. Before the kids and I moved to Italy, he had been here for months, alone. Maybe this affair with Giulia had started then, while I changed diapers at home.

Had I been inattentive? Not interesting enough. Not beautiful enough. Not sexy enough?

I thought of him with Giulia, her dyed hair and voluptuous body. That's what he loved…at least for now.

And what about me? Had I wandered and sinned because I felt alone and unloved? Was Henri's behavior a valid excuse for my straying? No. I needed to take full responsibility for my actions. I should forget Andrea. Nothing good would come from this affair. I should disengage; not for Henri, but for myself.

As I sat there in the darkened theatre, an image of Andrea's eyes appeared before me, brimming with empathy and love. Yes, love. Was I ready to give him up?

Chapter 46

In the middle of February, Henri had to go to the States for some high-level meetings. Robertson's was holding the convention in a luxurious golf resort in California. Henri didn't play golf and actually thought it was a silly waste of time. He would be gone for a week. That same week, Giada invited Lucie to go skiing in the Dolomites. Her family owned a chalet near Cortina d'Ampezzo. Lucie had never skied before but Giada assured me this wouldn't be a problem. Lucie and Francesca would both be in classes with a ski instructor every morning.

I remember how excited Lucie was. We outfitted her with ski gear and a new anorak. After Henri and Lucie left, the household felt different with just me and the boys. I simplified meals and felt relaxed. I realized that, although Henri wasn't actually home all that much, his looming presence put me on edge.

That week, the weather was almost balmy. We went to the park each afternoon and had picnic suppers on a blanket under the dining room table. I spent longer in the boys' room telling stories and singing their favorite songs.

Down at the station, early in the morning.
See the little puffer bellies, all in a row.

241

Hear the station master, blow his little whistle,
Chug–chug, choo–choo, off we go.

I spent every spare minute thinking about Andrea. How I wished I could bring him down to the house while Henri was gone. I would prepare a feast for him and we would drink wine and cuddle on the sofa. The boys would be charmed by Andrea and he would get on the floor and play games with them. At night, we would make love between smooth sheets and we would be *warm*.

I remembered the Dickinson poem that reflected exactly how I felt. That Wednesday, I read it to Andrea. We both longed for wild nights together.

Wild Nights–Wild Nights

Wild Nights–Wild Nights!
Were I with thee
Wild Nights should be
Our luxury!

Futile–the winds–
To a heart in port–
Done with the Compass
Done with the Chart!

Rowing in Eden–
Ah–the sea!
Might I but moor–tonight
In thee!

***

That week, we had a scare. I made good time driving up the mountain. After a long embrace and deep kisses, I held Andrea off and looked at his dear face. He was so pale from living in darkness.

"Let's sit in the sunshine a while. You need some color."

He agreed. We made cappuccinos and sat together in front of the window. The sun's rays poured in, warming our faces. Blue dots danced behind my closed lids. Andrea's hand felt warm and solid in mine. We'd only been sitting there a short while when Andrea pulled his hand away and hissed, "Sh-sh-sh."

I opened my eyes. He was holding up a hand, gesturing for me to be quiet. Moments later, I heard footsteps on the metal staircase outside. Someone was coming up. Andrea raced across the room and into the bedroom, gently closing the door behind him. I opened my satchel and pulled out a notebook. As I turned back around, I heard a knock and then Gabriella Gallo's voice. "Buongiorno, Kate. Are you there?"

I looked briefly around the room. Andrea's cup was on the table. I put it in the sink and then I opened the door.

"Ciao, Gabriella. *Che piacere.* How nice to see you." I tried to produce a sincere smile. My knees were shaking as I stood blocking the entrance.

Gabriella was bundled up in an old anorak and work pants. She probably was off to care for her chickens. "I've seen your car here, and I wanted to stop by and say hello."

243

"Well, hello," I said, smiling nervously.

"What are you doing here?" she asked. Gabriella was never one to mince words.

I repeated my oft-used lie. "I come up here to write. I'm working on a book. I need to get away from the distractions at home."

Gabriella raised an eyebrow. "Isn't it cold in there?" She gestured at my bulky clothing.

"Yes, you're right. It's cold, but I've got electric heaters to warm me."

She still looked skeptical. I blabbed on. "When I'm at home, I think I should do the wash or clean the stove. There's always a chore. When I'm here, I'm forced to write."

"Would you like to come up to our house later?"

"No, I've got to get home for the children. Listen, I better get back to work. Thanks for stopping by."

Gabriella shook her head and turned to leave. Hopefully, she just thought I was a nutcase.

"Thanks for coming by. I'll bring the children up for a visit soon," I shouted at her receding back. When I shut the door, I felt like a jerk. I hated lying to a friend, but I needed to protect Andrea.

After I was sure she was gone, I whispered to Andrea that the coast was clear. He came out of the bedroom, went over to the windows, and shut the blinds with a bang, plunging the room into semi-darkness.

"We have to be more careful. Someone across the valley could use binoculars and see us sitting here," he said.

"No one in the village of Cerro would be spying on this cottage," I scoffed. But I could see a spark of fear in his eyes and he was paler than usual.

"They are looking for me. I know it." Andrea paced around the table. He exuded nervous energy.

"Who are *they*?" I asked.

"You know…the family of the kid Massimo killed. The Greco family. They want to kill me. It's only a matter of time. They'll find me." He slammed his fist into his hand, again and again.

"What would you do if they showed up?" This was something we'd never discussed. The truth was, I didn't want to think about the inevitable future…Andrea returning to his real life, his father and his brother.

"I've got a bag packed. If I heard them come up from the road, I would climb out through the bedroom window. It's at ground level. I'd have to find a place to hide…" He stopped pacing and looked at me. "You know, I'm always listening. Even at night, I wake up at the least sound. I think someone is out there and I lie in bed waiting for them to race up those stairs and shoot their way in here."

"Maybe the two families will settle the argument. Could they negotiate a peace?"

"We've been fighting forever. It goes way back." He sighed. Then he reached out to me and I was in his arms. We clung to each other as though we were the only two people in the world.

Later, as we lay spooned in bed, I said, "I'm thinking about where you could go if they came to get you. At the top of the hill above the

245

cottage is a small tower. It's a chapel. You could go up there and hide inside. Marc got locked in one-time last summer. I managed to open the door with a knitting needle, but you could probably use a pen or pencil."

"If I made it out of here before they caught me." He flopped over on his back. "This inaction is driving me crazy. The days and nights last forever. Even with reading and my daily exercise regimen, time seems to stand still."

Andrea had told me about his routine. He did hundreds of sit-ups, push-ups and jumping jacks each day. He was fit with a slim, muscular body. He ate and drank sparingly and read everything I brought him. Sometimes when we were in bed, we'd read poetry together. Once we imagined we were like Catherine and Henry in *A Farewell to Arms*. We would be living together in a chalet in Switzerland, dependent on our mutual love. The rest of the world would be far, far away.

I grasped his hand. "If you escape from here, you will need money. I have money for you."

Andrea laughed. "You're going to support me? You'll be my benefactress?"

"Yes, I have money for you," I repeated. "It's in my satchel. I'll give it to you before I leave."

"I can't take your money…or more precisely, Henri's money."

"It's not Henri's. It's mine. I earned it."

I could feel Andrea studying my profile. "Giancarlo Bianchi gave me the money for visiting you and bringing you sustenance," I said.

Andrea squeezed my hand.

"When he gave me the envelope full of lire, I was angry. Initially I didn't want to come here…to participate in aiding and abetting a murderer. The money made me feel like a prostitute. I hid it in the bottom of my satchel."

Andrea's laughter was caustic. "There is some irony there."

"Yes." I laughed, too. "I suppose there is."

He turned to face me, his lips inches from mine. "Oh, my darling Kate. I am so sorry to have put you through all this, to have sullied your convictions by, as you say, 'aiding and abetting' me." He kissed me gently. "And yet, I am selfish. I love you. I want to spend every minute I can with you. I hate to think of your life away from me." He closed his eyes. "I'm sorry for this weakness."

Chapter 47

Alonzo came three times to paint me. In between visits, he painted from the photos he had taken. When he swooshed into the house, he reminded me of a swashbuckling pirate, complete with a wide-brimmed hat, black mustache and an evil grin. The children thought he was marvelous. Once, he brought a spotlight and black paper. He sat the children on a stool and traced their silhouettes that were projected on the paper. Later, he cut them out and made a collage of the profiles, then glued them on top of a canvas painted with a psychedelic rainbow of colors. Henri loved the collage and hung it over the side table in the entryway.

Alonzo was there for several hours each time. I found it hard to sit still. He didn't seem to mind if I changed positions ever so slightly. While he was working, he said nothing, and my mind would wander. What would we have for dinner? Had I washed Lucie's smock for school? Then I would think about Andrea and relive our last morning together. I would revisit each kiss, each conversation. Once when I was daydreaming, Alonzo asked me what I was thinking about. I blushed. I was sure this man could read my mind. After that, I was on my guard and policed my thoughts.

In the portrait, I am quite beautiful. I suppose all painters flatter their customers. I have a secret smile and my eyes are wistful. When

I look at the painting, it reminds me of that time; of illicit, passionate love; of deep loneliness; of unrelenting guilt. Alonzo managed to capture those fleeting emotions that must have raced across my face. Now, the painting hangs in my office at home. It is a reminder of another time, another life.

Alonzo gave me several photographs to keep. I put one in my satchel and gave it to Andrea on one of my visits. He was thrilled to have it. I planned on taking a picture of him with Henri's camera, but that never happened. So, the only image I have of him is tucked away in my psyche.

***

I made another friend at the park during the week when Giada was gone. I had seen the woman before. That afternoon, I was sitting on a bench knitting. She sat down beside me and introduced herself. Her name was Amaya and she had been born in Iran. She had three little boys, and Marc and Timmy often played with them. Her Italian husband was an engineer and worked in the Middle East for an Italian construction firm. He met Amaya when she was sixteen. They married, and he moved her to Verona. I think her husband was twenty years her senior. I met him only once. He was chubby and balding.

Although we came from different spots on the globe, Amaya and I had a special connection: we were both foreigners. Even though she had lived in Italy for years, she still felt apart. In retrospect, my relationship with Giada was similar. She was an outsider as well because she came from Milan and all of her family lived there. In

Italy at that time, families were very close. The lives of the Veronese women I met revolved around their parents, their siblings and the extended family. They had no need of a new friend who might move away. For example, in our apartment building, there was a young couple with a baby. The wife's parents lived one floor above, and the husband's parents lived one floor below. They had lunch with one set of in-laws and dinner with the other. Sometimes I heard them bickering in the elevator. There was a lot of togetherness, a lot of love and a lot of tension.

Amaya was heavy-set and somewhat unkempt, though she must have been a beautiful young girl. Although she wasn't that much older than me, she seemed a mature woman. Her husband continued to work in the Middle East and was gone for months at a time. Amaya was in charge of the family domain, which included a large house in Verona surrounded by gardens and a farm and vineyard out in the countryside. She spent her life running back and forth, taking care of minor problems and major disasters...all with equanimity.

Her house was decorated with heavy Italian furniture and Persian accents: Persian carpets and intricate wall hangings, velvet and bronze. One day Amaya invited me over in the afternoon for coffee. The boys ran ragged around the house. It felt as though a volcano was about to erupt, but Amaya smiled placidly and prepared what I call Turkish coffee. She served it in small cups with little square cakes. After we finished our coffee, a dark sludge of grounds remained at the bottom of the cup. Laughingly, Amaya told me she was a fortune-teller. I handed her my cup and she spent considerable time studying the coffee grounds. When she looked up, she avoided my eyes.

"What do you see?" I asked, a smile in my voice. I'd been up to Cerro that morning and I felt buoyant.

"Oh, never mind, it's not clear. I'll try with the next cup of coffee." She rose to wash out the cups.

"Is it bad?" I insisted.

"I'm not really a clairvoyant. I just dabble."

Sobered now, I kept pushing. "That fortune-teller at the park told me I would find great happiness, then death and unhappiness. Is that what you see?"

Her back was to me. At first, she didn't respond. Then she said in a quiet voice, "Yes, death and pain…but you will recover."

I ran my fingers through my hair and leaned my elbows on the table. *Death and pain.* All I could think of was Andrea. I would lose Andrea. They would find him and shoot him in retaliation. My lighthearted mood had turned grim.

Amaya turned, her expression to one of concern. "Don't believe my silly prophecies. It's just a game and means nothing. I shouldn't have said anything. I can see you're upset."

I laughed darkly. "You're right. It's just a game…nonetheless, life is a risky business. One spin of the roulette wheel can change everything."

At the entrance to Amaya's house were two large persimmon trees. When I left with the boys that afternoon, the fog had rolled in. The world was grey and opaque, but the bright orange fruit glowed on the tree. As I closed the gate behind us, I could hear the muffled plop of a heavy, ripe persimmon as it hit the leaf-strewn ground. I'm told persimmons symbolize transitions. And aren't transitions the very essence of our lives?

Chapter 48

I don't want you to get the idea that Andrea was a spineless namby-pamby. As we talked, I learned he had been raised in a strict environment. To me the Mafia family was like an exacting religion, with stringent rules and devotion to the familial cause. He talked about *omertà*, the Mafia's code of silence concerning criminal activity and a refusal to give evidence to the authorities. The feuding families seemed to be in accord on that point. The shootings and acts of revenge didn't involve the police. Either the carabinieri were unaware of these goings-on or they chose not to get involved...or they were in on it.

One day I brought scissors and cut Andrea's hair. As I worked, we talked about his life in New York. He had loved the freedom of being away from the constraints of his immediate family. He wasn't party to his uncle's criminal activities in New York City or in Las Vegas. Instead, he was allowed to attend college and live a normal life. He made friends with some guys and played soccer on Sundays, followed by drinks in a bar. Along with his accounting classes he took a creative writing class and a theatre class. The latter included tickets to several plays. He went to the symphony, attended Giants and Yankees games, and briefly dated a Jewish girl.

"Ah-ha. What happened to that love of your life?" I teased. I was crouched in front of him, trying to even out the two sides of his hair.

Andrea pulled me in and kissed the tip of my nose. "She wasn't as sexy as you."

"No, really, what happened?"

"Her father didn't approve of me. She was forbidden to ever see me again."

"Was she beautiful?"

"Ravishing…a dark-haired beauty." Then he pulled me in close again and we ended up in the bedroom before I'd completed the haircut.

***

Some days, Andrea wanted to discuss politics. We talked about the *Brigate Rosse*, the Red Brigade, that was terrorizing Italy. The left-wing terrorist organization was responsible for numerous violent incidents, including assassinations, kidnappings and robberies.

"They aren't much different from the Mafia," I said.

"They are. They're trying to destabilize all of Italy," Andrea responded.

"Your Mafia family performs brutal acts as well. They're violent and lawless," I countered.

"I can't defend the family's illegal affairs, but they aren't trying to destroy the entire country."

"Murder, extortion, stealing, I don't see the difference. Maybe Italians are particularly prone to crime." I pulled myself away and glared down at him.

His eyes flashed with amusement. "Are we having a fight?" he asked.

At that moment, I realized I did have a problem with his being a member of the Mafia. It was difficult to reconcile his family's activities with this person I loved. "I wish you could leave the Mafia and begin a life somewhere else…an honest, crime-free life."

Andrea looked deep into my eyes. I saw a flicker of desperation. "I wish that as well," he murmured. Then he pulled me down into his embrace.

Later, as he caressed the line of my hip, he said, "Someday I would like to return to the States and New York. I want to live there with you and stroll down Madison Avenue and through Central Park. We could go to the Metropolitan and the opera."

I stretched under his caresses like a contented cat. "I would love, love to stroll with you," I purred.

***

The second week of March was unseasonably warm. On Wednesday, I made my preparations early and took down the bags for Andrea before everyone was up. I had made lasagna the night before and I wrapped two squares in foil to take to the cottage. I'd also bought a bunch of daffodils and included some pieces of lemon pound cake.

I put on a blue-checked shirtwaist dress and a sweater. I felt light and airy as I drove up to Cerro. The days were getting longer, and the sun was already high in the sky. At the cottage, I raced up the stairs. I wanted to share this sunny, warm day with Andrea. He pulled open the door and we fell into each other's arms. Then he held me at arms' length. I twirled around. He'd never seen me in a dress. Usually I was bundled up like a polar bear.

"You look beautiful." His eyes were filled with tenderness. I suppose mine reciprocated. I felt intoxicated with the spring day and our love. I opened the blinds and the French doors. The soft air blew into the room. I gave Andrea the daffodils and he placed them in an empty jam jar on the table. They looked hopeful and sprightly. While he prepared espressos, I rummaged around in my satchel and brought out a college anthology of poetry. When we sat down by the open window, I opened the ragged book and turned to the Wordsworth poem about daffodils.

"I wandered lonely as a cloud
That floats on high o'er vales and hills,
When all at once I saw a crowd,
A host of golden daffodils;
Beside the lake, beneath the trees,
Fluttering and dancing in the breeze."

We smiled at each other when I'd finished. Everything that day seemed perfect. In the bedroom, we lay entangled on top of the

256

covers. We made love slowly and deliberately, giving sweet pleasure, breathing in each other's essence.

I drove home feeling satiated and ebullient.

Chapter 49

The following week the warm weather was gone, and I bundled up before setting out for the cottage. I'd been late taking the children to school. Lucie had lost her shoes somewhere in the apartment and it took fifteen minutes to find them wedged behind the sofa. As I got ready to go, Marina was cleaning up the kitchen and starting a pot of minestrone. When Timmy saw me putting on my coat, he began to cry. "Mommy. Stay home."

"No, sweetheart. I have to go. You'll have fun with Marina."

His face turned dark, and he wrapped his chubby arms around his chest. "I don't have fun with Marina. I hate Marina." He stamped a foot.

I crouched down and took him into my arms. "Timmy, what's going on? You always like your special day with Marina."

"No, I don't." He pulled away and burst into tears.

What was I going to do? I had to get going. I went into the kitchen and grabbed a lollipop from the jar on top of the fridge. Marina looked askance. She didn't approve of snacks between meals. But this was an emergency. I found Timmy in the bedroom. He had thrown himself on the bed and was bawling.

I sat and rubbed his back until he calmed down. At first, he wouldn't look at me. He kept his face turned towards the wall as his sobs turned to sniffles. Finally, he turned his head and looked at me.

I smiled. "Hey, buddy, would you like a lollipop?"

He nodded and sat up. Ah, the power of sugar. I helped him remove the wrapper. Then I picked up **Mr. Rabbit** and Timmy wrapped his arm around his fuzzy friend. Marc's train set was on the floor. I got down on my hands and knees and wound up the engine. I attached it to the train cars and clicked the switch. The train started chugging around the tracks. Timmy was mesmerized. I slipped out of the room, feeling guilty.

"I'm leaving," I yelled to Marina as I opened the front door. I rushed down the hall to the elevator and pushed the button. As I waited, I could hear Timmy crying again. But I had to go. He would be all right, I told myself. I punched the elevator button again and again. Nothing happened. Finally, I gave up and started down the stairs. On the ground floor, I met Signor Colombo. He wanted to tell me about the elevator. I knew this could be a long conversation.

"Sorry, **signor**, I can't talk. I've got an appointment."

"Well, signora, I hope it works when you get home with the children. It's a long trek up to the fourth floor."

"Yes, yes, so do I." I smiled as I slipped by him and headed toward the stairs to the parking garage in the basement.

Traffic was heavy driving through Verona. As I started up the mountain, I got behind a truck carrying livestock. A stench crept into my car, and the truck took forever to get up the hill. At every hairpin turn, it slowed to a snail's pace. It would be nearly 10:30 by the time I got to the cottage. I would only have an hour and a half with Andrea. I banged the steering wheel in frustration. Everything was going wrong that morning.

Up in Cerro, mist and light rain blurred my vision, as though I was driving through a cloud. As I drove up the lane, I couldn't see the cottage. The gates were open as I pulled into the parking area below. How had that happened? I always clanged them shut when I left. Had I forgotten to do it the previous week? Had I been in such a hurry when I'd left?

I parked, stepped out of the car and pulled out the two plastic bags I'd brought. Through the mist, I couldn't see the balcony above. I found the bottom step of the staircase and started up, holding on to the railing. At the top of the stairs, I approached the door, expecting Andrea to pull it open. My smile was eager, and I felt a little giddy.

Then I looked more closely. The door was partially open already. Panicked thoughts raced through my brain. What could have happened? Had they come? Had they shot Andrea? Was someone in there waiting to accost me?

"Andrea? Hello? Are you there?" I called out. I hesitated, then pushed the door. It swung open wider. I felt a slight breeze. "Hello?"

Silence.

"Andrea? Hello?" Half-expecting to be shot or grabbed, I stepped into the front room. It was empty. I looked into the small kitchen.

Empty. Slowly, I moved towards the bedroom. I was afraid of what I might find. "Andrea, are you, all right?" I whispered.

Silence.

The bedroom was empty. The covers were in a jumble on the bed. Then I saw the open window, the partly open shutters. Instinctively, I reached down and pulled back the covers, hoping against hope Andrea would be there, asleep. But the bed was empty. I looked in the corner, where his duffle bag had stood ready for an escape. It was gone. Andrea was gone. But where? Had he escaped the Greco family? Or had they carried his body away? I looked for blood on the sheets and on the floor. Nothing.

"Please, dear God, make Andrea safe," I whispered, choking back sobs.

I went back into the front room, looking for blood or signs of a struggle. There was nothing amiss. The empty jam jar stood on the dining table. In the kitchen, a square of dried up lasagna on a plate hadn't been touched. How long had it been sitting there? Certainly, several days. A fork lay on the floor. Maybe Andrea had heard a car and some voices. I could imagine exactly what happened. He'd dropped the fork and raced to the bedroom, pulled open the window, pushed open the shutters outside and raced up the hill, over the low fence and towards the chapel. Had they caught him? Or had he successfully hidden himself among the scrub pines and cypress trees?

I went back to the bedroom and stood at the window, looking up the hill. With the drizzle and mist, I couldn't even see the edge of the property. Quickly, I pulled the shutters and closed the window.

Then I got to work. I changed the bed with the sheets I'd brought from home. I took the extra blankets from the master bedroom and made up the single beds in in the second bedroom. I cleaned the bathroom and changed the towels. In the kitchen, I emptied the fridge and wiped it down. I went through the cupboards and threw out any foodstuffs. I swept the floor and arranged the chairs around the table. I carried garbage bags down to the car. I didn't stop. I kept moving. I didn't cry. At twelve noon, I drove out of the driveway and made sure the gates slammed shut behind me.

I cried all the way down the mountain. Between the rain on the windshield and my tears, the world was a blur. I had known this day would come. I had known Andrea would leave, and I would be alone again. But in spite of that knowledge, I wasn't emotionally prepared. I was adrift. My heart was broken. I felt sure I would never love anyone again, not like I'd loved him. And in my heart of hearts, I knew no one would ever love me as he had. I cried for myself and for my loss.

Chapter 50   2019

We're about to land in Italy. Lucie reaches over and takes my hand. "Hey, Mom. I bet you're excited."

I smile. "Yes, I am. That year we spent in Verona was a pivotal one for me...and for you...for our family."

She squeezes my fingers. "Because of Papa, right?"

I glance at her but can't read her expression. "Yes, and because of other things that happened while we were living there. I've been thinking a lot about the people we knew and the friends I made. Many of them are dead now."

Lucie nods, looking empathetic. "Well, I'm glad we could all come with you, although I've got to admit, I don't remember that much."

"Maybe it will come back to you when we walk through our old haunts."

***

We get through Customs relatively quickly. A member of the prize committee is there to greet us at the baggage claim. Signor Sartori is worthy of his name. He's wearing a well-cut suit, with elegant soft-leather shoes on his feet. He exudes class and bonhomie. Chattering away, he leads us to a van and directs the driver to load our luggage. Soon we're speeding along to the hotel. I have to admit

263

the streets are unfamiliar. Verona looks better than I remembered. In the intervening years, the city acquired money to spruce up decrepit buildings and renovate shops and restaurants.

The Gabbia D'Oro is a beautiful hotel located near the Piazza delle Erbe. The cozy lobby is decorated with Venetian furniture, luxuriant green plants and two parakeets in a gilded cage named, of course, Romeo and Juliet. My room is elegant yet cozy with a red, flowered chintz sofa and chair and a comfy-looking bed. I know better than to lay down. I need to keep moving or I'll crash. I take a shower and change into slacks and a sweater.

We meet down in the lobby and go for a walk. I had asked the hotel concierge for a map, but Lucie is guiding us using her iPhone. We stop every few minutes to check out a shop window, or a building or a passerby. Everything fascinates my grown children. They're engulfed in the magic of another culture. I feel proud walking among them, listening to their comments and hearing their laughter. How lucky I am to have four beautiful, intelligent children.

When we arrive at Piazza Bra, Tim suggests we take the time to tour the Arena. I remember doing this when he was a tiny tot.

"Yes, let's do that," Marc says. "I kind of remember the exterior."

We learn that back in the first century, gladiators and wild animal hunts brought in a crowd of onlookers. Today, the Roman Amphitheatre is used for opera and rock concerts. A poster informs us that Adèle and BTS will be playing there in the near future.

After the tour, I suggest we go down Corso Porta Nuova and check out our old apartment building and Lucie and Marc's former school. Much is the same as we walk down the boulevard, except the traffic is heavier than I remember. Our building looks the same. I try opening the entrance door into the lobby, but it's locked. You need to type in a code. No longer does a friendly doorman inspect who comes in or out. But it's probably more secure this way.

The café in our building is still there, but it looks shiny and spiffed up. There are tables outside on the sidewalk with bright umbrellas. We sit and order cappuccinos from a young waiter, who is both handsome and impatient. I ask him who owns the place and he says, "Signor Costa." I can't believe it. He would be eighty or ninety by now. He can't possibly be working in this café.

"Is Signor Costa here, now? I'd like to talk to him," I say.

"No, he took his daughter to the dentist."

Ah, the owner must be the older Costa's son.

The kid is getting annoyed with me. Marc and Lucie seem to be following the conversation. Tim looks perplexed and Drew is studying the menu.

My Italian is pretty rusty, but the young man seems to understand me. "I lived here many, many years ago and I knew Signor Costa then. Does his son own the place now?"

"No, signora, you're talking about his uncle, the old man. He's here. He's always here, sitting in the back." The kid gestures towards the door to the café. "Now I've got to get your coffee." He disappears through the door, and I follow him inside.

The interior of the café has changed, but it's the same layout. Way in the back at a small table is a crumpled-looking old man with a full head of white hair. He wears thick glasses and a blue turtleneck sweater. I go over and sit down in front of him. He looks bewildered.

"Buongiorno, Signor Costa, É Signora Joubert. Ti ricordi di me? La donna Americana? Do you remember me? The American woman." I hold out my hand.

His rheumy eyes light up and his thin lips form a smile. Without a pause, he says, "Certo. Sure, I do. You're the woman with the three little children."

"I'm here visiting with my children."

"How are they?"

"They're all grown up with children of their own."

"I remember you coming in for a cappuccino every morning with your little boy, the little blond one."

"Yes, I loved the coffee and the brioche."

"How long ago was that?" he asks.

"About forty-five years ago." I chuckle. "I was a young woman then."

He smiles and pats my hand. "You were so beautiful. I was in love with you. Did you know that?"

I raise my eyebrows in surprise. "I didn't know that. But it's nice to hear."

He chuckles. "Yes, I wanted to take you away from that husband of yours. He didn't deserve you. Che idiota. What a jerk." He raps on the table with his liver-spotted hand.

I smile. "You were a good friend. Back then your smile and friendly conversation were a balm to my low spirits."

I think about the terrible anguish I suffered after Andrea disappeared and then later when Henri…I remember stumbling into the café every morning and going through the motions of smiling and chatting with the regulars. I couldn't stand to go upstairs to the apartment where pain, loneliness and guilt reverberated through the empty rooms.

Chapter 51

When I got home, Timmy was not feeling any better. He had been crying off and on while I was gone. Marina gave me the evil eye when I rushed into the apartment. She was right. I had been a bad mother, running off when my child needed me. I felt his forehead and he seemed warm. Then I noticed he was scratching his tummy, so I pulled up his shirt. His chest and abdomen were covered with a red rash. That afternoon I took him to Dr. Petrini around the corner, and my diagnosis was confirmed. Timmy had chicken pox.

I was told there wasn't much I could do except let the illness run its course. I needed to prevent him from scratching the fluid-filled blisters. There was an Italian version of calamine lotion to smear over the sores. Several times a day, he soaked in a warm bath in which I dumped quantities of baking soda.

A few days later, Marc came down with chicken pox, and then Lucie. Those weeks seemed like an eternity. I was comforting and bathing one child or another, day and night. Marc got the worst case, with sores in his mouth. He couldn't eat hard food for days. I made puddings and milkshakes. I read stories and played games. At times the children were docile and took long naps. At other times they fought like baby tigers. Giada did some shopping for me, and Anna and Amaya brought over some prepared meals. I was grateful for their help, since I couldn't manage anything but my nursing activities.

During this time, I barely cried. I was too busy. Some child needed me every minute, twenty-four hours a day. Emotionally, I was a zombie. I didn't let myself think about Andrea. Was he alive or dead? Would I ever see him again? Entertaining these thoughts would have sent me over the edge. I was already strung out.

One day I opened the door and found a massive box, probably three feet by three feet. At first, I thought it was another gift of thanks from Alberto, but when I opened it up, there were boxes and boxes of De Cecco pasta. Then I remembered Adriana had told me weeks before that her office was ordering a train carload of pasta. She'd asked if I would like some boxes at a discount rate. I left it to her to decide the amount and shape. She'd sent me some of everything: spaghetti, fusilli, cavatappi, rigatoni, etc. Obviously, as an Italian mother of four, she figured I needed hundreds of boxes. I let the children play with the big box and entertain themselves piling the smaller boxes of pasta in vertiginous towers.

I didn't talk to Henri about my last Wednesday at the cottage, worried that I would fall apart if I initiated the conversation. Most nights I didn't see him, and in the mornings, I was too busy caregiving. On the weekends, he went to work. He claimed there was too much noise at home with the children crying and fussing. On the following Thursday, he came home from the plant at a decent hour. He was upset. I remember I was making rice pudding for the kids.

"Why didn't you tell me he was gone?" His voice had a sharp edge.

I acted dumb. "Who?"

"You know who. The killer. Andrea Mongelli."

I felt angry. How dare he talk about Andrea in that tone of voice. He didn't even know Andrea…and *my* Andrea wasn't a killer. I felt rage bubbling up. "Why do you care? You didn't want to know about all those trips I made at your behest these last four months. How dare you talk to me like that!" I was waving my wooden spoon around, and blobs of milky rice flew across the room.

Henri stepped back, holding up his hands. "Giancarlo asked me what you had found last Wednesday when you went up there. I didn't have an answer."

"Ah-ha. Your amour-propre was wounded." I laughed derisively. "You weren't worried about me, and if I'd been shot at by those Greco hooligans. No, you were worried about what Giancarlo thought of you."

"Come on, Kate. Was he there or not last week?" His mouth was set in a hard line.

I shook my head. My eyes filled with tears. "No, he wasn't there. I think he escaped through the bedroom window." Then realization dawned on me. I stared at Henri. "Why did Giancarlo ask you that?"

"Because they got a call from the Mongelli family. You're right. He did escape. He's making his way down south. No one knows where he is right now."

I pulled out a chair and sat down, hid my face in my hands and sobbed. Henri came over and tentatively patted my back. "I know these months have been hard on you. You've been very brave. I'm grateful. But it's over now. You don't have to go up there anymore. Don't cry."

I continued to sob, and Henri left the room. He didn't get it. He didn't have a clue…and that was for the best. His lack of empathy saved me from blurting out the truth.

***

The School of the Angels would not permit Lucie and Marc to return to classes until they no longer had any visible blisters. We had been housebound for several weeks. The children and I needed to get out of the apartment and get some fresh air. I knew the mothers at the park would not look kindly on my children playing with their darlings. Where to go? One bright, warm morning, I decided to go up to Cerro. Even though I didn't relish the thought of returning to the cottage, Cerro was a place where the kids could play outside without spreading chicken pox.

I packed salami and cheese paninis, fruit, juice and cookies. All three kids were super excited. They chattered happily as I drove up the mountain. Angst filled me as I approached the cottage, but I drove up to the gates, got out and pulled them open. Once parked, the kids tumbled out of the car. Together we climbed up the stairs and I opened the front door.

"Look, Mommy, it's just like we left it," Lucie said. She scampered around the table.

"Yes, it's just the same," Marc echoed.

They checked out the bedrooms and then they ran back outside. Soon they were playing a game Lucie made up. While they were busy, I searched through the cottage. I opened every cupboard. I looked under the beds. Even though I'd swept and cleaned that last time, I was hoping against hope I would find some remnant of Andrea. Some little object I could treasure. But there was nothing.

Later, I took the picnic basket and my knitting, and we walked up the hill to the grassy area for our picnic. The children gobbled down the lunch I'd prepared. It was the first time they'd been really hungry in weeks. While they played King of the Mountain on the rocks, I lay down on the blanket and looked up at the blue sky. Puffy clouds moved through the ether. I felt warm and a sense of calm flowed through me. I closed my eyes.

"Hey, Mommy." My eyes snapped open. I must have dozed off. All three kids were looking down at me. I smiled at their dear, little spotted faces.

"Mommy. Let's open the door to the chapel. Let's go inside," Lucie said.

"I've already been inside," Marc said.

"But I want to see inside," Lucie protested.

"Me too. Inside," Timmy said.

"Well, I guess we could do that. Let me get a knitting needle and we'll open the door."

We traipsed over to the chapel. While I fiddled with the needle, trying to jimmy the lock, the kids were jumping around. Finally, I managed it and pushed open the door. From inside came a whiff of chilly, musty air.

"Ooo…it's spooky in here," Lucie said.

"No, it's religious in here. You don't have to be afraid," Marc said with authority.

There wasn't much to see. Ten chairs in two rows faced a small altar. To the left, a stone staircase led to the balcony above. The kids started up the stairs to see what they could find, giggling with excitement. I walked over to the altar. Flowers were strewn on top. Getting closer, I found a bunch of dried-up daffodils. Underneath was a page torn from a book of poetry. I read,

"I wandered lonely as a cloud
That floats on high o'er vales and hills,
When all at once I saw a crowd,
A host of golden daffodils;
Beside the lake, beneath the trees,
Fluttering and dancing in the breeze."

Chapter 52

I slogged through the following weeks in robot-mode. I kept myself busy by taking excellent care of my children, cooking delicious meals and smiling non-stop. You remember the words to that old song, *laughing on the outside, crying on the inside*? I didn't allow myself to think about Andrea or of those few magical months. Often, I told myself I had been saved from perdition. I could have ruined my marriage and my children's future. Thank God Andrea was gone. Thank God I hadn't lost everything for a fleeting romance.

The weeks flew by. I made list after list, checking off each accomplishment throughout the day. At the park, I knitted diligently. I completed Timmy's French sailor sweater. Now he and Marc had twin pullovers. I talked animatedly with Giada, Amaya and Anna. I baked sugar cookies for them and gifted them in pretty, decorated boxes. In spare moments, I refinished an old chest that Henri's parents had given us. I sanded and painted out on the kitchen balcony. At night I wrote children's books about cute little animals and how they overcame adversity. There was the one about the white bunny, Hugo, who hides in his burrow. Eventually he conquers his fear of the world, ventures outside and makes new friends. Then there's the baby giraffe, Lilliput, who is teased by the other giraffes

274

and learns to be strong and to forgive. You get the gist. Much later, when I lived in Litchfield, I met the artist, Charlotte Jameson. She made those stories come alive through her adorable illustrations. I'm not sure if I became more famous from those books or from the novels. But I do know the effort of writing them was a lifesaver. Each evening when the children slept, I escaped into the imaginary world of my innocent baby animals.

On the first Wednesday after Lucie and Marc went back to school, Marina expected me to take off for Cerro. She was surprised when I made no move to leave. She was washing the windows in the living room. They were open, admitting a light, warm breeze. She washed the windows regularly. I don't think I've ever had such spotless windows.

That morning, I was on the floor with Timmy, putting on his shoes. We were going out to run some errands.

"You're not going to the mountains to write?" Marina's tone was ever so slightly sarcastic.

"No, I've got errands to run."

"You didn't write much on those trips," she said, polishing the glass with vigor.

What was she getting at?

"I looked in your notebooks to see what you wrote. So many pages were empty." She looked down at me with a sly, self-satisfied expression.

Why should I explain myself to this woman? What nerve to look through my satchel. I should have been angry, but I was still overcome with guilt. I murmured an excuse. "I stored my writings up in Cerro."

She shook her head and continued working. She didn't believe me, and I didn't care.

***

We had been in Italy for a year. It was time to re-up our cottage rental. I told Henri I didn't want to go back to Cerro. The thought of returning there filled me with dread. At first, he gave me a hard time, but eventually he relented and agreed to notify Signor Moretti. It turned out Moretti also owned a small apartment above the Lago di Garda. It was located on the property of a *Club di Nuoto,* a swim club, which included a pool, tennis courts and a restaurant. For a small fee, we could use the facilities. Henri would join us there in the evenings. The plan was to spend six weeks there. Then in August, we would join Henri's parents in Burgundy. I never wanted to see the cottage again. But I would miss the entire Peron family and especially my conversations with Adriana and La Mama.

***

I sat in the *chiosco ristoro* with Giada and Anna one afternoon. The tables were filled with mothers and grandmothers enjoying small cups of iced coffee or soft drinks. The fortune-teller was there with all her books and her little dog. She had a client, but she couldn't concentrate. The dog kept whining and jumped up on her lap and then back down. It was panting, its little tongue lolling out. The fortune-teller stopped her work, stood and held up her hands to silence us. Then, in a sonorous voice, she announced that something

276

bad was going to happen, that her dog sensed the danger. At first, we were taken aback. No one spoke. Then Giada started to laugh. That broke the ice and the women sitting around at the other tables began to talk again, their voices subdued.

"That woman is probably crazy," Anna said, rolling her eyes.

"She told Kate's future," Giada said turning to me, her eyes dancing. "What did she tell you again?"

I felt myself blushing. "I don't remember. Something about finding love and someone dying."

Anna scoffed. "That could be true of anyone. I hope you didn't pay her a lot."

***

As it turned out, the little dog was clairvoyant. That night at about nine o'clock there was a terrific noise and then a rolling and shaking. I don't know how long it lasted. Probably only a few seconds, but it seemed an eternity. I was sitting on the sofa with my legs pulled up under me. I had a glass of white wine on the side table. The liquid sloshed around and then the glass crashed to the floor. The open windows onto the balcony shook and banged shut. The picture of the children hanging in the entryway fell off the wall. I heard rattling from the kitchen.

I shot upright and then stood frozen, wondering what to do. What had happened? It felt like an earthquake. More shaking, shorter this time. What should I do? Should I wake the children and take them downstairs? We couldn't take the elevator. That would be dangerous. I went to the balcony and looked down. Hundreds of people were pouring into the street.

I went into the bedrooms. The kids had heard nothing. They were fast asleep. I went back to the living room and stepped out on the balcony. Now crowds of people were milling around and shouting. I saw flashing lights and heard loud sirens.

I didn't wake the children. We didn't leave the apartment. I told myself we would be all right. In retrospect, I let Fate take its course. If the building crashed down, so be it. I was depressed and felt an overwhelming inertia. This fatalistic reaction was selfish. Rather than saving my children, I let destiny take charge. I went to bed after consuming some of Henri's Armagnac and slept well. In the morning, Henri told me he had felt nothing. He had been in a car on the way to dinner with Giancarlo and Francesco. He said they were surprised at the hullabaloo when they arrived at the restaurant. He had not called me to see if we were all right.

The Friuli Earthquake had a magnitude of 6.5 and a maximum Mercalli intensity of X, which is considered extreme. In the following days, many people were afraid to go inside their apartment buildings, even though it was deemed safe. They slept in the park across the street and partied. Each night, I watched from the balcony. There were bright lights, laughter and music. People were relieved to be alive.

***

In the second week of May, Henri came home with a square white envelope. He tossed it on the kitchen table and went back to the bedroom to hang up his suit jacket. I dried my hands on a kitchen towel. With vague interest, I picked up the envelope and ran my finger under the flap. I pulled out a folded piece of card stock. It was a wedding invitation.

I gripped the card tightly. My knuckles turned white. I felt faint and collapsed onto a chair. The card announced the wedding of Sofia Maria Greco to Andrea Giuseppe Mongelli.

Chapter 53   2019

That night we have dinner in a nearby restaurant that the concierge suggested. I order ossobuco with risotto Milanese. It's delicious, and something I hadn't eaten for years. I almost lick the plate.

"That was fabulous," I say, and finish my glass of Bardolino.

"This restaurant was a great choice," Tim says. He had enjoyed a veal stew with mushrooms and polenta.

After the wonderful meal, we're all satiated and ready for bed. "What's the plan for tomorrow?" Marc asks.

"I don't actually have a plan. What would you kids like to do?" I say.

Drew laughs. "Right, we kids." He makes quotation marks with his fingers.

I raise my eyebrows and smile. "To me you will always be my kids."

"I'd like to do some shopping," Lucie says. "I want to bring back something for Chelsea and Carson. But there's also this organization in Verona called The Environmental League. I'd like to touch base with them. They've been doing some interesting work and I'd like to see if I can talk to someone."

Tim tops off his glass from the bottle of Soave. "There's this radio museum I'd like to see. You know, Marconi was involved with the first radio. I met a guy in New York who raved about the museum."

"I'd do that with you." Marc turns to me. "What about you, Mom? Does that sound fun, or do you want to go shopping?"

"I think I would be happy just wandering around and revisiting the past." I pause and looked at my dear children. They're all wondering what they can do to make me happy. "I would like to drive up to Cerro."

"What's Cerro?" Drew asks.

"It's where we rented a cottage when we first moved to Verona. We didn't have an apartment down in the city at first, so we spent four months up in Cerro. I'd love to drive up there and check it out."

"How long does it take to get there?" Lucie asks.

"Oh, probably forty-five minutes," I say.

"I'd go there with you, Mom," Drew says. "I don't have anything special I want to do."

"We'd have to rent a car or get an Uber," I say.

Lucie, ever the organizer, says, "Listen, why don't we all do whatever we want in the morning, meet for lunch and drive up to this Cerro place in the afternoon."

Marc sits forward in his chair and crosses his arms on the table. "What I remember about that place was this grassy hill we walked up. There was this tower and I got locked in. Heck, I was scared to death."

I laugh. "Yes, you were. I had the devil of a time getting you out."

281

"I remember that. You used a knitting needle. Right?" Lucie says.

Tim and Drew roll their eyes. Neither one of them remembers Cerro. Tim was too little, and Drew wasn't born yet.

***

We meet at one o'clock and share a couple of Quattro Stagioni pizzas. The concierge at the hotel has procured a nice Fiat. I sit in front with Marc. Lucie sits between her other two brothers in the back. Drew put Cerro Veronese into his phone's GPS, and he is able to direct us. This turns out to be a good idea, since I don't recognize the streets or landmarks. After all, I haven't been here for over forty years. But when we turn onto the SP6, I recognize the route. The road doesn't seem as zig-zaggy as in the past. We make our way up the hill relatively quickly. When we come out into the valley, I find I'm holding my breath. There is the village of Cerro, up on the hill to the left. Our cottage will be on the hill to the right. I direct Marc to turn right and we make our ascent.

New houses line the road, and at first, I don't recognize the turnoff to the cottage. Then I spot a house I remember on the corner of our lane. It looks the same, but it's almost completely hidden behind the tall cypress trees. We turn left. Where there had been open fields and scrub pine, there are now more houses on both sides of the road.

"There it is. That stone and stucco one behind the iron fence. Do you remember it?" My hands make tight fists in my lap.

"I do," Lucie says. She's excited. "But it seemed enormous back then. Now it looks pretty small. We must have been on top of each other in there."

"Me, too. I remember the balcony and those metal stairs," Marc says.

"How long did we live here?" Tim asks.

"For four months...but it seemed longer back then," I say. "There were empty fields around it. All these houses have been built since then."

Drew is inspecting the cottage. "It must have been pretty remote."

"Yes, it was. I was here with three little kids, no phone and a stroller to get around."

"That's nuts, what if one of us had broken a leg or there was a robber? How would you call the ambulance or the police?" Lucie asks.

"Somehow I didn't worry about any of that. I mean, cell phones didn't exist. If there had been a problem, I would have grabbed you kids and made my way down the hill to that restaurant in the village. They would have had a phone."

"Gosh, no phone and no computer. Lucie wouldn't have survived," Drew says.

"Ha-ha. Neither could you without your laptop," Lucie says.

"Why didn't we have a car?" Marc asks.

"We did, but your dad needed it to get to work. He left early in the morning and came back late at night. That's how things were back then."

"That sounds chauvinistic," Lucie grumbles. She was always a champion for women's rights.

We park the car and walk up the hill to the chapel. It's been spiffed up with glass panels and carved stone steps. I had forgotten the magnificent panorama of green hills and snow-covered mountains in the distance. While Marc, Drew and Tim go into the chapel, Lucie and I sit down on the rocks that used to be a favorite place to play. Lucie has been silent for much of the walk up the hill.

She looks over at me. I sense she has something to get off her chest.

"What's up, buttercup?" I ask.

She looks off at the view. "I know about Dad. I know how he died."

I pat her hand. "You've always known that. It was a car accident on the way to Venice."

"I've been talking to Francesca. She told me the whole story." Her voice is low and strained.

Giada died of cancer ten years ago, but I knew Lucie and Francesca had remained in touch all these years. Francesca had come to the States for an MBA and they had rekindled their childhood friendship. During that time, Francesca spent Thanksgiving and Christmas with us. I remember she and Lucie had skied at Sugarbush together.

284

"What whole story?" I turn to look at her. She's pale and her lips are quivering.

"She told me about how Dad died in that car crash, that he wasn't alone. He was with another woman." Lucie begins to cry.

I put my arm around her. "When did you learn this?"

"Just last week when I told her I was coming over," Lucie says. "Her mom told her years ago. I guess it was in the paper and everything. I feel so bad for you, Mom." Lucie turns and hugs me. Her tears wet my cheeks. "How could you stand it? The public humiliation?"

I take a deep breath. "It was a shock, but I'd had inklings he was unfaithful."

"Did you know the woman he was with?"

"Yes, it was the wife of a colleague. The whole thing was a mess. After he died, we left for the States." I gaze across the hills to the remote snowy mountains.

"But you were pregnant, right?"

"Yes, five months pregnant."

"That must have been terrible to think the father of your child was dead...and that he'd been screwing some other woman."

I hold Lucie's face in my hands.

"My darling girl, don't let the past consume you. I've been able to put it all behind me. So, should you. In life, we can choose darkness or light. I chose light."

Chapter 54

We left for the wedding on Friday morning. Henri had called Françoise and she had agreed to come down and babysit. She and Benoît arrived on the Wednesday. Henri and I gave them our bedroom and we moved into the study. The children were thrilled to see their grandparents. I left a list with the daily schedule and filled the fridge with the makings of several meals.

On the way to Naples, Henri and I talked more than we had in months. I had never asked him about Andrea's escape and Henri had avoided the subject. As we drove south towards Naples and the wedding, he told me the story. I learned Andrea had been surprised by the arrival of Luigi Greco, the bride's brother, and one of his henchmen. Andrea had climbed out the back window and made his way up the hill to the chapel.

"Do you know where I mean?" Henri glanced over at me.

I continued to look forward. "Yes, last summer the children played up there."

"He figured out how to get inside and stayed hidden there for a couple of days. Then he made his way down to Verona and someone from the plant picked him up."

"That was lucky," I said. My response was bland and unemotional.

"From there he was transported down south."

I took a breath. My hands were clenched in my lap. "I don't understand why he's marrying a Greco if they were out to kill him."

"Apparently, there were a lot of high-level negotiations going on. From the outside, it looks as though the two families made peace and they decided to seal it with an inter-family wedding."

"Oh, my gosh. This sounds so medieval. A king marrying off his daughter so they could enlarge their domain or form an alliance."

"Or to create a détente, so the fighting would stop," Henri said.

I raged internally. I couldn't believe Andrea would marry just to make his father happy and end a quarrel. He was a grown man with his own plans and desires. He couldn't possibly marry this Sofia like a dutiful son. It was primitive and antiquated.

"I can't see a son doing his father's bidding in this day and age. That's crazy," I said vehemently.

Again, Henri glanced over at me, as if appraising my reaction. "Did you ever talk to Andrea?"

I must have blushed. Hearing Henri utter Andrea's name caught me off guard. "Yes, sometimes. We had coffee and I talked about the children or my writing."

"I'm glad to hear that, Kate. I felt bad sending you up there. At least the man was appreciative and acted with propriety."

"Yes. He was an admirable gentleman," I said. My emotions were doing somersaults and I had a foolish desire to break out in laughter. *I was having a torrid affair, you idiot. Just like you and Giulia...the exquisite Giulia.*

287

As we drove, I thought more about Andrea's escape. "Did you ever learn how the Greco's found Andrea?"

"I don't know. Maybe they followed you?" Henri chuckled.

I shivered at the thought that I had led those men to Cerro and to Andrea.

***

In Naples, we stayed in a lovely old hotel. Our room had high ceilings and large French doors that looked out on the bay. Our car was parked in an underground garage. This was a necessity because, according to several acquaintances, a car left in the street would be stripped within the hour: wheels, windshield wipers, radio, you name it. Stealing and robbery were the norm.

That night we had dinner in the cavernous dining room. I remember we ate spaghetti alle vongole, fileted fish and some delicious, tiny strawberries. We sat at a table with the gang from Verona. I said little but I smiled a lot. Most of the time the men were talking business.

In the morning, after breakfast, we left for the bride's home. We were in four separate cars and formed a little cavalcade. After leaving the city, we took a twisting road through the countryside. Half an hour later, we turned off a narrow lane and entered a dusty farmyard. Several cars were parked there at angles. To the left was an old barn and a fenced-off area with pigs and chickens. To the right was an ancient stone building with a red terra cotta roof. This was the farmhouse.

We got out of the car and made our way across the yard, stepping around muddy potholes. We entered the house directly into the kitchen, a dark, low-ceilinged room with a large wooden table and rickety straight-backed chairs. At one end was an ancient open brick oven. A row of copper pots hung on hooks nearby. Beside them were braids of garlic and drying herbs. At the other end was a staircase leading to the second floor.

About twenty people milled around the room, drinking espressos. On the table was a bottle of grappa that the men poured liberally into their coffee. We formed a strange tableau, all these people dressed in their wedding finery cooped up in this dark, sooty kitchen. I didn't want to sit down in my new rose-pink dress, so I stood by the only window that looked out on the yard. I noticed everyone was paying homage to a squat, bald man standing by the staircase. I figured this was the father of the bride. Two men who seemed to be his bodyguards lounged against the counter.

After a half hour, the crowd hushed, and the bride appeared. She descended the stairs in a billow of white satin and lace. She was a sturdy girl, with a voluminous chest. A Madonna-inspired veil covered her light brown hair. She wasn't glowing, but instead looked as though she was irritated by something. Her father came over and took her hand, and our little crowd applauded. She deigned to smile to her admirers. On her other side appeared another rotund individual that I guessed to be her brother. He leaned over and kissed her cheek, and the crowd applauded again. This was Luigi, the guy who had been up at Cerro chasing down Andrea. Now they would be brothers-in-law.

We all headed back across the dusty farmyard to our cars. Sofia and her father settled themselves in a black Mercedes and took the lead. We followed along. The cars snaked their way through a valley and then we began our ascent up a steep hill. Above, I could see stucco-walled houses with red-tiled roofs. Their green shutters were closed against the sun. The houses seemed to cling to the steep mountainsides. The road was narrow as we wound our way up. At the top, we arrived at a small piazza. Around the square were several shops, a bar/café and the unadorned façade of a Romanesque church.

The cars parked at random and we all got out. Most of us walked to the church entrance, but I noticed several men went into the bar. They skipped the wedding mass all together. Henri took my arm, and we went up the steps and into the dark interior of the church. It was cool inside. Filtered light came through the stained-glass windows. The church was unadorned, with a stark crucifix behind a simple stone altar at the front.

Andrea stood there with another man. They were conversing and didn't see us come in. Henri led me to a spot on the right-hand side. We sat down and awaited the entrance of the bride. I could see Andrea's profile as he turned to face the door.

Chapter 55

The wedding mass was a long affair. I stole looks at Andrea's profile and back. He stood tall and straight like a guard at Buckingham Palace. The priest gave a homily that seemed directed at these two families. He said marriage required forgiveness and acceptance. He asked that this union be blessed by both families, that the Grecos and the Mongellis live in peace and concord. I suppose through confessions, he knew a great deal about the family rivalries.

Once told they were man and wife, Andrea and Sofia kissed chastely. I turned away and studied the window depicting the beheading of St. John the Baptist. It was simplistic and bloody.

At the end of the ceremony, we poured out of the church and loaded back up in our cars. We followed the black Mercedes down the mountain and across a valley to the Palace of Caserta. I had not been familiar with this palace that rivaled Versailles in size and grandeur. While the photographer took pictures of the couple in the royal gardens, we all stood around and waited. The Gelati Bianchi men smoked, while their wives chatted. Giulia Ferrari and Signora Bianchi discussed their summer vacations. The Ferraris were going to Mallorca and the Bianchis had rented a villa in Ibiza. I nodded as they talked. Here were two families off to Spain, while the Spaniards would probably take their holiday in Italy. That was the way to keep the European economy running.

"What are you planning, Kate?" Giulia asked.

"We've got a place near the Lago di Garda and then we'll be going to France to my in-laws," I answered, thinking Giulia probably knew all about it already.

"That sounds like a wonderful time for your children. The air at the lake is excellent for their health," Signora Bianchi said.

"Yes, at least they won't be in Verona with all the traffic and noise," Giulia agreed.

And you will have my husband to yourself, I thought.

***

After what must have been thousands of pictures, we again got into our cars and followed the Mercedes to a renowned restaurant. As we entered the dining room, a full orchestra was playing a well-known Napolitano song. The hall was enormous, and we were joined by a couple of hundred people. It was a lively affair with booming music and an animated crowd. The Italians love to talk and laugh. The air vibrated with their voices.

Again, we were seated with our Bianchi crowd, as though we were a tight little family. I would have liked to mix with the other guests, but this wasn't to be. I was seated between Henri and Avvocato Ricci, the lawyer I had met at the Christmas party. He had more stories to tell about his son's adventures in the States. That summer they would again be traveling to visit national monuments and go hiking in the Rockies. The man seemed to have an exceptionally close relationship with his son. When the second course arrived, Signor Ricci changed the subject.

"You were helpful to Andrea Mongelli. Without you, he might not have been here today to celebrate this happy event."

I felt uncomfortable with this comment. "I believe you might have been helpful as well. Do you perhaps work for the Mongellis as well as Giancarlo Bianchi?" I toyed with the sweet and sour fish on my plate, not looking up.

"Ah, signora. You are most perspicacious." He chuckled. "Yes, I encourage arbitration and compromise." He sipped his champagne and muttered," Someone has to clean up after the elephants."

Later, Andrea's father visited me. He had craggy features, with a prominent nose and dark, deep-set eyes. He was thin, almost emaciated. He looked like a war-ravaged, angry version of Andrea. It struck me the two of them were like the before and after of a twenty-year bout with cancer.

He eyed me suspiciously, yet he shook my hand and thanked me for helping his son. How much did he know about what had transpired in the cottage? What was I to say? *You're welcome. It was a pleasure.* I felt guilty and exposed. Perhaps he viewed me as a loose woman who had provided for all of his son's needs. And was he wrong?

***

The dancing had started. After Andrea danced with Sofia, other couples joined them on the floor. We had finished the sweet and sour fish and were on to a slice of buffalo mozzarella, sprinkled with a fruity olive oil. I didn't have much of an appetite, but I ate a bite of the fresh cheese. Simple as it was, it tasted sublime. I watched the dancers and then glanced up at the head table on a dais. Andrea and Sofia didn't seem to be communicating. Andrea drank a glass of wine and poured himself another. Sofia looked unhappy. Could those be tears on her plump cheeks?

I twirled my wine glass, wishing all this was over. I wanted to go home to my children and make an effort to regain my old life…and my sanity. Again, my eyes were drawn to the head table. At that very moment, Andrea turned and looked directly at me. Our eyes locked. Was my heartache visible? He had an expression of pain and tenderness. I caught all that in one quick glance. Then he got up and came around behind Sofia and stepped down onto the dance floor. He was coming across the room towards me. Was he going to ask me to dance? I couldn't do it. Not here. Not surrounded by all these people.

A terrific explosion cracked through the air. As I watched, Andrea fell to the ground. Pandemonium broke out, people screamed. Henri grabbed my arm and pulled me towards the door.

Chapter 56   2019

The prize committee sends a van to pick us up from the hotel. The ceremony is scheduled for four o'clock. I had debated long and hard on what to wear. I decided on a deep blue sheath and a blue, pink and grey Hermès scarf. I wore my pearl and diamond earrings. My white hair was in a low bun. Lucie had seen to my hair and helped with my make-up as well. She's quite the artist, although she doesn't often wear make-up herself. She applied concealer and blue eyeliner and a natural foundation. I thought I looked pretty good for an old girl.

We arrive at the Palazzo Barbieri a few minutes early. The mayor and several city officials welcome us. There's lots of hand-shaking and big smiles. A small retinue of photographers and journalists is on hand to record the moment. Drew, always the gentleman, takes my arm and we ascend the stairs. More people are waiting in the ornate entrance hall. More bows, handshaking and smiles. Then we're led down a corridor with shiny parquet floors, tapestry hangings and gold-painted woodwork. We arrive at a large rococo-style room. A thick red and gold carpet covers the floor. Extravagant crystal chandeliers hang from the ceiling. Against the walls are crimson silk settees, and behind them hang Baroque tapestries depicting gods and goddesses at play. A podium is set up at one end and about two hundred gold and velvet chairs are arranged in neat rows. Already half the chairs are filled, and people are coming in behind us.

We're led to comfortable satin-covered armchairs in the front row: me, Marc, Tim, Lucie and Drew. We settle into our chairs and wait for the ceremony to commence. I've prepared a few words, but I don't want to talk at length. At last Signor Sartori comes to the podium.

"Welcome, everyone, to this great day when the city of Verona honors Katherine Joubert, author of the bestseller Verona With Love. Her novels have put Verona on the map and the entire town has benefited from the popularity of her books. Tourists come for the Arena, they come for Juliette's balcony, but they mainly come to visit the beautiful city depicted by Signora Joubert. She writes with simplicity and clarity. Her characters seem to step out of the pages of her books and become our friends. The two bestsellers Verona With Love and The Verona Caper were adapted for the cinema and brought film crews and famous actors to our city. The economy is booming. Restaurants and hotels are packed. We owe Signora Joubert a debt of thanks. Her love of our city has made us proud. For this reason, we are presenting the Verona Literary Award and the Honorary Citizen Award to Signora Katherine Joubert."

Signor Sartori beckons me forward. He pronounces a myriad of compliments. Then he hangs a medal around my neck, hands me a key to the city and a small package wrapped in silver paper. I thank him profusely, smile and then turn to the audience.

"Thank you, Signor Sartori and the award committee. I am honored and touched by this recognition of my novels and my life's work of bringing Verona's beauty to the written page. I spent a pivotal year in Verona that colored my life. I made many friends and acquaintances, and suffered loss, but I have grown through those experiences."

I speak for a few more minutes. When I finish, there's a round of applause. I survey the room. Some hands shoot up with questions.

A man in the front asks, "Signora Joubert, do you base your characters on actual people you knew?"

"No, my characters come from my heart and soul. But undoubtedly, they sometimes speak in the voices of people I have met."

A woman on the left: "Often your characters face difficult decisions. Are they reflecting your own life experiences?"

"Yes, and my characters learn to accept and grow from the consequences of their choices. I believe that in life, you need to fall and pull yourself back up. Adversity and wrong decisions can be healed through love, relationships, friends, or even a chance encounter. Through adversity you grow stronger. Your world expands and deepens."

I answer several more questions and take a sip of water from the crystal goblet someone thoughtfully placed on the podium. Another hand shoots up.

"While you were living in Verona, didn't your husband die in a car crash?"

I nod. Where is this going?

"Wasn't there another woman in the car?"

I pause and take a breath. "Yes, I was told he was not alone." My eyes sweep down to my four children, lined up in the front row. Tim and Marc look shocked. Drew looks sympathetic. Lucie has tears in her eyes.

"So, when you speak of adversity and suffering through loss, you're probably thinking about this man who cheated on you, right?"

At this point, Signor Sartori gets up and cuts the Q and A short. As he is speaking, I look out at the crowd. The faces are blurry and indistinct. My gaze travels down the rows, then is drawn to a man with a full head of grey hair. He sits towards the back. His eyes seem to drill into mine. They are deep brown with flecks of gold.

I feel like I might have a heart attack right there. I know those eyes. Although crow's feet surround them, and deep wrinkles mark his cheeks, I know the man's face. How could it be? Andrea had been shot and killed decades before. Who is this man with my Andrea's eyes? I look away and realize that Signor Sartori has asked me something.

"Scusi, I'm sorry...again thank you for this great honor," I babble.

At that moment the doors open, and waiters come in, carrying glasses of champagne and trays of biscotti and hors-d'oeuvres. I am soon swamped with people who want to shake my hand and tell me how much they love my books. I keep trying to look over their heads

298

at the man at the back. I can't tell if he's still there. People are shaking the children's hands and chatting. At last the crowd ebbs and I can draw a breath. A waiter brings me a glass of champagne and I take an unladylike gulp. Then I look across the room again. The brown-eyed man is still there, seated in his chair.

"Mom, look who's here!" Tim says. He's glowing. Pierre stands beside him.

"Félicitations, Madame. C'est un moment inoubliable," Pierre says, bowing slightly.

"Merci, Pierre. Thanks so much for coming. I know Tim is thrilled to see you."

We exchange a few more pleasantries, and then I spot Lucie and Francesca seated together on a settee. The two of them have plans to have dinner together tonight. I walk over, hug Francesca and chat with her. Then, building up courage, I walk towards the back of the room. I feel drawn there, as if by a steel cable.

I lock eyes with the seated man. He stands with the aid of a cane as I approach. We face each other.

"Is it you?" I ask.

"Yes, it's me." There are tears in his eyes.

I take a deep breath. "I thought you were dead. They told me you died." My tone is accusatory.

"Yes, the family thought it was best."

"But why didn't you tell me?"

"I was in hiding."

"Where?"

"In Switzerland. I'm a Swiss citizen now."

Tears of happiness and frustration well up. "You've been alive all these years. Surely you could have contacted me?"

"It was too dangerous, for me, certainly, but also for you and your children. They knew I had been hiding in your cottage. They were keeping track of you. Only recently my brother died, and the matter has finally been put to rest." He looks across the room and then back at me, his face flushed. "When I heard you would be here, I had to come, though I didn't know how I would be received." He reaches into his inside jacket pocket and pulls out the photograph I had given him years ago. It's yellowed and creased. "You've always been next to my heart."

I feel light-headed. "I've got to sit down."

At that moment, Drew comes over. He takes my arm. "Are you all right, Mom?"

I look from one man to the other. Andrew has the same eyes, the same thick, dark wavy hair, the same build...the same name. Can he see that this is his father?

"Let me sit down," I say. Then I pat the seat beside me. "Drew, sit for a moment. I want to introduce you to an old friend. This is Andrea Mongelli. Andrea, this is my son Andrew."

They shake hands.

"I am very glad to meet you," Andrea says. Tears shimmer in his eyes. "Your mother is a very special person, indeed."

Drew's eyes widen. "Yes, she is. Were you friends back when she lived in Verona?"

"Yes, we were friends," Andrea says simply.

"Well, glad to meet you." Drew frowns and then turns to me. "Listen, Mom, Tim, Pierre and Marc have plans for dinner. Do you want to go, too?"

"No, I think I would just like to go back to the hotel and have an early night. This has been a big day."

"I'll go back with you, then."

"No, go with the guys, I really want some quiet time this evening."

He hesitates. "Okay, if you're sure?"

"I'm sure. The prize committee will drive me back to the hotel."

Drew smiles at Andrea. "Well, as I said, nice to meet you." He stands up and goes to join Tim, Marc and Pierre at the door.

Andrea reaches over and takes my hand. His feels warm and familiar. "When was he born?"

"In November...the fifteenth."

His eyes crinkle and he breaks into a tremulous smile. "I am so happy. I have a son. And I have found the love of my life."

Dear Reader,

Verona With Love is set in the mountains of Verona and in the city proper. I lived there as a young mother with three children. In that sense this book is a quasi-memoir. The backdrop represents the Italy we knew in the 1970s. However, the family that I portray in the book is NOT my family. I've created children that are physically and emotionally very different from my own children. Henri, in NO WAY, resembles my former French husband. Henri needed to be an egocentric, insensitive individual to explain Kate's unhappiness in her marriage.

Many of the people I portray in the book are combinations of Italians we befriended. A few resemble actual acquaintances, but I've changed their physical appearance or provided them with a new personality. Andrea is a total fabrication, but it was fun to imagine this passionate love affair.

I hope you enjoyed Verona With Love and were transported to the marvelous country of Italy.

Happy reading,

Deborah Rine

Made in the USA
Columbia, SC
15 October 2022